About the Author

Lorna lives in rural Essex and is married with two sons and two stepsons. Having worked in a private hospital for twenty-five years, she now spends her time writing and sailing and has published four children's books. Lorna is also a great animal lover. This book was inspired by bed-time stories told to Lorna by her grandmother, Beanie, who was brought up on Milldown Farm on the Scottish Borders.

Milldown

Lorna Uglow

Milldown

Olympia Publishers
London

www.olympiapublishers.com
OLYMPIA PAPERBACK EDITION

A CIP catalogue record for this title is
available from the British Library.

ISBN: 978-1-80074-735-7

The Thorburn family are my ancestors. The friendship between Eve
Simpson and Beanie is factual; all other characters are fictional. Apart
from the Thorburns, any resemblance to actual persons, living or dead,
is purely coincidental.

First Published in 2023

**Olympia Publishers
Tallis House
2 Tallis Street
London
EC4Y 0AB**

Printed in Great Britain

Dedication

Dedicated to Robina Walling, née Thorburn
30.07.1892 – 01.12.1964
and her beloved daughter, Ella Fair Walling
16.02.1919 – 18.10.1921
who died and was buried in Cork, Ireland.

And to my youngest son William Thorburn How
Who bravely fought leukaemia for eighteen months,
But sadly, passed away peacefully at home.
03.02.1975 – 24.05.2022

Prologue

Dublin, 1905

"Killian, you're not going off on that boat with shoes covered in mud! Killian, get back here."

"Ma, they'll be dirty again before I get down the lane."

"Bye, ma. Killian, come on, we'll miss the boat."

Brandon and Ronan sprinted off down the lane ahead of Killian, and sure enough their boots were soon clogged with mire.

"Killian, come on."

The wonderful smell of the Irish countryside was something the three boys knew they were going to miss over the coming months spent working on the arable pastures of Scotland.

The season would be challenging but by the end of the summer the yields would be harvested and new crops planted, and the boys would have some much-needed money in their pockets to share with their family.

"Ronan, where are you off to?"

"Ah no, it's Cara, she's mad in love with you, Ronan."

Cara, with her long, dark hair and bright blue eyes, ran towards the boys like a young filly, her long ponytail swishing behind her. She was a child but on the brink of adolescence, shy but pushed by a desire to befriend Ronan.

Ronan blushed, knowing his brothers were not wrong in respect of her feelings towards him. They elbowed him and roughed up his hair, moving off, leaving him to say his goodbyes. Cara had shown him so much attention over the past few months it was embarrassing. He was glad to be getting away, but he didn't have a bad bone in his body so felt obliged to acknowledge her. Being the youngest of the three brothers, his interest in the opposite sex was slightly puerile. He was especially shy to have to speak to Cara in front of his older brothers, who he knew were certainly not naïve when it came to the art of seduction.

"Go on, Ronan, give her a quick kiss and we'll be on our way."

Brandon was always the one to tease.

Ronan's blush intensified as he faced Cara with a slight discomfort in the pit of his stomach, hoping fervently that she would not expect a kiss.

"We're off to the Scottish Borders for the season. I'll see you when I get back." He turned to follow his brothers but Cara touched his arm.

"Ronan, will you write?"

"I'll try, Cara, but we'll be mad busy."

With a less than enthusiastic farewell, he raced after his brothers without a backward glance, leaving Cara to stare dolefully after him.

The docks at Dublin were, as expected, crowded and bustling with the noise from horse-drawn carts, angry young men and livestock ready to be transported to England. Ships were being loaded and unloaded whilst young boys in caps ran errands for anybody offering a tip. The brothers were jostled and cussed at but managed to find the *S.S. Kilkenny* and board straight away.

The steam ship was two hundred and seventy feet long with bunks below for the first-class passengers and below that room for the transportation of cattle to the docks at Liverpool. The boys however would stay on deck, seated under the tall funnel that already spewed out smoke. The weather was mild enough, and preferring their own company they would mull over their anticipated adventures whilst appreciating the sea air.

Their spirits were high and their banter loud as they watched the crew prepare to sail. The ship sat upon the River Liffey, which separated the north from the south of Dublin before opening out into the Irish sea with its fickle reputation for churning waters and high winds.

As they sat, relieving their boots of the clogging mud they had accumulated along the way, they planned their journey from Liverpool to Berwickshire, which in itself would be an adventure. They fantasised about all the girls they hoped to meet along the way and the nourishing food that they would enjoy over the coming months on the farm, for their Irish diet did not fulfil their expectations of a hearty meal.

Suddenly they became aware of a commotion, with people pointing towards a barge progressing slowly towards them with its stern low in the water. On top of the open flatboat, wooden kegs of ale, which they assumed was Guinness, rolled and collided with each other precariously, the odd one slipping overboard. *The Vartry*, owned by Guinness, was in serious trouble. The one-man crew was seen to be making a valiant attempt to steady his vessel, securing the wayward kegs and adjusting his course, but to no avail.

The barge suddenly veered to starboard, the icy waters of the Liffey pouring over the gunnels, flooding the hold below. Now, recognisably beyond help, the boys watched transfixed, as *The Vartry* slipped unceremoniously beneath the murky waters of the river. The barrels were left bobbing up and down around the frantic bargeman, whose arms were now flailing in the air as the water threatened to engulf him. The turning tide, which would interfere with any rescue attempt, began to take the kegs filled with ale slowly and indifferently upstream from whence they had come.

The barge had sunk within minutes. The boys, as well as the onlookers, were powerless and could do nothing but spectate. Captain Jones of the *S.S. Kilkenny* however, who had seen the disaster unfold, leapt into action, ordering lifeboats to be lowered to pick up the desperate man and as much of his cargo as was possible. A cheer from the docks went up and caps were flung into the air as the shaken bargeman was hauled, drenched and dripping, into a lifeboat. The wayward barrels however made a leisurely escape upriver and were mostly left to their own devices. The boys soaked up the spectacle, which would be their last memory of Dublin before setting foot on English soil.

Chapter 1

Milldown

Although there was a chill in the air and a gentle drizzle was descending on the land around the farm, inside the kitchen was warm and the smells enticing. A large pot stood on the range with a simmering pea and ham soup that slowly bubbled and thickened, the huge bone having been split to intensify the flavour. Fresh bread was taken out of the stove straight to the table in readiness for the imminent arrival of the boys.

Each spring, labourers from Ireland or the Hebrides would arrive at Milldown to help with the manual work involved in the running of the farm, in return for their keep and a handsome handshake at the end of the season. The work involved long hours in tough conditions, cultivating the land before planting corn, oats and other crops. The invaluable team of muscular draft horses ploughed, pulled wagons and hauled manure.

Large barns stored hay, housed the milking cattle and other animals and also the farm equipment. The brick- built barns were numerous, serving three hundred and sixty-five acres of mostly arable land. They were built running downhill towards the mill pond, where chickens and geese ran freely, their noise a constant reminder that this was farming country. As on any farm however, animal husbandry was not always without tragedy.

"Ellie, put another loaf in the oven, and Beanie, go and see if your father is all right; he's been up all night with Queenie."

"Okay, mum."

Queenie, one of their draft horses that worked the land, had developed a wound on her withers where her harness had rubbed a sore. Beanie had administered several soap and sugar poultices to draw the infection but the horse had made no improvement over the past few days. In fact, her condition had worsened overnight: her neck and jaw seemed to have stiffened and she shuddered if you touched her. Her ears stood erect and she had begun to sweat. The light chestnut hair had darkened with perspiration over her flanks, whilst the white flash down her face looked dull and grey.

"How is Queenie, Dad?"

"She's not good, Beanie. I'll go and call the vet; you stay with her."

Beanie seemed to have a connection with all the animals. She understood what her mother called "the way of the world", in that farm animals were reared for food and had to be slaughtered, but as long as they were treated with respect and kindness during their lifetime, she was okay with that.

Queenie however was not, in Beanie's eyes, to be tarred with the same brush. Beanie stroked the neck of her favourite horse and whispered to her, looking into her large brown eyes, at the same time noticing the stiffness in her tail, her strange stance and the onset of laboured breathing. Tears filled her eyes, as deep inside she knew that this horse, who had been so hard-working and mild-mannered during her lifetime, was not going to survive. She accused herself of not doing enough, not changing the poultices often enough or giving over as much time to care for her as she should have done.

As Beanie comforted the mare, she heard raucous laughter outside which filled her with a deep resentment, thinking the disturbance disrespectful to her horse. She left the stable quietly to confront the three offending boys.

"Keep your voices down; there's a sick horse in here. Go into the kitchen, my mother's expecting you."

Her tone was intimidating, so Killian and Brandon skulked off to the farm kitchen. However, Ronan followed Beanie back into the barn. Beanie couldn't bring herself to speak to the boy but allowed him to caress the horse's neck. He stood directly in front of Queenie, blowing softly onto her muzzle whilst holding her head steady. The horse stood still; her breathing seemed to relax slightly and Beanie's temper subsided.

"You have a way with horses."

"I always have." He was not bragging, simply stating a fact. He examined the sore on the horse's shoulder and questioned Beanie about the progression of the infection.

"I'm no expert, but I think your horse has tetanus. I've seen the same back home; I'm so sorry."

Ronan looked genuinely concerned by the condition of the horse but also had a sympathetic eye for Beanie.

"You're doing a fine job comforting her. Is she going to see a vet?"

Beanie was fighting back tears and had to look away, allowing herself to dry her eyes and nose. She sniffed loudly but retained her composure.

"Yes, my father has gone to call him."

"Do you want me to stay with the horse?" asked Ronan. "I think there's no doubt she'll be put down. It'll be harsh for you to watch; I'd gladly stay."

Beanie really appreciated the offer but felt she would be letting Queenie down if she wasn't there for her at the end.

"I'll stay. You must be starving. Go along, there's food for you in the kitchen."

"I'd rather stay, if it's all right with you."

Beanie reluctantly conceded, looking directly at Ronan for the first time. He was young, with untamed hair and had a roguish ruggedness about him that Beanie found attractive.

The smell in the barn was sweet and fresh. The horse had a thick layer of straw underneath her and a hay bag hanging, sadly untouched. The rug she was so used to hung loosely over her back and haunches. The open barn door allowed the smell from the fields and sea to waft through, so Queenie was at ease with her surroundings. Ronan continued to whisper to the mare, whose eyes became heavy as if she were getting sleepy and her head and neck dropped. Beanie wondered how this boy, who knew nothing of her horse's nature, could have such a calming effect on her. She noticed his hands, broad and chafed, obviously used to manual work, but now so tender.

"Robina." Her father's voice startled her and she jumped. "The vet is on his way; your mother needs you in the kitchen."

Beanie's father came into the barn, his stride purposeful, making her stomach churn at the thought of the vet coming and the consequences of his visit. She did as she was told, however, but assured Ronan that she would be back soon to take over from him.

When Beanie had gone from the stable back to the kitchen, her father told Ronan that the vet would not in fact be coming, as he was carrying out an emergency caesarean section on one of the hogs on a neighbouring farm. This meant the kindest thing to do was to shoot the horse. Beanie's father was as distressed as Beanie but had been forced to shoot animals before and was capable of doing it quickly and humanely. The horse's nostrils had become dilated and her breathing now increasingly rapid.

She was going into respiratory failure, so the sooner he could end her life, the better.

In the kitchen the boys were tucking into their bread and soup, unaware of the tragedy unfolding outside. Beanie's mother Helen asked Beanie to go and check on their lodgings, as the boys would need a rest after their long journey. Work could start in the morning.

"Take towels and sheets and make sure a fire is lit. Thank you, darling."

Beanie wondered why her sister Maggie couldn't have done that particular chore, as she was just chatting away to the boys. However, Beanie grabbed some towels and sheets and was about to go to the lower floor when a gunshot cracked through the air. She dropped everything and collapsed, kneeling on the floor in front of the press, head in hands. There was no doubt as to what had just happened. Her father had wanted to spare her the agony of seeing the horse shot.

Rushing back through into the kitchen, she was brought to a sudden standstill as all eyes focused on her. She was bewildered, not knowing whether to sob or scream in anger. Her mind was made up for her as Ronan entered the kitchen, looking extremely solemn.

"I told you I would be back. She's dead, isn't she?" yelled Beanie.

Ronan froze as the accusations came flying at him. Beanie was distraught, not knowing where else to vent her unleashed emotions.

"Robina, go to your room."

Her mother, shocked at the outburst and embarrassed by Beanie's behaviour, made it quite clear that she was to leave the kitchen immediately.

"Sit down, Ronan. She's upset. Here, have some soup; help yourself to bread."

Ronan's face was red and he was unable to speak or eat, for that matter. His brothers tried to lift the atmosphere but failed miserably, as no one had anything to say. The boys finished eating, voiced their appreciation and made their apologies for leaving. Beanie's father, who had returned to the kitchen, offered the boys a dram of malt whiskey but they declined. They went to their rooms, upset and morose, thinking that the months ahead of them were in no way going to be the fun summer days that they had looked forward to for so long.

Chapter 2

Milldown

Milldown Farm was situated at the head of the dramatic natural gorge of Milldown Burn, overlooking Coldingham Bay. Col Mill, lower down the cliff, was supplied by the burn, which in turn was regulated by the sluice gates at Mill Dam. The working mill itself was on three floors. The upper floor, or bin floor, housed rows of sacks containing customers' grain waiting to pass down to the second floor through the hoppers to the millstone below. The freshly milled meal was then stored on the ground floor, ready for Mr. Jamieson the miller to receive his patrons. Adjacent to the mill was the large granary store.

Several of the young men from the village and from Milldown cottages either worked on the farm itself or helped Mr. Jamieson at the mill.

"Have you seen Beanie today?" asked one of the lads who had a crush on her.

"Aye, she's been down here. I think she's gone to the bay to collect the rent from the beach huts."

"Thanks, Mr. Jamieson. I'll pop down and see her."

"Don't you be long now; there's sacks to be filled and the yard wants sweeping."

Andrew ran off with a leap and a bound, happy in the knowledge that he was going to see his Beanie. He saw her in the distance, walking slowly to one of the beach huts on the far side of the bay. Seagulls screeching overhead and waves crashing on the shore made it futile to shout. Stooping to tie his lace, he looked up to see a young lad strolling down the path towards Beanie. He stayed low to the sand as he watched the boy catch up to Beanie and they started talking. Beanie stood back defensively from the youth, who was a good head and shoulders taller than her, causing Andrew to wonder what they had to say to each other. He saw Beanie shake her head and move still further away, making him think that maybe he should intervene. However, he decided to leave them and reluctantly returned to the mill.

"Beanie, I'm so sorry about your horse. I never would have taken your place, but your father acted quickly and was adamant he didn't want you there."

"Well, you should have come to get me anyway. What stopped you?" Her voice was loud and deliberately provocative.

As soon as the words were out of her mouth, Beanie knew that she had let herself down again. She blushed and turned away, slightly ashamed of her own conduct, but by the time she looked back, Ronan was sauntering back up the path to the farm, leaving Beanie once again with tears in her eyes.

Beanie sluggishly followed Ronan but not before stopping off to have a word with her brother John, who was tilling in the lower field. His two horses obediently dragged the heavy plough behind them, building up a sweat. Flocks of gulls screeching above were landing in the deep furrows for the newly exposed food on offer.

"Beanie, I've got such a thirst. Would you go and fetch some water, please?"

"Oh, you're always thirsty, John, get it yourself."

John's face fell but Beanie rescinded and with a smile as if she had been joking, which she hadn't, went up to the farm to get John a drink and a snack.

"Mother, I'm a bit worried about John; he's got an unquenchable thirst."

"He's doing hard work, Beanie, that's all."

"I think there's more to it than that. He's complaining about other things too, like tingly fingers, and he thinks he may need spectacles."

"Ah, Beanie, don't fret. Take the boys their lunch for me. I've put bread, cold meat and cheeses in the basket. Could you put some apples in there too?"

Beanie did what was asked of her, reluctantly taking the food to each of the boys in turn. When it came to Ronan however, her nerves were jittery, but he had an infectious smile and a glint in his bright blue eyes that almost made her blush.

"So, you're talking to me now, are you, Beanie?"

Thankfully Ronan had a big heart and was not planning on making life difficult for her. She handed him the contents of the basket and teasingly told him that his skills at muck spreading left much to be desired.

Over the following weeks, Beanie and Ronan became good friends and both indulged in a mild flirtation. They both preferred to work with the livestock, so their working hours coincided. They were up early feeding the horses and cattle and mucking out stables and barns. Eggs had to be gathered and the chickens tended to. They worked well as a team. It fell upon Killian and Brandon to work mostly on the land alongside John. With the division of labour settled, the farm began to run efficiently once more, the weather improving daily.

The boys spread compost on the fallow fields to aid spring growth, which would be cut later for silage. A large silo stood in the farmyard to store the damp grass which would be left to ferment to feed the cattle in their pens over the autumn and winter. The fermentation process was accelerated by adding molasses which also acted as a preservative. This was Ronan's job today whilst Brandon and Killian were planting potatoes, a job they were well used to!

Back at the farm that evening, the meal went without issue. The boys were jovial and Beanie and her sisters took great pleasure in teasing the Irish lads. John however looked tired and troubled.

"Are you all right, John? You're looking a little peaky."

"I'm okay, mum, I just need an early night. Can you pass the water, please?"

As Mrs. Thorburn passed the jug of water to her son, she exchanged glances with Beanie. His thirst had certainly increased and he was constantly excusing himself to go to the privy. They all left the table and went outside, as the evening was mild, but John went to his room. Brandon also went to his room but returned with his fiddle in rare good humour. He started to play, strumming the instrument and stamping his foot. The music was lively and the girls found it hilarious. They were all larking around when Andrew appeared with a fierce look on his face. Beanie had known Andrew since childhood, never much caring for him, and she didn't appreciate this uncompromising young man strutting up to the farm now and spoiling the atmosphere.

"Beanie, can I have a word?"

Beanie was reluctant to give him the time of day but she was aware that he had a crush on her, so walked over and stood before him.

"Beanie, you shouldn't be hanging around with these paddys; you'll get yourself a bad reputation. They're no better than tinkers. I saw you on the beach today, and I wasn't the only one."

"You weren't the only one who saw what, exactly?"

"You two on the beach."

"Ronan and I exchanged pleasantries. What else do you think you saw?"

Andrew was beginning to get the gist that he was not going to be able to put Beanie in her place.

"I don't appreciate this lecture, Andrew. You have no right to speak about our farm hands like that, and you certainly have no right to insinuate any misbehaviour on my part."

Beanie turned her back but Andrew followed. The music had stopped and the group were, without exception, looking towards Beanie. Andrew reached her and swung her around by her arm. She was livid, being shown up like this in front of her siblings.

Ronan stepped forward, seeing Beanie in an awkward situation, and having heard the comment about he and his brothers being tinkers, was understandably infuriated. Beanie knew Andrew was a fit, well-built youth and had heard rumours of him inciting brawls in the village, so was reluctant for Ronan to confront him. Ronan's brothers however seemed to have conspiratorial smiles on their faces.

"Andy, is it?" Ronan stepped closer. "Do you have a problem with any of us here?" Ronan spoke respectfully with no hint of intimidation, calmly waiting for a response.

Beanie stepped forward to intercede, but before she could utter a word, Andrew had thrown a punch which was swiftly blocked by Ronan, who remained expressionless. Brandon and Killian stood back, arms folded, with no intention of interfering.

"Killian, Brandon, please don't let them fight." Beanie's plea fell on deaf ears.

Ronan stood calmly, seemingly without a care in the world, making the spectators wonder what exactly his game was. Andrew's face was red by now and perspiring, but he had started this confrontation and would have to finish it if he didn't want to lose face. He certainly had no trouble in the village getting the better of the would-be local heroes but there was something about this Irish lad that he didn't like the look of. He threw another punch with as much force as he could muster but it was blocked as swiftly as before.

"Finish it, Ronan."

Killian had a smirk on his face that Beanie thought hid a sinister threat.

Although Andrew was an ass, she got the feeling that things were getting slightly out of hand and felt somewhat concerned.

The whole stand-off had only taken a matter of seconds but to the onlookers it had seemed longer. However, it was all to come to a very swift end. Ronan did nothing more than effortlessly throw a lightning punch to Andy's jaw and he crumpled like a sack of potatoes.

Beanie had no desire to rush to his aid, so Ellie and Maggie did the honours. Beanie went to Brandon and asked him to take Ronan and Killian inside. She went back to speak to Andrew, who was by now sitting up with the help of Ellie.

"Andrew, was that really necessary? Please don't come up to Milldown in the near future unless it is to apologise."

With that she turned her back and left Ellie to help Andrew to his feet. The boys were in the kitchen with Beanie's father William, getting an unembellished lecture on the reasons why not to resort to violence. However, when Beanie explained that it was definitely in self-defence and also defending her honour, the whiskey came out of the cupboard and a large dram was poured for each of the boys, which this time they did not refuse. The boys did not reveal however, that Ronan held the lightweight boxing championship title in his home county of Wicklow. He was also involved in illegal fist-fighting, which was commonplace in the country villages of Ireland, and he had earned himself quite a nice little nest egg from the sport.

Chapter 3

Wicklow

Wicklow, just forty-two kilometres south of Dublin, was known as the garden of Ireland. The surrounding countryside, with rolling mountains, pristine beaches and forested areas, was a glorious place to live. However, when you had nine siblings, as Cara did, there was never an occasion put aside for frivolous activities. Life was hard. Her father, a postman, did well to keep a roof over their heads, but each member of the family had to contribute in some way if they were able, merely to exist.

Cara, the eldest, was coming up to fifteen and had been placed into service; she was to start the following Monday. She was a sweet girl and was a great help, taking some of the pressure off her mother in the raising of her younger siblings, but now her leaving home was in some ways a blessing. It meant one child successfully reaching adulthood, one less mouth to feed and some money brought home at the end of each week.

"Cara, darling, have you packed your bag already?"

"Yes, Mum, just a few shifts and a shirt."

"Have you packed enough raggedy cloths?"

Her mother meant, had she enough rags for when it was her time of the month. When there were that many girls in the house, a bucket was always kept in the privy to soak rags in salt water, ready to be washed and dried for re-use.

"Yes, Mum, I can look after myself."

"I know you can, my darling. I'll miss you, for sure I will."

Cara kissed her mother's cheek, unable to miss the look of exhaustion on her face.

"What is it, Mum? You're looking tired; are you all right?"

"I'm fine, my darling, just, I think there's another bairn on the way."

"Oh, Mother, what will you do? You can barely cope now."

"I suggested putting it to nurse but your father won't hear of it. I could just about afford to pay someone to take it off my hands if you helped a bit with your wages, but your father says we'll manage; we always do."

"I'm sorry, Mother. I'll help as much as I can."

Cara felt miserable and the weather certainly didn't help. The heavens had opened, churning up mud, splattering the house and damaging some of the precious vegetables growing out back. The chickens, bedraggled and cold, went to their coup for shelter. Flint, the dog, sprawled on top of a large bale of straw in the barn where they kept the milking cow. Large puddles started to accumulate in the yard outside and the water butt overflowed. Sheep could be heard bleating their disapproval whilst the river beyond was flowing frantically, the level rising by the minute.

Usually, the River Dargle was a playground for children and dogs alike, but today the speed at which it was flowing made it treacherous. The rain pounding on the roof tiles and lashing against the windows was frightening the younger children; even Cara was beginning to worry. Her father was not yet home and the sky had darkened, creating a foreboding atmosphere in the house.

Cara and her mother repeatedly crossed over to the window to watch the storm and to look for Cara's father, Mick, but there was no sign of him. By now the noise of the Dargle was intense, smashing against rocks with increasing ferocity, carrying debris in its wake.

"I don't like the look of this, Cara. Take the children upstairs and read to them."

But before Cara could muster her siblings, an old apple tree in the yard split noisily and fell across the chicken coup. A flurry of feathers shot out of the coup, followed by the fowl, which sprinted off in all directions, squawking and flapping their wings, their spindly legs splayed, trying to avoid the larger puddles.

"Holy Mary, Mother of God!" Cara's mother was as fearful as the rest of them, herding them all up the stairs as fast as she could. From the upstairs window she could see the Dargle suddenly breach its banks, sweeping old Mrs. O'Donnell's house into the water. The house slid down the bank, boulders preventing it from becoming completely submerged or drifting off downstream. They prayed that the old woman had made it to safety as water flooded the ground floor. The noise from the storm did nothing to block out the screaming from the children, who were terrified, not really knowing why, but their fear was contagious. Conor, snatching a book from Liam, sent him flying off the bed to bang his head on the dresser, adding to the overwhelming sense of distress in the room.

The water had now reached the top of the Dargle bridge, making it perilously unstable. However, Cara's father appeared on the other side and looked like he was going to attempt a crossing. Cara's mother, Mary Ellen, began to pray fervently, making the sign of the cross over and over again at the sight of her husband in such a hazardous situation. He slipped stepping onto the bridge, then warily placed one foot in front of the other whilst edging slowly forward, holding tightly onto the slippery rail with both hands.

Spray from the torrent soaked him to the skin in seconds. They could see him looking at the sunken house and hoped he wouldn't try to be a hero and go in after Mrs. O'Donnell, but he did just that. Stepping off the bridge with the utmost care, he made his way down the bank to the upstairs window of the stricken house. They watched him bang loudly on the window then smash a pane of glass with his elbow. Calling inside, he seemed to be satisfied that the house was empty so began his ascent, using fallen branches to cling on to. He had just managed to scramble back up when, with a wrenching, splitting noise, the bridge gave way.

Reaching his house, he burst through the front door, kicked off his boots and flung his coat to the floor, then raced upstairs to check on his family. His eyes, blurred from the water dripping from his hair, scrutinised his children. They were all accounted for. His wife fell into his arms and he held her tightly whilst smiling at his precious children. The boys with ruddy cheeks and runny noses, the girls poorly dressed with dishevelled hair, all looking up to him for direction. His heart, still pounding from his exertion, was full of pride and thankfulness. His wife, with hands on his warm, strong chest, relaxed into his embrace; he was her life and soul.

It was the first time that Mick had noticed the frailty of his wife's body. Once so firm and shapely, it now seemed delicate, without substance. He looked into her eyes and the expression he saw looking back at him was almost ethereal. The children had taken their toll on her body; she looked so much older than her years.

"Come on now, let's all have a nice, warm cup of tea. We're all safe; now mind your mother and let's get you all downstairs."

He moved to follow the children but as he did so his wife

collapsed.

"Mary, Mary Ellen! Oh God; Cara, can you help me get your mother onto the bed?"

The children started wailing again but were mostly ignored, except for Liam, who was still holding his head after the bump, his nose streaming, his sleeve in full use as a handkerchief. Cara helped her mother onto the calico-and-straw mattress then covered her with a thick, rough blanket before picking Liam up and comforting him. The younger ones tried to get on the bed with their mother but were turned away by their father, who herded them out of the bedroom and down the stairs.

The woozy feeling that Mary Ellen was experiencing slowly subsided and her vision started to correct itself. The sickness and the high-pitch buzzing in her ears that had overwhelmed her initially however, persisted.

"Mick. Mick, are you there? Can you see to the children? I'll be all right in a minute." She spoke to an empty room, aware of the quick, light beating of her heart.

It was not the first time that Mary Ellen had fainted recently and Mick was becoming concerned.

"Cara, take your mother the tea. I'll give the children some bread and dripping to tide them over."

That night Mary Ellen lost the child that she had been carrying so begrudgingly. She prayed over and over again for forgiveness, believing herself to be a sinner. For the feeling of relief that had flooded over her when the lifeless foetus had slithered from her body was absolute.

It was the last prayer that Mary Ellen ever prayed, for she passed away the following evening in Mick's arms. The doctor wrote "postpartum complications" on the death certificate, but Cara knew that her poor mother's frail body had given up every essence of her being to nurture her children. She had never been robust.

Cara's engagement as scullery maid was terminated, as she now had to step into her mother's shoes to take on the responsibility of caring for her nine siblings. Her father was inconsolable and started to drink heavily every evening, becoming withdrawn and uncommunicative, putting his job at risk. The priest, who visited regularly, was unable to bring peace to the household through sermon or through prayer. Life had grown even darker.

Chapter 4

Milldown

Mondays at Milldown were always busy and the boys were up early. The majority of the animals had been fed or turned out and the stables had been cleaned by the time Mr. Thorburn suggested that they take the trap into Duns. They had to pick up supplies and maybe check out a Shire horse that was for sale nearby. After the death of Queenie, they were short of a working horse and a Shire would be a good addition to the team. Killian and Ronan volunteered to go with Mr. Thorburn, or Will, as he wanted to be called, to check out the new horse, whilst Brandon said he would help John, who was still working in the lower fields. They set off in the trap, taking the scenic route across the cliff top, Dandy the pony picking up a brisk trot.

Out to sea, the charismatic St. Ives luggers seemed to glide effortlessly into view across the choppy waters of the North Sea, nets cast to scoop up the inexhaustible supply of herring. The luggers, with their distinctive rust-coloured sails and gaff rigging, followed the herring shoals, circumnavigating the shores of Britain until their capacity was reached and the barrels of salted herring were unloaded at Lowestoft. Only then could they make their way back home to Cornwall to their loved ones, carrying presents for the children, a stick of rock perhaps or a small toy from a far-off place.

Beanie always looked forward to their arrival off St. Abbs

Head, knowing that their women folk, who followed the trawlers, would be waiting in Eyemouth to start gutting, salting and packing the catch into barrels. In previous years, Beanie had gone down to the harbour to chat to the vibrant hard-working women who waited patiently for the boats to come in before they could start their work.

Whilst they waited, they would be constantly knitting for themselves and for their men folk. Jumpers were knitted in a tube on several needles supported by a belt at their waist. The arms were knitted on last so that when they were worn out, they could easily be replaced. Patterns were handed down from mother to daughter, each child proficient at knitting by the age of five. New patterns were learnt from remote villages, causing rivalry and one-upmanship amongst the knitters.

Before the gutting began, the women would wrap their fingers in rags, or clooties, as they were called, to protect themselves from cuts from the sharp gutting knives. Cuts made painful by the salt were commonplace and infections could put an end to a working season. Each woman was able to gut and pack thirty to fifty herring a minute. This year was to be no exception, the boats on the horizon heralding their arrival.

"Mother, I'm going into Eyemouth. Would you ask one of the boys to come and pick me up when they get back from Duns?"

"Ay, I will. Could you see if Uncle Ralph has a haddock or turbot for me, please? I'll make a nice fish pie."

"Yes, mother. It will be nice to see Uncle Ralph."

Beanie set off across the fields towards Eyemouth. It was a fair jaunt, but the sea breeze was cooling and the familiar paths always a pleasure to walk. She looked out to sea and thought that there was no place on earth that she would rather be.

Small trawlers coming out of St Abbs' harbour mingled with the Cornish luggers amicably, each going about their day's work knowing that there were fish aplenty for all. Uncle Ralph, a local fisherman for the past thirty-five years, was amongst them and Beanie knew that she would be given the pick of his catch, whether it be turbot, haddock, cod, crab or lobster. The herring, or silver darlings as they were known, were left for the barrels. The majority of the cod, however, was sent by wagon up to Edinburgh to be sold at the markets there. Her good mood changed, however, the instant she saw Andrew coming along the path towards her.

"Beanie, how are you? We've missed you down in the village. What have you been up to?"

Beanie knew the question was innocent enough but thought that what she had been up to was no business of his.

"I've been up to nothing in particular. How about you?"

Punched anyone recently, she thought, but did not voice her musings.

"I've just been down to the beach. Would you like to take a walk with me?"

"Oh, I'm sorry, Andrew, I'm off to meet my uncle, can't stop."

Andrew's heart sank. It was clear by the way she flounced off that there was no future there. Never mind, he thought, there were plenty more fish in the sea, and Ellie had been quite attentive when that Irish gypsy had landed him a punch. There was no doubt in his mind that Ronan hadn't heard the last of that little fiasco, but that would have to wait. The question was, should he go straight up to the farm to seek out Ellie or bide his time?

Eyemouth was buzzing. The docks were lined with barrels

and farlins, into which the herring would be poured ready for the gutting process to begin. Large tubs of salt were awaiting the gutted fish after they had been graded. The packers would rouse the fish – that is, turn them in the salt time and time again before packing them tightly into the barrels, ready for transportation. It would be the packer's job to cook breakfast and lunch for the girls, whose hands remained wrapped in clooties, their oilskin aprons covered in guts and scales. The girls also put salt on their hands to get a grip on the slippery fish, increasing the risk of painful damage to their palms and fingers.

When Beanie eventually arrived at Eyemouth, the women belonging to the boats were idly waiting for the next luggers to sail in with their catch. Once the catch was landed, Beanie would stand no chance of chatting to her friend, as their work was fast and furious. The noise of their chatter and the screeching of the gulls was intoxicating as she took in the raucous atmosphere and greeted some familiar faces. She was looking out for one in particular: a young girl of similar age to herself, maybe sixteen or seventeen, who had been working in Eyemouth for the last two seasons and whom Beanie had befriended.

"Have you seen Nessa?" she asked a ruddy-faced older woman dressed in the familiar short-sleeved top, striped long skirt and oilskin apron.

"She's down by the last farlin, my darling, see, she's wearing a dark blue head scarf." Her sing-song voice made Beanie smile; however hard they worked and under such laborious conditions, these Cornish women always seemed to be happy.

"Nessa!" Beanie shouted, walking towards her friend and exchanging a hug.

Nessa fortunately hadn't yet started gutting so was clean and fresh. They knew they didn't have long, as three luggers were gliding towards the dock.

"Nessa, how are you? Are you still seeing Peter?"

"No, don't mention that name. I'm seeing one of the lads on *The Mist of Morwenna*. The lugger coming in now – see him waving? James is his name. He is quite as tall and handsome as your brother John; I've been seeing him for some time now. How is John, by the way? I had my eye on him not so long ago."

"Oh, I don't think he is well, but my mother keeps brushing it under the rug. You'll see him next weekend. I was thinking of having another ceilidh in one of the barns next Sunday, if you and some friends would like to come up to the farm?"

The young Cornishmen had good voices and plenty of sea shanties to sing if there was a beer in their hands. It made for a good party, a tradition Beanie had started a couple of years ago, with the consent of her father, who provided the beer.

"That will be great, Beanie. We've a hard week ahead of us, so we'll be ready for a shindig. Are you seeing a lad?"

Before they could catch up with one another, one of the luggers docked beside Beanie, and the skipper started to empty the quarter cran baskets directly into the huge wooden farlin in front of Nessa. Beanie felt quite squeamish seeing the shiny silver fish slide from the basket, some of which were still twitching, their mouths wide open, gasping for a last intake of air.

The awaiting women instantly crowded round and started gutting the fish with their futtles, the gutting knifes, grading them by sight and tossing them into the relevant tubs for rousing. The packers stood by, ready to do their job, which, if done properly would protect the salted fish from any movement that could cause damage during transportation. Beanie stood watching in amazement as the mound of shiny silver darlings was processed, gulls screeching above, hoping for a morsel, although even the guts were barrelled for use as fertiliser on the fields.

She knew that there would be no time for more chatter so left her friend Nessa in search of Uncle Ralph. He was further along the harbour wall, next to a stack of empty lobster pots. Rugged and red-faced, he greeted Beanie with a cold, wet, salty kiss on the cheek. His strong forearms and broad hands were working nimbly with his nets, mending a hole and getting rid of the detritus caught in them as he leant leisurely against the harbour wall.

"Take what you will, lassie. I expect your mother is waiting for the pick of the catch."

"Ay, she is that. What's on offer?"

"There're two nice haddock you can have. Now be on your way; I've no time for chitter-chatter."

With a wink and a smile, he wrapped the fish in paper and sent Beanie on her way. Scottish men seemed to have no time for small talk.

She left the harbour, taking the road up to the cliff path, daydreaming as she walked, head down, as the incline was steep.

"Beanie." A shout from the path ahead made her glance up and to her surprise she saw Ronan, bareback on top of a huge black Shire horse, at least seventeen hands tall and very handsome, with white feathered hocks, huge bright eyes and a white muzzle. He tossed his head, acknowledging Beanie. His huge hooves, polished and well shod, stomped precariously close to Beanie's unprotected feet.

"Ronan, who is this?"

"This is Captain, your new Shire horse. Your father asked me to try him out. We found a bridle to fit but no saddle with a large enough girth."

Beanie couldn't help but laugh at the sight.

"Come up here, Beanie. I'll give you a ride back home."

Ronan indicated the dry stone wall for her to climb onto so that she could mount the horse behind him. She had absolutely no fear when it came to riding horses, bareback or saddled. She was used to both but felt more than a little uneasy hopping up behind Ronan. She did what was asked of her, however, with a mischievous smile, clinging onto the fish whilst mounting the colossal horse.

"Walk on, Captain." The horse obeyed, suffering no encumbrance from the weight on his back. He walked with a rolling gait, but with such a broad back, the two riders were balanced and relaxed.

"Beanie, we haven't had time to chat lately. We've been fierce busy, but I wanted to tell you that I've had a letter from back home. There's been a serious flood in Wicklow. My mother's house is okay, but farmsteads locally have been devastated. Your father has given me permission to take two weeks off to help with the clean-up. I'm the one who has volunteered, not my brothers, as I have another reason to go home. I have a ticket to a boxing match at The Theatre Royal Dublin. My trainer bought the ticket for me and I'd surely love to go. Tommy Burns will be fighting Jem Roche for the World Heavyweight title."

If the names were meant to mean anything to Beanie, they didn't.

"I'm not going for a week, so I can help with the best part of the harvesting. Will you be missing me at all?"

Beanie, clinging onto Ronan with her one free hand, thought about the question before answering and surprised herself by her response.

"Well, Ronan," she said, smiling, a twinkle in her eye, "I think I will."

"I was hoping you would say that, Beanie. Walk on, Captain."

Chapter 5

Milldown

The work on the farm was now intense and involved everybody in different ways. The wheat and barley were being cut and tied into sheaves, the grain stalks being placed so as to keep the grain heads off the ground whilst still in the fields prior to collection for threshing. The sheaves were assembled into stooks and scattered round the arable pastures to dry for several days, weather permitting. Lush grasses were cut, moist with sea spray, ready to be taken by horse-drawn wagons to the silo.

Preparations in the lower fields continued, making ready the pastures for planting the next batch of cereal crops. John was drilling one of the last fields, ready for sowing the winter wheat and barley. His two strong horses pulling the plough kept their pace as John lost his footing and stumbled.

"John, let me take over for a while, will you?" Brandon shouted.

He had seen John lose his balance and knew something was wrong. He ran briskly across the furrows and caught up to John, instantly noticing the stream of perspiration running down his brow from underneath his flat cap.

"John, let me finish up here. You haven't had a break all day, man."

John didn't look pleased that his awkwardness had been noticed but thanked Brandon and walked off up to the farm, going straight to the kitchen sink to quench his thirst.

"John, darling, I'm going to call Dr. Murray. There's no denying that something is not right with you."

"I'm all right, Mother. My age is catching up with me, that's all."

John, the eldest of Helen and William's four children by ten years, was still a young man, next in line to run the farm. He was quite insular, not courting a young lady as one would have expected of a man in his late twenties. Being reserved, he liked his own company, always happiest out in the fields with the horses.

"I'll go to my room, Ma, don't fuss. I'll just rest a while."

Helen was not content to let this go another day so made a call to Dr. Murray, who promised a home visit soon.

Captain turned out to be a true character. He was visibly happy at all times, pleased to be harnessed and put to work. He integrated with the other farm horses and pulled his weight with obvious pleasure. It was Ronan's job to teach him the ropes. This was a job which came as second nature to him, as Ronan had a strong passion for horses and worked with them back home.

To reward Captain for his hard work, Ronan got into the habit of riding him bareback each evening down to the beach. Captain loved nothing more than trotting along the shoreline in the cool of the evening, scattering the gulls and bobbing his head to the odd dog that had come down to the beach for the same purpose. Beanie would often accompany Ronan, perching herself up behind him, enjoying the respite from work and also the chance to be alone and close to Ronan. They had become the best of friends, working in the stables together a lot of the time, for it was Beanie's job to oversee the horses, their tack and harnesses and also their feed. Ronan would keep the farm equipment in good working order.

It was after a ride along the shore that Beanie and Ronan returned to the farm and saw Dr. Murray's two-cylinder Model F Ford car parked in front of the main steps leading up to the front door of Milldown. The front door only being used on special occasions made Beanie wonder if something was seriously amiss.

"I'll see to Captain, Beanie. You go and see what's wrong."

Beanie jumped off the horse onto a wall, as the drop would have been too great for her to do otherwise. There was an unusual silence in the house, creating an unhealthy atmosphere. The door to John's room at the top of the first-floor landing was closed but murmured voices could just be heard from within. Beanie went to the kitchen, the hub of the house, to see if anybody knew anything. Ellie and Maggie sat at the table with their mother, Helen. Their father was with John and the doctor.

"Oh, Beanie, don't look so worried, darling; the doctor has just come to check on John."

Helen tried to conceal her concern from the girls but her eyes betrayed her. They sat quietly, waiting for news. It was given by the doctor, who wore a troubled expression as he entered the kitchen, followed by William.

"Mistress Thorburn, or can I call you Helen?"

"Helen of course, Doctor. Please sit down."

"Helen, your son, I think, has diabetes. Now, I can't be sure, so I'll run some tests. In the meantime, he should rest, and perhaps you girls could mollycoddle him a little. Keep him off sweet foods, Helen; no sugar at all, but increase his fat intake. I always find that bacon is a good source of fat. I'll call you as soon as I have some test results."

With that, the doctor shook hands with Helen and bade the

girls farewell, carrying his bag and a sample of John's urine back to his car. At the surgery, the diagnosis was confirmed after boiling John's urine with Benedict's solution. It immediately turned brick red – he had diabetes mellitus.

John's diagnosis put a damper on Beanie's plans to throw a barn party, but her father encouraged her to carry on as normal and invite her friends as planned. Both she and Ronan went ahead and decorated one of the empty barns, the one furthest from the house, because of the anticipated noise. Fresh bales of straw were laid out to sit on and several bundles of reaped corn, tied with ribbon or decorated with the odd wildflower, were hung from the beams. To congratulate themselves on a job well done, they decided to take Captain out, so strolled up to the stables. As they were brushing Captain down and putting his bridle on, they heard a muffled giggle from one of the stables. Guiltily, Ellie stepped out of the stable, followed by Andrew.

"Ellie, what on earth do you think you are doing?"

Andrew's snigger inflamed Beanie's anger.

"I thought I asked you not to come up to the farm, Andrew, unless it was to apologise for your behaviour. Could you please leave?"

At that point, Ellie's temper flared. Refusing to let go of Andrew's hand, she confronted Beanie.

"It's all right for you to get up to who knows what with Ronan, out on that horse all the time when you should be pulling your weight. But when I want a bit of fun, it's a different story!"

Ellie's face had turned red with anger whilst Andrew just stood with a stupid grin on his face, his arm going protectively around Ellie's waist. Ronan stood back, not wanting to ignite a sparking fuse.

The stand-off was unbearable, so Beanie turned and went

back to harnessing Captain, her anger simmering to boiling point. Climbing onto the stable door, she mounted Captain and dug her heels in, making Captain jump into action. Outside, she trotted off towards the beach path, not waiting for Ronan.

Trotting through the foam on the shore line, the wind in her hair, Beanie soon calmed down and began to feel tearful. She hadn't liked arguing in front of Ronan and she hadn't liked Andrew, with his smug face, touching her sister. She made an impulsive decision to go and find Nessa. She wanted to get away from everybody, including John, whom she loved dearly. She was finding it increasingly difficult to watch his condition deteriorate, which it had done over the last few weeks.

Eyemouth was peaceful, the evening sun shimmering on the water reflecting a mackerel sky. The trawlers, now at rest, bobbed gently against the harbour wall, their halyards clinking an incessant tune. The women, who had washed and finished their fish supper, now sat chatting and knitting. Halcyon days, thought Beanie. Nessa waved and Beanie urged Captain forward until she towered over her friend.

"Beanie, lovely to see you. Are you coming down or shall I come up?" she joked.

Beanie laughed and dismounted to talk to Nessa whilst Captain stood quietly by, taking in his surroundings, his ears standing tall, eyes alert.

"The barn is ready for a ceilidh, but I can't say I'm in the right mood to enjoy it."

"What's wrong, Beanie? I thought you weren't looking your usual happy self. We're all really looking forward to a get-together. There're quite a few of us planning on coming up to the farm."

"Oh, it's nothing really, Nessa, I'm so happy to see you all, but John isn't well, and Ellie has taken up with a boy from the village that I've had a bit of trouble with. I'm hoping he won't come to the barn, but I'm guessing Ellie will invite him if only to annoy me."

"Ah, we'll soon sort him out. Don't give it another thought. Who's this fine beast?"

Captain was becoming impatient and nuzzling Beanie's shoulder.

"This is Captain and he's telling me he wants to go. I'll see you up at the farm tomorrow, around seven."

The harbour wall, conveniently close, enabled Beanie to mount Captain and be on her way. Deep in thought, she didn't initially notice Ronan by the dry stone wall at the end of the harbour.

"Will you be going my way at all?"

Beanie, roused from her thoughts, laughed when she saw Ronan waiting for her, not in the least bit cross at having been left behind in the stables with her sister and Andrew.

"Leap up behind me." She steered Captain over so Ronan could mount, leaving Beanie up front in the driver's seat.

"Beanie, I'm so sorry about John. Maggie explained he has diabetes. I know how precious your siblings are. I lost a younger brother, Ambrose, last year from the whooping cough. It tears your heart out, sure it does. My mother just prays and prays for his soul. It's a hard thing to watch."

With that, Ronan's arms went round Beanie's waist, holding her close, his face tickled by her long auburn hair. It was for his own comfort that he hugged her, but Beanie needed it as much as he did. She found the pressure of his strong arms around her reassuring. She basked in the sensation of warmth and security, the motion of Captain's stride making his embrace almost sensual.

Chapter 6

Milldown

Sunday was a day of rest. The women folk had prepared the vegetables for Sunday lunch the day before and baked bread, so their day would be free to congregate outdoors, exchange gossip and have a laugh. There was no washing on the clothes lines and no chores to be done save feed and tend to the animals.

Ronan, Killian and Brandon were up early, taking the pony and trap into Kelso to the nearest Catholic church, their faith dictating their attendance. They would attend mass and accept Holy Communion, the taking of bread and wine as symbols of Christ's body and blood. Their religion was deep rooted, their prayers said in earnest. Returning to Milldown along the cliff tops, the boys discussed the havoc that the flood had caused back home. Ronan was leaving in the morning and would see first-hand what damage had been done to their smallholding. He knew Cara's farmstead had suffered the brunt of the storm but did not know as yet that she had lost her mother.

On their return from church, the boys were invited to take Sunday lunch with the family but only after mucking out the stables and cowsheds. Beanie had already fed the animals with the help of Maggie, who told her that her beau, Todd, would be coming to the barn party that evening. Maggie, the youngest of the sisters, was not as attractive as her siblings but she had the most beautiful nature. She had been walking out with Todd for some months and had found a very good friend in him. He thought the world of her and it was understood that they would marry one day. Beanie only hoped she could find the same good qualities in Andrew, if he were to become serious with Ellie, which she very much doubted, as he had a capricious nature.

The lunch was both delicious and plentiful, the aromas having drawn the boys into the kitchen before time.

"Can we help in any way, Mistress Thorburn?"

"Och, Brandon, you're well acquainted with me now; you can call me Helen."

"That's kind of you, Helen. Will I be setting the table for you?"

Killian didn't know if Brandon's enthusiasm came from a newly found sense of etiquette, or if it was his impatience for lunch. Either way, Killian found it amusing.

"Brandon, did you not get your porridge this morning? You'll make a mighty fine housewife."

"Now, Killian, don't tease. Here, put the serving spoons on the table, please."

Helen enjoyed the boys' company and took pleasure in feeding them up. They had arrived looking quite puny and pale, but the long hours spent in the fields had tanned their skin and put some muscles on their torsos.

"Sit down now and tuck in. Here, John, you sit next to Ellie; William, head of the table as usual."

The large joint of beef was carved at the table by William whilst everybody helped themselves to the vegetables, huge Yorkshire puddings and gravy. The warmth and the smells in the kitchen added to the opulent atmosphere and everyone tucked in whilst enjoying the jovial banter. Apple pie and custard, all homemade, followed, at which point John excused himself, took a glass of water and went to his room. The lively atmosphere was dampened and a sadness fell over the kitchen. John's illness was weighing heavily on everyone who knew and loved him.

Time slipped pleasantly by but the finishing touches to the barn had to be finalised, so the relaxing sanctuary of the kitchen was left abandoned, not before having been spotlessly cleaned by all who had enjoyed the abundant home-grown produce.

Trestle tables covered in starched white tablecloths sprinkled with wildflowers were set up in the barn for food and drink, and the boys brought a few instruments down to the venue to practise their Celtic tunes. Brandon had his fiddle, Ronan the Bodhran and beater and Killian had a flute. The large Bodhran, or drum, was Ronan's prize possession and was always kept in its leather case to protect the stretched animal skin that created such a distinctive sound. It was played held upright on the lap of the musician, who would be seated whilst banging out a tune. The weather was balmy, perfect for their shindig, so whilst practising on their instruments their mood lifted, as they looked forward to meeting new friends and having some relaxing time.

The girls, having finished preparing the tables, went to get themselves ready. They each had a distinctive shade of blond hair, Beanie's being the darkest with streaks of red amongst the auburn. They had made a conditioner from chamomile, and Maggie and Ellie took it in turns to wash and treat their hair with it, believing the chamomile would enhance their corn-coloured locks and perhaps make them a little fairer.

Beanie added vinegar to her rinse, as it brought out the red streaks in her hair, making it glow like polished copper. They dried and brushed their hair using a brush with a silk scarf tied over the head of it to make their beautiful tresses shine. Pleased with the results, they went on to dress in clean blouses and trousers or dungarees – skirts were not appropriate for a barn party.

"Have you invited Andrew, Ellie?"

"Yes, why do you ask? Are you jealous, Beanie?"

Maggie could feel the sudden tension in the room and was disappointed that the camaraderie between the sisters had ended and bad feelings had surfaced.

"Come on, you two, no bickering. I thought we were going to have some fun tonight."

"Well, Beanie needs to mind her own business. Andrew is a perfect gentleman and I happen to like him even if Beanie doesn't. You make it perfectly obvious that you don't like him, Beanie."

"I'm sorry, Ellie; perhaps he will prove me wrong."

Beanie thought otherwise but decided to keep quiet so as not to spoil the evening. They trotted off down to the barn in high spirits, each looking forward to a little flirtation. Beanie especially looked forward to chatting to Nessa, who was in many ways far more worldly wise than Beanie or her sisters.

The music from the barn was exhilarating, the Bodhran beating out a frenetic pulse in time with the rhythm of the flute and fiddle. The girls were delighted, the barn looked beautiful and the guests had begun to arrive. Several of the young men from the village came, bringing chocolates or flowers for the girls. William had donated a keg of beer for the boys and the girls had made an elderflower cordial. Loaves of freshly baked bread, cheeses and meats were laid out for all to help themselves. The party had all the hallmarks of being a great success.

Andrew arrived and made a beeline for Ellie, who, by the look on her face, thought she was the cat who had got the cream. Beanie scowled. Nessa sauntered in next on the arm of James, with seven or eight of the young fishermen from the luggers and a few familiar faces amongst the girls who worked with Nessa. Each girl was wearing a colourful, long skirt and fresh blouse, their red hands the only thing giving way to the fact that they were working girls.

The party grew loud with excited chatter and the intense music. Nessa introduced Beanie to James, who immediately took his leave to get a beer. Standing next to Andrew at the trestle table, James noticed Andrew was fidgeting with a pocket knife that he nervously turned round and round in his hand. James turned his back on him, taking an instant dislike to Andrew, who looked to be more than capable of causing trouble.

"Nessa, James is very handsome. Does he live near you in Cornwall?"

"Our families are friends; we've grown up knowing each other. Our fathers have worked on the same trawlers for years and now my brothers work with James. It makes for a simple life. How about you, Beanie? Is there someone special?"

"Well, I have become friends with Ronan, the one playing the drum, but I don't know if we are anything more than friends."

"He looks nice. You'll have to let him know that you're interests run further afield than just horses."

Beanie laughed, hoping that Nessa might give her a little advice on that subject.

"I'll get my boys to play and sing for a while – that will give you the opportunity to spend some time with Ronan." With that, Nessa got up and shouted, "An Culyek Hos," or "Cornish music now, please." Nobody understood the old Cornish language except her friends, who did as they were told and got out their guitars and flutes, taking over from the Irish lads. The Cornish vocals were amplified in the old barn, enticing the guests to get up and dance.

"Beanie, introduce me to Ronan; he's coming over."

Nessa made a great fuss of Ronan, who explained that he was going back to Ireland in the morning. As he spoke to Nessa, he couldn't take his eyes off Beanie, who blushed and fidgeted.

"We've a wagon of barrelled cod going up to Edinburgh tomorrow morning. Would that help you on your way?"

"Oh, that would be grand. What time should I be ready?"

"I'll talk to the boys and let you know later, but it will be around five a.m., to catch the early markets."

With that, Nessa excused herself to join James, who was helping himself to bread and cheese.

"I'm sorry you're leaving tomorrow; did you say you'll be gone for two weeks? There's still so much work to be done, and with John being unwell it's going to be a push to get the harvest in before the weather breaks."

"I've told William that I'll stay on two weeks longer into September to get things finished. The threshing and winnowing has already started, but there will still be planting and hedge trimming to do. Beanie, do you want to take a walk?"

Ronan took Beanie's hand and led her off up the cliff path to the top of the gorge to take a look across the ocean. The sweep of Coldingham bay, with its row of beach huts, was lit by the low evening sun, which glinted off the peak of each dawdling wave. A woman was throwing a ball for her two dogs, which raced across the sand to retrieve their quarry.

"Beanie, I have something for you. I made it myself."

Ronan gave her a delicately plaited leather ring which he deliberately placed on her right hand to save any confusion.

"It's a friendship ring, Beanie. Do you like it?"

"I love it, Ronan. That's so kind of you."

She looked up into his eyes and before she had time to think about it, Ronan had planted a soft, warm kiss on her lips. She swayed, slightly disorientated by the pleasure she felt, the hair on Ronan's forearms that she clung to awakening the desire that she felt for him. Ronan put his arm around her to steady her, then, after taking one last look across the bay, he guided her back towards the party.

Their absence had not gone unnoticed by Andrew, who had been eyeing Ronan all evening, much to Ellie's displeasure. She was under the impression that it was Beanie he was watching and jealousy was stirring her anger. Andrew's blood was boiling, thinking that a peasant such as Ronan could fancy his chances with a beautiful, well-bred girl like Beanie. Thankfully his attention was taken by a new, shrill noise approaching the barn. William had taken it upon himself to contribute to the atmosphere by resurrecting his old bagpipes. He was parading between the cowsheds towards the party in his kilt, attempting to play a recognisable tune. Whistles and claps of appreciation greeted him as he did a turn inside the barn then stopped for a beer.

William was a popular member of the community and most of the party knew him well. He drank his beer and chatted to the Cornish lads about their catches then was about to leave when Andrew stopped him.

"William, can I have a word?"

"Mr. Thorburn, if you don't mind, Andrew. Yes, what can I do for you?"

"Wil... I mean, Mr. Thorburn, I don't like to think of Beanie getting into any sort of trouble, but I saw that Irish boy leading her away from the party and they haven't returned yet."

"Don't worry yourself. Beanie can take care of herself, and as for Ronan, he is a good lad. I'm very fond of him."

"Well, I only thought…"

William blew into his bagpipes and the noise drowned out Andrew's protestations, but walking back up to the farm he did feel a little uneasy, as he had noticed that Ronan and Beanie were becoming a little too fond of each other. His apprehension was not born out of a dislike for Ronan or thinking that he was not good enough for his daughter, rather it was an uneasiness about what would happen after Ronan returned to Ireland.

Reaching the farm, he put his bagpipes to one side and was about to pour himself a wee dram of whiskey when he heard Helen's distraught voice.

"William, John's had a fall. He said he missed the last step on the landing; it's his blurry vision. I checked his legs and saw numerous patches of dark brown skin everywhere. He's also got an ulcer on his foot from a blister that he rubbed two weeks ago and it won't heal. I'm worried, William. Should we call the doctor?"

"I'll see to him, Helen. You make sure all the girls come in safely by ten thirty latest."

William's face as he entered the kitchen later said it all. John's condition was deteriorating. He'd call the doctor in the morning. Ten thirty came and went and only Maggie had returned and gone to bed. Ten fifty and Ellie returned in a bad mood and she too went to bed. Finally, Beanie crept in at a quarter past eleven, clutching the dirty tablecloths, and William's temper, fuelled by Johns' condition, flared.

"What time do you call this, my girl? Do you want to get yourself a reputation as a hussy?"

Beany was shocked, as her father never shouted. Tears filled her eyes, and she looked to her mother for support, but none came. She could see that they were both anxious, but surely not on her account? She had done nothing wrong.

"Father, someone has put a knife through Ronan's drum and we were trying to sort that out and clear up."

"So, you're telling me you didn't leave the party and go skulking off with Ronan to get up to who knows what?"

"We went for a walk, Father."

"Go to your room, Beanie, and we'll have to see if we want Ronan back on the farm or not. Now go on upstairs."

Chapter 7

Wicklow

Edinburgh was a fascinating city, especially seen from the upstairs window of the electric tram on which Ronan was riding. It was energising, busy and vibrant, the architecture unfamiliar and exciting. The monuments and the castle towering overhead looked foreboding, menacing even, conjuring up visions of historic misdeeds, battles and beheadings. The industrial revolution was responsible for blackening the facades of the buildings, the furnaces spewing out smoke and soot, unchecked for so many years.

Studying the buildings looming up towards the castle, Ronan was completely unaware of the underground vaults over which he travelled. He had no idea of the squalor in which a small populace of Edinburgh's inhabitants had existed in the past. The Blair Street Vaults had been built in the eighteenth century under nineteen arches of the South Bridge beneath the Old Town. The vaults were dark and damp with no running water or sanitation.

Originally, they housed taverns and workshops, but in later years, when the conditions became intolerable, the city's most destitute moved in. Many rooms had housed up to ten people, the conditions incubating a hotspot for murderers and criminals alike. Some speculated that they were used by body-snatchers to store their victims overnight. One could only imagine the whiff of decomposition that must have permeated the air.

Waverly Station, situated between Old Town and New Town, was where Ronan picked up the steam train to Liverpool via Carlisle. He was reluctant to leave Edinburgh, with its intense sense of history and the vista of finely dressed families promenading along the wide paths in the park beneath the castle. His country upbringing had kept him virtually oblivious to the wonders of the world outside of Wicklow. The furthest he had been was Dublin, apart from his farm work in Berwickshire. He was beginning to get a taste for adventure but was well aware that his limited education would not get him far.

The journey by train down the west coast was very pleasant and relaxing after the early start from Milldown. His head nodded and rolled, his shoulders slumped and he slept. A loud whistle woke him. Befuddled and stiff, he had reached Liverpool. The crossing would take about six hours, getting him into Dublin around ten p.m. He would then have to hitch a ride from a passing wagon, or Shanks' pony would take him home.

"Mary Beth, where's Kathleen? Sister Leonella will be coming by for the lace any minute now. Where is Kathleen?"

Kathleen was where she usually was, in the barn, chatting to the milking cow whilst tatting, her shuttle flying from right hand to left over the thread held between forefinger and thumb, then under the thread at a speed which looked unattainable due to the breadth of her hands. Kathleen, now twelve, had Down's Syndrome and was the apple of her mother's eye.

"She's got the face of an angel," her mother would say, and Sister Leonella seemed to agree. The nun had taken Kathleen under her wing from birth and had taught her at the convent with her five siblings over the last twenty years or so. Kathleen was short in stature and ever so slightly chubby but a kinder heart you'd not find anywhere in Ireland. The nuns had taught her lace-making, or tatting, from an early age and she was now as proficient as any of the other girls at the convent and better than her two sisters.

Her work was sought after and worn by the wealthiest women across Europe. The nuns provided the silks and cottons and bought the finished pieces of work from the girls to be sold on, thus creating a cottage industry that would provide an income for some of the poorest families in Ireland. Kathleen had been working on a christening robe to be worn by the granddaughter of the Mayor of Dublin, and she was very excited to show Sister Leonella.

"Kathleen, darling, have you finished the piece now? Let me see; did you keep the cloth across your lap as I showed you to keep it clean?"

"I did, Mammy. See, I've finished it. It's so beautiful."

Kathleen spoke with a slight lisp, as her tongue was marginally large in her mouth due to her condition. She showed no sense of modesty as she delighted in the finished garment, her beautiful oval eyes shining with happiness as she held it up.

"Oh, Kathleen my lovely, it's surely the most beautiful christening gown I've ever seen. Just wait until Sister Leonella sees it. It's grand, for sure it is."

Kathleen glowed with pride as she lay the gown down for the nun to collect. She had no expectation of self-profit from her work, as the money went straight into the kitty. It would mean they could buy some much-needed supplies when they received payment for the gown. Times had been hard, as they had lost precious vegetables and grain in the flood. They were expecting Ronan to arrive that evening – another mouth to feed, if that were possible.

"Mary Beth, pop down to the grocery store and get me two

tins of corned beef. Fiona will put it on my tab. We'll have a nice hash for Ronan when he arrives."

Patricia, Ronan's mother, started to prepare a baked potato and apple pudding made from cider, apples, butter, sugar and potatoes. She was extremely resourceful when it came to feeding her husband and six children. They may not have had a varied diet, but she saw to it that they never went hungry. The nuns often contributed to their meagre supplies in return for help from the children in the convent gardens, where they grew many crops and kept chickens.

His homecoming was a happy event, but as he arrived so late in the evening, the meal was served the following day, after which he got straight down to mending fences, digging over flood-damaged vegetable plots and generally tidying up the smallholding. Kathleen never left his side, as Ronan was her favourite brother and he indulged her with good humour and handmade gifts.

As they sat eating an apple from the orchard, Cara came into sight, walking towards them. Ronan's heart sank, as he wanted to get on with his work and did not fancy Cara's naïve attempt at flirting with him. As she got closer however, he noticed a detrimental change in her demeanour. It wasn't until she was upon them that she spoke.

"Ronan, I heard you were coming home. How have you been?"

Ronan couldn't believe his eyes. Cara had lost her youth in the short time that he had been away. Her hair, tied back at the nape of her neck, looked lank and unclean. The wisps that usually tickled her cheeks so prettily hung in cloying strands. Not waiting for an answer to her question, she continued.

"Ronan, would it be at all possible for you to come and help me clean up after the flood? There's been a lot of damage, you see, and I haven't the time to see to it myself."

"I will, Cara. Shall I come by in the morning?"

Kathleen, who was quietly listening, suddenly spoke up.

"Cara's lost her mammy, Ronan. That's why she's so sad."

With that, Cara's eyes filled with tears, and she turned quickly and left.

Returning to the house, Ronan kicked off his muddy boots at the door and went to find his mother in the kitchen.

"What's happened to Cara, Mam? She looks like she's been pulled through a hedge backwards."

Patricia, who was preparing potato boxty to fry on the griddle for lunch, looked up and saw the concern on Ronan's face.

"Her mam died of exhaustion, and Cara's been left to pick up the pieces. Her dad's taken to the bottle and the wee ones are going hungry."

Kathleen stood at the door, listening, and on hearing that the children were going hungry burst into tears.

"Kathleen, darling, it's not as bad as all that. Look, I'll make a large potato farl and you can take it over with some bacon. Would you do that for me, darling?"

Kathleen stopped crying and wiped her nose on a clean white handkerchief edged in lace pulled from her pocket.

"I'll go over tomorrow, Ma, and clean up for her. Does Sister Leonella know what straits they're in?" asked Ronan.

"The convent provides what they can, but Cara's father is in such grief he's turned against his religion. He's told their priest he's not welcome."

"Oh, that's a bad state of affairs for sure. I'll see what I can do tomorrow."

Ronan hadn't been at home longer than a day before the weight of the world seemed to settle on his shoulders. Seeing Cara so destitute had pulled on his heart strings. He knew that life could have been so different for her. He also knew that she had had aspirations of a relationship with him, a thought that had not been so displeasing before the flood and the death of her mother. But now, her youth had been lost under the weight of responsibility that now engulfed her, and her freedom, so precious, was harnessed.

Ronan and Kathleen went the following day with eggs, a large potato farl, bacon and apples from the orchard. The children, or at least six of them, gathered round to see if the visitors had brought any food. Two sisters just a year or two younger than Cara had gone into service, which slightly eased the burden. Cara stood at the mangle, trying to push sheets though, but being absentminded, she was draping them in the mud at her feet.

"Here, let me do that, Cara. Kathleen, get a bucket of water and rinse the ends that are muddy."

Cara looked down at the mud on the ends of her sheets and her eyes filled with tears.

"Cara, go feed the children. We'll finish the sheets."

Cara took the food without speaking and went into the kitchen, followed by her brood. Ronan and Kathleen finished the washing and hung it on the line and over bushes to dry.

"Kathleen, you go and see if you can help inside. I'll start outside."

Ronan mended fences, cleaned out the barn and saw to the milking cow, which had no drinking water, then mucked out the chicken coup. He removed debris from the vegetable patch and added it to the mound of accumulated waste that he would burn later.

Returning to the kitchen, he found everyone tucking into the crisp bacon and potato cake.

"Cara, where's Flint? He's usually in the barn with the cow."

The room went quiet.

"Flint panicked in the storm, ran onto old Mr. Doyle's land and he shot him. Said he was worrying the sheep."

Cara had no more tears, but Kathleen, on hearing about the dog's demise, willingly gave up her own.

The following day after doing chores for his mother, Ronan went back to help Cara, this time without Kathleen, who had gone up to the convent. The house was quiet and all he could hear was the birds singing and the cow mooing from the barn. The day was a hot one so he went into the barn to check that the cow had water. She had overturned the bucket, so Ronan replenished it. He was about to leave when he saw Cara down by the river, which, meandering along, tickling the tendrils of weed, bore no resemblance to the torrent that had caused all the damage.

"Cara, would you be wanting any help with anything?"

Cara turned but remained silent, her hand dipping in the water.

As Ronan walked slowly down the bank towards Cara, a vision of Beanie crossed his mind and the kiss that they had shared and what it had meant to them. A nervous twitch in his stomach warned him of the situation he was walking into but he couldn't seem to turn away. Cara's demeanour was inviting in a seductive way and Ronan was being drawn in.

"Cara, where are the children?"

Ronan was conscious of why he had asked the question and he felt ashamed. He wanted the two of them to be alone, uninterrupted, the lapping water creating a false sense of security as time stood still. He no longer felt in control of his emotions, his misgivings redundant and Beanie no more than a figment of his imagination. Cara had bathed since he last saw her. Her hair was clean and fell freely down her back, her blouse loosely open at the neck.

He instinctively knew that she was aroused as he sat down beside her and for the first time, she looked up into his eyes. She was young, fresh and pretty, conscious of the sort of comfort she craved as she pulled Ronan's head down and kissed his lips tenderly. She was fully aware of how this union would climax, but life had been so cruel and so hard for such a long time that she would give in to this one tumultuous carnal pleasure that would offer her complete liberation for so brief a moment in time. Her staunch morals and her all-consuming religion were forgotten. She was oblivious to her despair as she relaxed under the weight of his body, her mind floating in a void.

Chapter 8

Wicklow

Ronan's boxing trainer had organized an illegal bare-knuckle fight that was to take place on a remote farm on the outskirts of Wicklow. His opponent, no older than himself, was hard-faced with attitude, but Ronan was not daunted. He was already fighting a battle with his conscience after what had happened with Cara. How could his base physical desire prevail over his moral and religious doctrines, and how, when he thought so much of Beanie, could he have done such a thing? He was profoundly ashamed, which, in the face of the fight, pumped him with adrenalin. There were few spectators, but he saw large sums of money exchange hands, which gave him further impetus to fight ferociously. Each youth had a handler offering surreptitious advice and motivation. Ronan needed neither; his body and mind were prepared for this fight.

They fought in bare feet and naked from the waist up, firstly having been searched for concealed weapons by each other's handler. It was reminiscent of a cockfight as the boys let rip. Eye to eye, they threw punch after punch with no sign of pain. Ronan was more agile, ducking and diving, avoiding each cuff with the grace of an athlete. Blood soon dripped profusely from his opponent's upper eyelid and nose, whilst Ronan had only a small tear to his lip.

Neither boy showed any signs of tiring as blow after blow

damaged their faces. Drool dribbled down from their mouths and their breath was now coming in gasps. The crowd cheered for each blow that connected and cussed at a missed opportunity. Twenty minutes passed with no winner, until Ronan's last punch connected with his opponent's left ear and the boy went down.

Relief flooded over Ronan's battered body. He had triumphed, but his pleasure was short-lived, as his opponent did not get up off the ground. His handler stood over him, pouring water onto his face but his eyes, half open, remained vacant. The crowd seemed oblivious to the young boy, as money was rapidly changing hands with scowls from some and howls of delight from others. The boy's condition was of no concern to any of them.

Ronan's handler, Jim, tried to pull him away, but he was determined to make sure that the unconscious boy was recovering before he had his own wounds tended to. Impatiently, Jim went to collect his winnings before the crowd dispersed, knowing that his debtors would in no time become invisible in the crowd and scatter without paying if the opportunity arose. Having collected a tidy sum, Jim, who was both handler and trainer, returned to Ronan, pushing a wad of notes into his hand. Seeing his opponent's eyes roll back into focus, Ronan, content that he hadn't inflicted any permanent damage, returned home alone.

"In God's name, Ronan, what have you done to yourself?"

Ronan's mother was none too pleased to see the state of her son and Kathleen burst into tears.

"It's nothing, Ma. I fell out of a tree."

"And what would you be doing up a tree, may I ask?"

"Saving a cat." He winked at his mother, who knew only too well what he had been up to.

"And was the cat called Jim, by any chance?"

His mother's sarcasm made him smile.

"Did you save the cat, Ronan?" asked Kathleen.

"I did that, and she's away back with the little girl who lost her."

Kathleen looked up at her brother. He was her hero, and she gave him a big hug.

Having had his cuts and bruises tended to by his mother, he pushed some money into her hand and went to his room. Lying on his bed, he reminisced about what had happened between himself and Cara. His eyes closed and his body lurched as he relived the unrestrained desire that had infiltrated the depths of his being, relieving him of all conscious thought. Now the pain and regret that he felt in the total disregard of Cara's wellbeing overwhelmed him and he sobbed. He felt no desire to return to help her or her siblings. He couldn't face her and wondered how he could escape the responsibility he now so begrudgingly felt. After all, wasn't it she who had initiated the sexual act?

He stayed at home for the following few days, labouring from dawn till dusk as a form of self-flagellation. His conscience was so tormented that one afternoon, he crossed the field at the back of his house to the antiquated Catholic church that nestled into the coppice on the edge of the hamlet and stepped into the confessional.

"Bless me, Father, for I have sinned."

As he sat, head down, he studied the mud clogged on his boots and shame once again swept over him. How lowly he felt here in Ireland, the land of his birth, sat in a confessional, covered in mud, having to confront his own depravity. He remembered Milldown and how happy he had been over the last months. He thought of Beanie and Captain and relived the bareback canters across the sands of Coldingham Bay, of being free of responsibility and free to fall in love with Beanie.

The priest's voice startled him out of his reverie.

"What is your sin, my son?"

"Forgive me, Father, for I have sinned. I did not come to church last week. I have used bad language and I have been fighting." The next words stuck in his throat.

"Three Hail Marys and four Our Fathers."

"That's not all, Father. I have compromised the reputation of an innocent girl."

"That's a far more serious confession, my son. What do you intend to do about it?"

"I don't know, Father. I have no profession, nothing to offer her."

"Is it someone in our parish?"

"I'll not give her a bad name, Father. It was my fault I lost control of my senses."

"You were weak, my son, but God will find a way to forgive you. You must do penance. Let us pray." Ronan shut his eyes and grasped the bridge of his nose as if for comfort as he and his priest prayed.

"Will you read your bible and pray each day for clemency?"

"I will, Father."

"You must apologise to this young girl and seek her forgiveness. Does she need financial assistance?"

"I'm sure she does, Father."

"Then you must be charitable; help her as much as you can."

"I will, Father."

"You have been cleansed of your sins. Go in hopes that you will not sin again."

Ronan was dismissed and left the church via the font in

which he himself had been baptised. He left a donation then retraced his footsteps across the fallow pastures back to his homestead.

Jim was waiting for him on his return, chatting to Ronan's mother, who was wearing a scowl that Ronan recognised only too well. She had no time for Jim, although she was only too pleased to accept the money that was offered after a fight.

"Ronan, don't forget the fight in Dublin now. I've two tickets for The Theatre Royal, Jem Roche fighting Tommy Burns for the World Heavyweight title. Day after tomorrow."

Jim looked excited but Ronan's mood was dampened by his shame and anxiety.

"I'll not forget, Jim; I'll be going straight back to Berwickshire after the fight."

"That's the first I've heard of you leaving, Ronan. Will you not stay a while longer?"

"I can't, Ma, I have to get back to Milldown or I'll not get my wages. Jim, I'll see you Friday; there's something I must take care of before I leave."

"I've a proposition for you too. We'll chat on Friday."

Ronan left his house knowing he must put things right with Cara before going back to Scotland. Head down and hands in pockets, he took off across the field with a reluctance that threatened to turn him in his tracks and have him running for the hills.

Cara was milking the cow when he arrived, and thankfully she was surrounded by several of her siblings. She looked happy, which Ronan hadn't expected. She was singing, "Hi bonnie lassie can you milk a coo, pull it by the udders and moo moo moo," making the children laugh, which made his apology seem somewhat detrimental to the prevailing mood. It had to be done though, for he would find no peace of mind until he had cleared the air between them.

"Cara, can I have a word?"

"Of course, Ronan, I'll be right with you. Gracie, can you carry the bucket into the kitchen for me? You can all have milk and an oatcake."

With that, the children followed Grace into the house and left Cara alone to talk to Ronan.

"Ronan, I'm so pleased you're here. I've been waiting for you to come and see me; do I get a kiss now?"

Her bright, hopeful eyes tugged on Ronan's heart strings, but he had to say what he had come for.

"Cara, about the other day…"

"Oh, Ronan, I'm so happy. Since my mother died and my father has taken to drink, I've been at my wit's end. I haven't known how to cope on my own, but now we are together I feel I can manage the children and the farmstead. You won't go back to Scotland now, will you?"

"Cara, I have to go back or I'll not get my wages. They're expecting me; I'm leaving on Friday."

With that, Cara burst into tears and ran into the house. Ronan followed but she had gone upstairs. The children were silent, watching to see what Ronan would do, the little ones at the table still eating oatcakes, crumbs falling everywhere. Ronan decided to follow Cara, who had shut the door to one of the bedrooms.

"Cara, can I come in?"

There was no response, so Ronan let himself in quietly. Cara sat sobbing quietly on the bed.

"Ronan, you can't leave now. I can't manage on my own – I thought you loved me."

"Cara, we've never mentioned love. We're far too young to

be thinking of that. Perhaps in a few years, but I can't support you and your family now."

"But Ronan, we do love each other, and I don't want to be without you now. I know I'm young, but I have the children to look after, and what if there's another on the way?"

Ronan's stomach summersaulted. He had not thought of the possibility of Cara being pregnant. Why hadn't he? He had thought that what they had done was a mistake, a sin maybe, but he hadn't considered that there may be consequences. His inexperience with females and the force of his spontaneous passion had left him oblivious to potential repercussions. His thoughts hurtled this way and that. Was it possible that Cara may have intentionally tried to trap him? He didn't think so. What would his brothers say, and his mother? Panic flooded over him, and when Cara reached out to touch his cheek, he pushed her away.

"Cara, I have to go. I can hear one of the children crying; you'd best go down."

Ronan ran down the stairs, left a wad of money on the table and walked out of the kitchen door. He didn't look back.

Reaching his home, he pushed past his mother and Kathleen and went to his room to pack. His getaway was imminent, his thoughts in turmoil.

After staying the night at Jim's and having a couple of whiskeys, they set off to Dublin for the fight. The city was alive, buzzing with excitement around The Theatre Royal and all the way along Hawkins Street. Inside, people stood around the ring, shouting with anticipation as the room filled and bets were placed. There were seats for four thousand people and every one occupied. The purse was a staggering seven thousand five hundred dollars, the odds seven to two on the American Tommy

Burns. However, the crowd was with their native Irish lad, Jem Roche. The assembly were whipped into a frenzy of patriotism as Roche stepped into the ring and the orchestra struck up "The Boys of Wexford", the spectators joining in the chorus.

Finally, Burns followed Roche into the ring with a band of followers who hustled around him whilst rules were explained and the competitors cautioned. Last-minute details were ironed out, gloves were checked, the ring emptied and the bell rang. Cheers erupted, deafening the spectators, whose heads, because of the surge forward towards the ring, were being pushed through the ropes, their faces animated with blood lust. The fight got off to a good start, each man agile, their muscles glistening under the lights. Large leather boxing gloves were held high, protecting their faces as they pirouetted around the ring, occasionally throwing out an insignificant punch as if testing the waters.

It was difficult to see either one's advantage until Tommy Burns, after only eighty-eight seconds, threw a punch which connected with Roche's left ear and jaw, and he went down. He seemed to be out cold as the referee counted him out on ten. Staggering to his feet, Roche teetered for a moment, looking bewildered, as if he would fall again but stayed upright long enough to warmheartedly congratulate the winner.

Chapter 9

Milldown

By the time Ronan set foot on Milldown Farm again, John was in hospital. He was on a strict sugar-free diet and had been put on an input and output fluid chart. His weight had plummeted, even though his appetite and thirst were insatiable, and the ulcer on his foot had not healed. His prognosis was poor. William and Helen were frequently at his bedside.

Ronan arrived ill-humoured and exhausted after missing his connection at Carlisle and having to walk several miles to the east of Edinburgh in order to pick up a wagon heading his way. The episode with Beanie staying out late after the ceilidh was forgotten, and Ronan's Bodhran had been repaired by the local saddler, who had found a suitable skin. They had yet to test the sound. Killian and Brandon had been working flat out with the help of the local workforce and were in need of a rest. They were delighted to see Ronan poke his face into the kitchen that evening, and although the ritual teasing and ruffing up of his hair took place, they could see that Ronan was in no mood for jokes and let him go straight to bed. Brandon and Killian followed; they could catch up in the morning.

A low Scottish mist hung over the dew-covered fields of Milldown when the boys first got to work. The hot summer days were fading, the nights drawing in and it was now imperative to cut enough of the mixed grasses from the fallow fields to pack the silo to create sufficient food for the cattle to overwinter. Soon the calves would be weaned and put into the barns for the season and would need the nourishment to fatten them up. Beanie had cleaned and prepared the barns and was now anxious to see Ronan, whom she had missed so much. She longed to harness Captain and go for one of their rides across the sands of Coldingham Bay with its backdrop of beach huts and orderly fields.

The morning had a chill to it as she crossed the furrows in search of Ronan. He was in the far field with Killian, drilling and sowing the winter wheat and barley, gulls screeching overhead. Her stomach lurched as she got no reaction to her approach.

"Ronan, it's great to have you back. Did you have a good visit home?"

"I did, thanks, Beanie."

That was it. No further conversation. Her heart sank. Had she misinterpreted his feelings towards her? She was wearing the friendship ring that he had given her and now began to wonder, as she turned it nervously on her finger, if it indeed had any meaning at all. Killian shrugged his shoulders, suggesting to Beanie that he had no clue as to Ronan's mood.

"Shall I bring the two of you a hot drink? It's so cold and damp this morning."

"Oh, that would be grand, thanks, Beanie." Killian accepted for both of them, as Ronan's head remained downcast, intent on the planting.

"What's got into you, Ronan? Has the cat got your tongue?"

"It's nothing, Killian. I've a lot on my mind."

"Well, would you be wanting to share it now? Did something happen back home?"

"It did, but I don't want to discuss it. Would you leave me be and let me work?"

The day passed slowly and mainly in silence. Brandon came to work with them later and got the same sombre vibe from his brother, causing concern, as Ronan was normally the exuberant one. Thinking something must be wrong at home, Brandon broached the subject, and after a day of hard labour and mental anguish, Ronan was ready to talk.

"I've done something so stupid I can't bring myself to talk about it."

"Ronan, I'm sure you can't have done anything we haven't already done with brass knobs on. You're the good one in the family, Ma's darling. Now, let's be having it. What have you done that we can't put right?"

Ronan was close to tears as he confessed his sin to his brothers. He had violated a vulnerable young girl who he knew had feelings for him. He had put at risk her future and that of her siblings, who were now under her care, for their father was now indifferent to the needs of his family. What if she was carrying his child to add to the family's wretchedness?

"Ronan, firstly from what you have told us, it's highly unlikely that she's pregnant. You are as inexperienced as she is and stars have to align to conceive. Secondly, it seems that it was she who made the advances; you didn't force her, and although that is certainly no excuse, you are young and easily led, as well we know."

Brandon tried to make light of the situation but Ronan was inconsolable. The fact was, he did not want a future with Cara. His heart was elsewhere – had he scuppered his chances with Beanie?

After the day's work, the boys walked slowly back up to the farmyard. Beanie was in the stable harnessing Captain, and when she saw Ronan, her heart leapt.

"Ronan, Captain has missed you. Do you fancy a breath of fresh air on the beach?"

"Go on now, Ronan; you'll have to put this behind you."

The brothers were in agreement and cajoled Ronan into taking a ride with Beanie.

Feeling slightly relieved after making his confession to his brothers, he leapt up behind Beanie and they headed off towards the bay.

Seated so closely behind Beanie with his thighs tightly against hers however, a now familiar feeling overcame him. Confused by his arousal, he slid back and let go of her waist. The comfort she had felt evaporated and a chill draft separated them. Had this been a bad idea so soon after his union with Cara? Were these sensations he was now feeling in the pit of his stomach in response to his closeness to Beanie, or were they evoked by a memory of the time spent with Cara?

The ride was uncomfortable and Ronan was relieved when they got back to the stable.

"That was grand, thanks, Beanie."

With that, he left Beanie alone in the stable to rub Captain down, brush out his fetlocks and settle him down for the night. Amazed at the speed with which Ronan had left her, Beanie strolled back to the kitchen, baffled and forlorn.

"Ellie, did Ronan come through here?"

"No, I haven't seen him at all today. Why, have you lost him?"

Beanie wondered if her sister's innocent comment was close to the truth. Had she indeed lost Ronan? She went to her room, in no mood to chat.

In the village, new sewerage pipes were being laid, which

caused much excitement, as this meant the end of the garden privy. However, it also meant that some of the casual labourers that Milldown relied upon disappeared for better pay and more regular work, digging trenches for the pipes. This put extra pressure on the migrant workers up at Milldown, especially as John could no longer participate and William was often at his bedside, not overseeing the running of the farm. Brandon, Killian and Ronan did more than their fair share and were very much appreciated by the family, who regularly shared large roast dinners with them.

The autumnal mists and heavy dew now made work a little more uncomfortable. The steam threshers had done their work and the mill was in full production and heavily stocked. The silo too had reached capacity and the barrels full of fish guts had been spread on the fields, fertilising them ready for winter planting. It was now time to separate the calves from their mothers and get them into the barns for the winter. Beanie found this a stressful time, as the mothers and calves did not like to be parted and the noise was distressing. She decided to go into Eyemouth for the day so she didn't have to listen to the doleful mooing of the cattle, which sometimes went on for several days.

Harnessing the pony to the trap, she took off to pick up her friend, Mistress Evelyn Simpson, daughter of the renowned Dr. James Simpson, who was experimenting with the use of chloroform as an anaesthetic. Bonardub, Evelyn's family home, was on the road to Eyemouth so didn't inconvenience Beanie in the least, and she always enjoyed Evelyn's company.

Evelyn was well read with a wicked sense of humour, recounting tales of how her father had experimented with chloroform on one of her younger brothers in the garden, testing his reflex to pain under anaesthesia with a simple prod or touch of a needle, then watching him stumble around under the apple trees in the orchard recovering from the effects of the chloroform.

"I remember my father laughing, saying, 'Look, Evie, we're going to validate Newton's theory of gravity as well as the success of chloroform if he knocks an apple off the tree.' After that, his favourite saying was, as the moon falls to earth, so does the apple fall from the tree. Meaning to him, it's a sure thing."

Eyemouth, now relieved of the frantic seasonal fishing, returned to its leisurely pace of life. Uncle Ralph sat on the sea wall with his nets as Beanie approached.

"And what is it that you want today, Beanie darling? Did I tell you what I saw this morning from far out to sea? I saw Beanie's blue bloomers hanging on the line to dry." It was a standing joke that her bloomers were so large they could be seen like a flag blowing in the wind.

"Oh, Uncle Ralph, that's an old one. You've not even been out fishing this morning."

Beanie sat beside her Uncle Ralph, and the two passed the time of day together whilst she waited for Eve to finish her shopping. When she returned with her purchases, Eve handed Beanie a book.

"What's this, Eve?"

"It's a biography of my father. I thought you might like a copy – it's just been published. I've signed it for you very formally, Evelyn Blantyre Simpson."

"Thank you, Eve, I'll treasure it. I'm sure your father will be famous one day."

"Well, I enjoy writing and he seems to be a good subject."

Beanie covered Eve's legs with a rug and they set off for home. There was a silence to the afternoon. It was dull, misty and there was a chill to the air. The sky was clear, a subtle shade of grey, and a heavy haze loitered over the sea, obscuring the surf. The one tree protruding from the grounds of Milldown Farm in the distance was swathed in fog. Eve, thankful to be home, said her goodbyes to Beanie, who set the pony off at a swift trot. The pony knew the road and hurried at her own pace, wanting the reward of a warm stable and sweet hay at the end of her journey.

Reaching the farm, Beanie was brought up short at the sight of the now familiar car belonging to John's doctor. Her heart sank thinking the worst, so she hurriedly settled the pony into her stall and went to the kitchen. The sombre faces and the tears in her mother's eyes said it all. John had passed away peacefully. The doctor was conveying his sympathies to all, William thanking him for his excellent care with a shake of his hand. Although the outcome of John's illness was a foregone conclusion, the shock was overwhelming. Once the doctor had left, the family came together round the large kitchen table to console one another. After a period of mutual solace, Beanie left the kitchen, walking past the hat rack. She took John's flat cap to her bedroom. She had her own way of mourning and wanted solitude to come to terms with the loss of her brother.

The weather outside reflected the mood she was in. The evening was dark, rivulets of condensation trickled down her windows and the tall glass panes overlooking the sea to the front of the house almost bent with the force of the intermittent gusts of wind. A knock on her door made her jump.

"Beanie, the horses are unsettled. I don't know what's spooked them. Will you come and calm them with me?"

Ronan spoke quietly in reverence to her feelings and waited patiently for her response. She opened the door and he could see that she had been crying.

"I'll go myself if you'd prefer, Beanie, no trouble."

"No, it's all right. I'll come."

The horses were restless, moving around their stalls, their ears raised, hearing something inaudible to humans or simply sensing something in the air. Whatever it was, they were soon calmed by the comfort of familiar voices.

"Beanie, I'm so sorry about John. I'll stay on for a while until the farm is settled for the winter."

"Thank you, Ronan." She turned and would have left the stable, but Ronan touched her arm.

The closeness of his corn blue eyes and his tussled hair evoked a familiar longing. She stood still, waiting, not knowing what would follow until his broad hands took her waist, his lips coming to rest on hers. The kiss seemed to last forever and it left Beanie with a sense of tranquillity. The outside world had evaporated, leaving her at one with Ronan, the horses she loved and the sweet potpourri of smells in the barn. The moment however, was short-lived.

Chapter 10

Milldown

A loud, persistent whistle broke free from the fog, filling the night with a sense of foreboding. It wasn't clear at first where the noise was coming from. It seemed to be all around them, startling the horses once again. Ronan and Beanie rushed from the barn in time to see a flare illuminate the clear sky above the layer of fog, which still clung to the sea's surface. Another flare followed, arching over and falling like a star into the soft miasma.

"Beanie, it's a ship in distress. Tell your father to phone the Lifeboat Station. Hurry."

Beanie rushed to the house to find that her father was already on the phone.

"Ay, ay, I'll do that, no worries." Her father was receiving instructions over the phone with a look of dread etched on his face.

"Beanie, they're sending a wagon of life-saving equipment from Eyemouth along the coast road. There's a boat gone aground off St Abbs Head on the Ebb Carrs rocks. The horses will tire; it's a four-mile journey and the wagon will be heavy. We're to have another horse ready to take over. Hitch Captain – go now, quickly."

Ronan had heard the directive and ran with Beanie back to the barn. Of all the horses, Captain was not only the strongest but also the calmest of the horses, ready and willing to take instruction. They harnessed him quickly and walked him out into the cold night air. His breath was coming in snorts, anticipating an assignment; the siren still pierced through the electrifying atmosphere.

The coastal road could be treacherous at night, especially in the weather conditions they were facing with limited visibility. Captain would be at risk of slipping, or worse still, which filled Beanie with trepidation. Time seemed to stand still. Captain pranced with impatience, pirouetting around Ronan, who held him back; the horse knew that he was going to be asked to perform a task. Then, over the sound of the siren, they heard the approach of pounding hooves. Captain pulled on his bridle, throwing his head with agitation, alerted by the noise, but instead of stopping, the four-wheeled wagon sped by. Lathered and panting, the poor horses, galloping on the uneven terrain, were to get no respite.

Ronan launched himself on top of Captain and said he would follow on to see if he could help. Beanie, shouting over the sound of the persistent wind and siren, refused to be left behind so leapt on top of a gate and up behind Ronan. They set off in poor visibility, Captain sensing the urgency.

From Round Hill on top of the cliffs, the fisher folk of St. Abbs, brought from their homes by the siren, understood what had happened. A steamer had ploughed straight into the jaws of the perilous Ebb Carrs, a semi-circle of jagged rocks just under the sea's surface. The lighthouse at St. Abbs Head, which in clear skies could be seen for twenty-one miles out to sea, was that night redundant under the heavy blanket of fog. The steamer, which stood no chance under the heavy swell, had ejected its deck cargo of solid wooden pit props on impact and now lay stricken and broken on top of the rocks.

When Ronan and Beanie arrived on the scene, rocket after rocket was being launched from the wagon, carrying lines to be attached to the stricken boat; all fell short. Cries for help could be heard faintly, as the noise from the steam whistle and the booming surf of the North Sea was deafening. The nearest lifeboat was coming from south of Eyemouth, five miles away, so had not yet arrived.

The second lifeboat was having to row from Skateraw, Dunbar, fifteen miles north, a four-hour journey. The oarsmen, sweating in their oilskins, pulled on the oars as one, thinking only of the lives of the men relying on them for salvation. The sea was churning but the brave crew did not falter. Their arms ached, sweat and sea spray obscuring their vision as they put all their strength into each stroke, relying on the helmsman alone for direction.

As suddenly as it had started, the whistle from the steamer stopped as the sea flooded the stricken ship's furnace. Cries for help could be heard more clearly then, but the rockets carrying the lines to retrieve the crew continued to fall short of the wreck by as much as four hundred yards. Orders, screamed out over the melee of the tempestuous night, were frantically observed by the rescuers, who were balancing precariously on the slippery, jagged rocks, but to no avail. Fishermen and women on the cliff tops prayed fervently for their fellow mariners but alas in vain. Beanie wept as she prayed for the sailors' souls as, one by one, they slipped into the freezing, hostile underworld.

When the first lifeboat arrived from Eyemouth, the sea was silent. Sixteen seamen had lost their lives. Never giving up however, the brave crew of the lifeboats continued to search in ever-worsening conditions, rowing against the boiling swell of the sea and colliding with the treacherous pit props that rose on the crest of each wave then fell catastrophically close to their boats. One made contact, severing a finger of one of the crew, the sea salt making the wound excruciatingly painful, but with total disregard for his injury, he rowed on.

An easterly swell was sweeping the lifeboats shoreward, a course the heroic men had to fight. It was imperative that they stay out beyond the wreck for their own safety so were frantically pulling on their oars. Several times they were at risk of sinking in the melee, the fog still hindering visibility. Over the sound of the crashing waves, they could hear the noise of buckling metal and splitting wood, telling a gruesome tale.

The search seemed to go on for hours once the Skateraw lifeboat arrived, but inevitably all hope of survivors faded and the crews had to concede defeat. The weather conditions and the threat from the pit props, which came like battering rams on the crest of each wave, was too grave a risk to the lifeboat men themselves. After a final sweep of the site with lamps scouring the surface of the white-washed waters, the boats turned to head for home.

The crews were exhausted, defeated, bruised and battered, both mentally and physically. The urgent commands that had been franticly shouted from the wagon ceased and slowly the sombre men began to pack their equipment back into the wagon. The fearsome power of the sea had won. The poor horses that had been left unattended were white with frothy sweat and stamping their hooves, throwing their heads up and down in frustration and fear, the whites of their eyes glowing in the blackness of the night.

Ronan and Beanie walked to a lower part of the cliff where they could see the shoreline more clearly, whether in the hopes of finding a survivor or merely to offer another prayer, they weren't sure. They stood in silence, the fog still shrouding the wreck.

"Beanie, look, there – don't you see? I think it's a seal in trouble."

A head could be seen with frantic eyes, struggling in the surf, throwing his head upwards for breath. Pit props rammed the animal, pushing him under the water again and again, and then he was lost.

"It will be all right. It's a seal – it can swim out to clear water."

Beanie was unconcerned for the seal; they were resilient and quite common, combing the harbours locally for fishy titbits thrown from the trawlers. Her thoughts were with the lost sailors. But when the animal resurfaced close to the shore, they could see that it wasn't a seal but a large dog. He stumbled out of the surf, his first instinct to shake the water from his coat. However, his legs were too weak. They buckled and he fell, white surf overwhelming him again, dragging him unwillingly back into the sea's relentless grip.

"Beanie, he's in trouble. I'm going to get him."

Ronan ran awkwardly over the rocks towards the dog but the animal was full of fear. He struggled to his feet and slipped past Ronan, running precariously up the cliff path away from what he perceived to be danger. The dog was huge, black with a white flash on his chest. It was an eerie sight, the black dog running out of the dark water, seemingly fleeing the wreck. If he had been on board the steamer, he would be the only one to survive that night.

It was two in the morning when people started to disperse, and Ronan gave up on the hopes of finding the dog after a brief search. They mounted Captain and headed home, exhausted and despondent, but Ronan couldn't forget the dog. He had been magnificent, powerfully built with a sleek coat, a Great Dane, thought Ronan, who decided he would resume his search in the morning.

Ronan's perseverance the following day proved fruitful, as above White Heugh Bay, north of St Abbs Head, Ronan saw the dog again. The dog's large, frightened eyes watched Ronan's slow approach. Ronan knew not to rush up to him, so sat himself down at some distance from where the dog lay, exhausted and fearful. Sitting quietly and not making eye contact allowed Ronan to edge towards the animal without spooking him. He lay, subdued and suspicious, his muscles still twitching from exhaustion.

Ronan edged towards him, talking softly, and although at one point the dog readied himself for flight, he didn't seem to have the energy. Soon Ronan was close enough to hold his hand out, offering a piece of cheese. He watched the dog's nose twitch as he sniffed the cheese, his tongue coming out to lick his lips, spilling salty drool. He was obviously starving. He took the cheese and raising his eyebrows, searched Ronan's hand for more. Luckily Ronan had brought with him a selection of treats to tempt a suspicious animal and soon the dog was eating out of his hand calmly.

Ronan spoke to him while he was eating, and the dog relaxed slightly. Having brought a rope in the hopes of finding the dog, Ronan quietly slipped a noose over the dog's head. The dog made to stand but his legs were still too weak. They sat for a while looking out to sea. The fog had not cleared completely, but Ronan could now see clearly the outline of the wreck, its back broken across the Ebb Carrs rocks.

"I think we'll call you Carro, after the rocks. What do you say, boy?"

Ronan very slowly led the dog back to Coldingham, across the cliff top. They dropped down to the beach where all the locals, including Beanie's family, were surveying the devastation caused by the wreck. Pit props bobbed up and down across the surface of the sea, interspersed with debris from the steamer. Small parts of the ship lay on the beach but no bodies had been recovered. People were subdued, each drawn into their own thoughts, but the dog seemed to lift spirits. A middle-aged man approached Ronan and fussed over the dog, explaining that he had just lost one.

"I'm wondering if he came off the wreck. Do you know anything about it?" asked Ronan.

"Yes. It was a Danish steamship out of Libau, bound for Grangemouth, so I'm told. *The Alfred Erlandsen*, carrying pit props. What a tradgedy – sixteen men lost. Those rocks have claimed more than one ship over the years."

"It was a sad night, for sure, but at least one survivor." Ronan stroked the dog's head

"I could take him, if you like. I'm from over at Kelso. He's a fine beast; off the ship, you say?"

Ronan liked the man and the dog's reaction to him, so agreed to let him go. As the man walked off however, the dog looked back, and Ronan was suddenly unsure of his decision to part with him.

"His name's Carro. Can I visit him soon?"

"Ay, that you can, and you can bring him some food too. He's going to take some feeding!"

Beanie could see that Ronan was reluctant to let Carro go, but she put his mind at rest, explaining that the man was a titled land owner, having a good reputation as an animal lover and horse breeder, having plenty of ground for Carro to explore.

Walking back up to the farm, Ronan took Beanie's hand.

"I'm sorry I've not been myself since coming back from Ireland. I didn't have a good visit."

"What happened?" But Ronan would say no more on the subject, so Beanie let it go.

Back up at Milldown, they all sat round the kitchen table to discuss the funeral service for John. He would be buried at Coldingham Priory, where the family had attended the Church of Scotland services for years. The mood was sombre. Helen made a large pot of tea and put a plate of scones on the table.

"Does anyone have a preferred hymn?"

The choice was open to discussion but the most popular hymn they all agreed on was "For Those in Peril on the Sea", not only a favourite of John's but a fitting tribute, they thought, to the men so recently lost in their waters.

The service the following Tuesday was well attended. The Thorburn family were well liked in the village and although John had been a quiet man, he did have many friends. The conversation was mainly about the Danish steamer that had gone down and the brave lifeboat men from Skateraw who had, by the time they got home, been rowing for ten hours. The men wore long black coats and bowler hats, the women, also in black, wore high-neck laced shirts, three-quarter length jackets and long skirts, their large hats almost obscuring their faces whilst keeping off the light drizzle that fell from the heavens.

Later, tea was served at Milldown, with a dram of whiskey to warm the men. Issy, the maid, served some finger food and Dr. Murray said some kind words about John, and a final glass was raised to the memory of a loving son and brother.

Chapter 11

Milldown

Killian and Brandon were due to return to Ireland within the next couple of days so were working hard in the fields, doing last-minute repairs and clearing ditches. Issy, the maid, was sobbing in the pantry, as she had developed a fierce crush on Brandon, who had shown little or no interest in her at all, even though she had flirted madly with him in the barns whilst milking the cows.

The day was fine, a cool breeze coming off the sea conducive to getting the clean sheets on the line to dry. They had been through the mangle and Beanie volunteered to peg them out. The basket was heavy and she nearly tripped; she left the kitchen with a muffled curse. There were three washing lines in a row, as there was always a full basket of wet clothes to be hung out.

Beanie got the first row of sheets hung and was pegging out the second row when she noticed feet peeking through from the other side of the washing, moving along the line as she did, the body obscured. A mischievous smile brightened her face, thinking Ronan was playing a game with her, about to leap out and shout boo at any moment. She continued pegging as a hand slipped over hers, playfully toying with her fingers. She reciprocated, their fingers entwining seductively. She moved slowly, enjoying the warm feeling of his hand touching hers until she got to the end of the line.

"Andrew, what the hell are you doing?"

Her face reddened with both sheer anger and embarrassment, and to make matters worse, she saw Ronan watching this game play out.

"How dare you touch me! I thought I had made it quite clear that you were not welcome up here."

"That's not what your touch was telling me, Beanie. Come on, give me a kiss; you know you want to."

Andrew had not seen Ronan watching his every move. If he had, he would not have been so bold, but Ronan bided his time, waiting for Andrew to completely overstep the mark.

"Andrew, get off me."

As Andrew grabbed Beanie's wrist and would have forced his lips on hers, she gave him a resounding slap across his cheek. He raised his hand as if to retaliate, only to find his arm twisted up behind his back in a painful armlock.

"I think Beanie has made it quite clear that she is not in favour of your attention, Andrew. Do you have to be told twice?" Ronan's voice was quiet and composed.

"I was just leaving, that is, if you would release my arm."

"That's grand. Shall we walk a while?"

Ronan's tone was taunting and by the look on Andrew's face, he didn't need to be pushed much further before there would be another fight. Beanie touched Ronan's arm, signalling that he should just let Andrew go. She didn't want to have to explain to her father that there had been another altercation between Andrew and Ronan. Andrew wrenched his arm away from Ronan and stormed off towards the mill.

"Ronan, I could have taken care of myself, but thank you anyway. I think he has an ulterior motive in trying to seduce all the Thorburn girls – he wants to take over the running of the farm now John has gone and my father is not getting any younger."

"Well, you can't blame a boy for trying, but I would question his approach."

Beanie smiled but her mood for the day was impaired.

"Let's take Captain and go for a ride. He's not been working today and he could do with the exercise. I'll show you my favourite place."

They harnessed Captain and walked slowly away from the farm. Some of the workforce gave speculative glances but Beanie was not in the mood to be intimidated. They walked past St Abbs Head and West in Thrile Bay, then headed inland to where Beanie went when she wanted some solitude. The gorse was still heavily flowered and made a beautiful yellow backdrop to Coldingham Loch. The loch, which was spring-fed, covered twenty-two acres and was stocked with plump rainbow trout for those who cared to fish. However, fish were plentiful from the sea, so the trout were left mainly undisturbed.

Dismounting, they tied Captain to a log with a long enough rein to enable him to graze. They sat on a sandy bank on the north side of the loch closest to the sea. Gulls were squawking overhead but otherwise all was tranquil.

"Ronan, what went wrong on your visit home? You never told me."

"I never did, did I? If you must know, it was trouble with a local lassie. She's had some rare bad luck and I felt obliged to help her and her family clear up after the flood. She's just recently lost her mother and there's a large brood of siblings that need her care. Her father has lost all sense of responsibility and taken to drink, so it's fallen heavily on her shoulders to take charge."

"So why did that upset you?"

"Well, let's just say she wanted a little more from me than I wanted to offer."

Although not quite the truth, Ronan was not prepared to confess the whole truth to Beanie at this time, but having put two and two together and come up with five, she thought she knew what had most probably occurred, or some of it at least. They were quiet for a while, Ronan looking pensive and distant.

"Ronan, are you involved with this girl, I mean, romantically?"

"No, Beanie. I know that's what she wants but I don't feel the same way. You must know I have feelings for you."

Beanie blushed but hearing him say that filled her with a sense of elation. Her attraction to him was without doubt fierce and she longed for them to be closer. She lay on her back, looking up at the wispy clouds scudding by, dreaming of what could be.

Ronan lay next to her. They could hear Captain munching on the grass. The mood was relaxed as the sun's rays danced across their faces, warming them. The tragedies of the last few days disappeared in a sleepy bed of lethargy until Ronan leaned over and kissed her. The kiss was timeless, the two of them lost to the outside world, their minds empty in a blissful union. His hands explored her body, and she had no qualms in giving herself freely. As her arousal soared, she lost all sense of self- preservation, giving herself entirely over to Ronan's desire in the knowledge that he was her protector and would not harm her. Suddenly he caught his breath and separated himself from her.

"I'm so sorry, Beanie. I didn't mean for that to happen."

He sat up and frowned, leaning on his knees, hand on forehead with a look of self-loathing distorting his handsome features. Beanie composed herself and put a hand on his leg.

"Ronan, don't say sorry; we were both participants. There's nothing to be sorry about."

"I should have been more respectful, Beanie. What would

your family say if they knew one of their labourers was taking advantage of their daughter? In fact, what would Andrew say?"

"Ronan, you did not take advantage of me and don't make light of it. Please don't describe what just happened in those terms. I thought it was beautiful. I have no regrets and I don't blame you for anything that happened. It will be a precious memory when you have gone back to Ireland."

Suddenly, out of nowhere, the tears fell. The thought of Ronan leaving Milldown was inconceivable. He had been her very best friend over the summer and now her lover. She didn't ever want him to leave.

"There now, Beanie, don't cry."

His arms went round her and she sobbed, not only at the thought of him leaving and the loneliness that she would feel but also for the loss of John that suddenly overwhelmed her.

As they sat quietly, watching the rippling waters of the loch, the sun brightened, illuminating an old, charred wooden pole jutting unnaturally from the water. It looked out of place – certainly not the remains of a tree, more like something that had been placed there for some purpose. It was burnt; maybe it had been struck by lightning in some past era. Their thoughts, however, were elsewhere, so they had no enthusiasm to speculate further as to its origin. The sun suddenly went behind a cloud and the day turned overcast and cold.

"Come on, Beanie, dry your eyes now. We'd better get back and feed the horses."

Ronan helped Beanie to mount Captain, then he leapt up behind her so that for the leisurely journey home he could embrace her. Both pensive, their thoughts differing wildly, they made their way back to Milldown.

On arrival back at the farm, Brandon and Killian were

waiting anxiously for Ronan.

"Ronan, Kathleen's been taken into hospital. Ma doesn't say how bad she is but she wants us home. We're leaving shortly. You're to stay and help William for a couple of weeks, unless something happens to Kathleen. As soon as we know anything, we'll run into Bray and phone."

Ronan was shocked by the news and had to leave Beanie to see to the horses. He helped his brothers to pack and then reluctantly bade them farewell. Ellie had volunteered to hitch the wagon and take them into Dunbar, from where they could get another ride into Edinburgh. Their work for the summer had finished and they had been handsomely recompensed. Ronan could now finish the planting and help out wherever necessary. He was invited to join the family for dinner that night, and although feeling a little lost without his brothers and worried about his sister Kathleen, he tucked into a large roast lamb supper with apple crumble to follow, giving Beanie several surreptitious admiring glances.

That night, Beanie sat on her bedroom window seat, becoming melancholy about John's death. She read from her book by Longfellow, romantically wishing that she could conjure up John's spirit to fill a void in her heart as she read:

Then the forms of the departed
Enter at the open door
The beloved, the true hearted
Come to visit me once more.
With a slow and noiseless footstep
Comes that messenger divine,
Takes the vacant seat beside me
Lays his gentle hand on mine.

And he sits and gazes at me
With those deep and tender eyes,
Like the stars, so still and saint-like
Looking downward from the skies.

Tears fell again as her heart was wrenched with sadness and a sense of loss. She had loved John with his quiet, good manners and fondness for his family, his dour sense of humour and his whole-hearted love of the farm. Life would go on but with an eternal sense that something was missing. From outside, Ronan watched her ethereal form framed in the window, a candle flickering in the background. He could sense she was mourning.

Chapter 12

Wicklow

"Where's Ronan?"

Patricia was beside herself. The minute the boys walked in through the door, after being away for so long, she was shouting. Kathleen was being disruptive in the hospital, constantly asking for Ronan.

"Ma, he's staying in Berwickshire to finish off the autumn planting. Don't forget he came home for a while – he owes the family another couple of weeks."

"Why couldn't one of you have done that? You know your sister only wants Ronan when she's not well. Are you mad, the two of you?"

Brandon and Killian braced themselves for the ear-bashing that they knew was coming. Of course, they should have thought of Kathleen's reliance on Ronan when she was not well.

"Sister Leonella is due any minute – get rid of your muddy boots will you; were you born in a barn?"

Patricia's husband, a short, stocky man with dark, greased back hair and dark glasses, was reading a paper at the kitchen table, trying to block out the hullabaloo.

"Will you stop your clucking, woman? I'm trying to read; can't you see?"

The homecoming was pretty typical, their father trying to ignore the goings on in the household and their mother in a constant flap. There was a knock on the door and Sister Leonella made her entrance in her long, flowing, dark habit, her face shrouded in white, perspiring a little from her long walk from the convent. The bottom four or five inches of the habit she wore were damp, slightly mud-stained and looking worse for wear.

"Will you look who's here?" Sister Leonella walked straight over to the boys and gave them a hug.

"Are you back for good? Kathleen will be so pleased to see you. I've heard from St. Vincent's Hospital – they are going to release Kathleen tomorrow. She's made a miraculous recovery. The sisters and I prayed for her last night and lit a candle; God has answered our prayers."

"Oh, Sister, she's not got the consumption then?"

"No, Patricia, you mustn't worry so, just a chest infection. She's nearly back to normal; her chest is a bit rattly still but she'll be fine. They'll be glad to see the back of her though; she's not been the best of patients, but she's made some fine lace, you'll be pleased to know. It's already been sold. Here, my dear, you take this. It will come in handy, sure it will."

Patricia took the money but not without noticing her husband Ambrose surreptitiously looking to see how much was handed to his wife, but Patricia quickly tucked it away in her pocket.

"I'll get you a drink, Sister. You chat to the boys."

Sister Leonella sat at the kitchen table, much to the annoyance of Ambrose, who turned slightly in his chair and continued to read.

"Brandon, come and tell me how the summer went for you in Scotland. Was the work hard?"

"It was good, Sister. We were with a fine family. A nice farm on the cliff top overlooking the sea. Three hundred and sixty-five acres. It kept us busy, for sure, but we were fed well and treated like part of the family."

"That's grand. Will you get work next year?"

"I think so, for they lost a son while we were there. He died of the diabetes, so he did."

"Oh, that's a shame."

Patricia came in with a pot of tea and biscuits enough for the boys as well, which was unusual, as they were normally only offered to visitors. Ambrose at this point got up and left the room without a word or a backward glance; he couldn't stand chit chat.

The following day, Killian hitched the pony and trap and took Patricia to pick up Kathleen from St. Vincent's Hospital.

"Cover your nose and mouth when you go in, Killian. Here, take my handkerchief; I don't want you getting the consumption, now."

Patricia had an inbred fear of consumption, as it had been known to wipe out whole families once it took hold. She refused to go in to collect Kathleen herself so waited with the pony. Kathleen came out in a rare bad mood, sulking and pouting all the way home.

"Kathleen, take your clothes off for me now, darling. I'm going to wash the whole lot. Go and get changed now, be a good girl."

As soon as they got home, Kathleen was washed from head to toe and put into fresh clothes. Patricia's fear of consumption was not altogether irrational and she took all precautions to keep it from her door.

Now spotless, Kathleen sat quietly in better humour, getting on with some more lace making. The concentration it took kept Kathleen calm, as sometimes her behaviour could be quite contrite.

"Where's Ronan, Ma?"

Kathleen loved her brother and couldn't understand why Brandon and Killian were home without Ronan.

"He's got a bit more work to do and then he'll be home, darling."

"Cara wants to see him, Ma. She's waiting for him."

"Well, you can tell Cara he won't be long. Now come over here and give your mammy a cuddle, then you can make me some pretty lace, there's a good girl."

The following day, Brandon and Killian went to Kilcavan, where there was an active slate quarry. The slate was used as roofing for houses and factories. It was also ground to a powder to be mixed with paint for use on boats. The quarry often offered casual labour but there was no hiring at present. However, it was good to get out of the house and away from the women. Another option for the boys was to go down to Wicklow Port, where they were reinforcing the harbour and foreshore with a grant from the British government of twenty-two thousand pounds.

A new North Pier was also being constructed, which would allow more commercial trade to take place, increasing employment, which was so badly needed in the area. Here they had better luck and were taken on as brickies, starting the following day. They celebrated with fish and chips eaten out of paper, a rare treat. Whilst they were in Wicklow, they took the opportunity to phone Ronan at Milldown and let him know that his sister, Kathleen, was on the mend but missing him. Helen answered the phone, delighted to hear from the boys and said she would pass on the message and that all was well with them.

That evening after supper, Kathleen asked Killian if he would come with her to see Cara. She was anxious to tell Cara that Ronan would soon be home and didn't like to walk the distance alone in the evening. Killian obliged and the two set off,

Killian chasing Kathleen, making her scream with delight, even though it caused a coughing fit.

Cara was feeding the chickens when they arrived whilst several of the children were playing marbles in the dirt. The youngest, Liam, was clinging to the hem of her skirt, whining, although Cara seemed not to notice. She looked vacant and slightly unkempt but smiled when she saw Kathleen.

"Hello, lovely, how are you, darling? Are you feeling better than when I saw you last?"

Killian couldn't help admiring her spirit under such adversity.

"Cara, you're looking fine. How do you do it with this lot to keep you busy?"

Cara blushed, her spirits lifted by the compliment; they were few and far between these days.

"Ah, Killian, you're too kind. Look at me – old before my time."

"I'll have none of that; you're as pretty as the day is long."

Kathleen forgot the purpose of her visit, sitting down on the dirt to play marbles with the children.

"Killian, would you like a drink?"

"That would be nice, thanks."

They went into the kitchen, not bothering to remove their shoes, as the floor had obviously not been swept in days.

"Sit down, Killian. Would you like some ale or elderflower water?"

"I'll just have water, thanks, Cara."

Sitting at the table chatting, they were suddenly silenced by a sound from the back of the house.

"Is someone sick, Cara?"

"No, that's my dad. He's been drinking. He's lost his job.

I'm in dire straits."

With that, the tears fell. Her shoulders hunched over as she covered her face, unable to cope with the embarrassment of her position. Killian got up and went to her side, pulling her to her feet and holding her close. His heart was breaking. Cara was young and pretty; she should be enjoying life with parents who cared for their children. It had all gone wrong when Cara's mother had died.

"Cara, shall I go and see to your father?"

"Please don't, he's in a terrible state. I don't know who to turn to."

"Let me go to him, Cara. Maybe I can talk to him."

Killian followed the noise to the back of the house, where he found Cara's father collapsed on the floor, an empty whiskey bottle next to him. He was incoherent, and by the state of his trousers it was clear that he had soiled himself. Killian turned him on his back and tapped his face. His eyes opened to reveal a yellow tinge to the whites of his eyes, dribble running from the side of his mouth.

"Cara, I think we need to get a doctor – he's in a bad way."

"The doctor has washed his hands of him, Killian, as he won't stop drinking. The priest won't come either, as my father has been abusive to him. I can't cope with him and the children."

"Have you no other relatives nearby?"

"None that would lift a finger to help."

"Don't worry, Cara. I'm going to help as much as I can."

That was the end of Killian's job. Brandon went off the following day by himself to Wicklow Port to explain that his brother was no longer available to work.

Patricia, although sympathetic, was not prepared to take on the care of any more children. She made three large boxty breads and some potato soup for Killian to take over to the children but that was all she was prepared to do. By the time Killian arrived, Cara had managed to clean her father up, but he was still in a state of collapse. She had a look of indifference that Killian found disconcerting.

"I think he may have had a stroke, Cara. I'm going to fetch the doctor."

The doctor later confirmed that Mick had suffered a stroke and was unlikely to recover. He had sclerosis of the liver and was suffering from malnutrition. There were no beds available at St. Vincent's hospital but he could get him a bed in the fever hospital. Cara agreed to let the doctor take him away in the wagon, which Killian thought was an undignified departure, but it was Cara's decision. Cara had loved him in her youth, but now she felt nothing but a deep-seated resentment that his demise was self-inflicted and she loathed and despised what he had become. Killian stayed, trying to reassure the children and clean the room in which their father had collapsed. Although unspoken, they each knew they would never see Mick again.

Chapter 13

Wicklow

Having been brought up by a nurturing mother, Killian, as well as his siblings, had been blessed with a compassionate nature, so the thought of Cara trying to run a house and look after her family tugged on his heart strings. It had been suggested by the nuns that three or four of the children would benefit from being taken into their care; however, Cara would not let that happen at any cost. She had heard rumours of abuse in the convent. Her mother would have turned in her grave at the thought.

Killian made it his business to visit Cara each day to offer support and friendship. He saw himself as an older brother, hoping that she would find her feet and become independent, but she soon became totally reliant on him. She dreaded him leaving in the evening, for the loneliness weighed heavily on her and the children ran riot without Killian's guidance.

"You're getting yourself in deep there, Killian. I hope you know what you're doing."

Patricia began to worry that her son was taking on the responsibility of Cara's dysfunctional family, and in her eyes that was a monumental mistake.

"It's all right, Ma, I'll help her until she can cope. She's lost both of her parents, don't forget, and the children are a right handful."

Killian slowly began to see an improvement in Cara now that

she had a small amount of time to call her own. Her hair regained its lustre and the clothes she wore were clean. She had a smile each time Killian arrived, greeting him with a drink and a home-made biscuit. He chopped wood, dug over and replanted the vegetable plot, cleaned the chicken coup and the barn, generally getting the family back into a routine, something that had been missing for some time. The two oldest sisters, Orla and Geraldine, were in service so brought home a salary at the end of each month when they got a day off, and there was also money that her father had left hidden under a board in the Jacks.

"Don't go, Killian. Read me another story."

"I'll read you one more, Liam, if you put your head down next to Conor and go to sleep."

The stuffed mattresses were laid out one next to the other on the floor, four in a row for the youngest boys. Now their father had gone, there was an extra room for the girls.

"Now, you be good lads. I'll see you tomorrow."

Killian had to admit that he was becoming attached to the children and he saw no harm in it. He popped his head into the girls' room and said goodnight to the three sisters, who were enjoying their new room, which meant not having to share with the boys.

"Killian, will you have a drink before you go? Or take a stroll? It's still light."

Killian knew that Cara was reluctant to let him leave, but he thought it best to get home or his mother might have something to say.

"Oh, Killian, could you just carry a bucket of water to the cow? My back is aching something fierce."

She looked so pretty and youthful with her dark, shiny hair wisping round her cheeks. Killian couldn't help feeling a strong attraction to her.

She put her hand into the small of her back, stretching out the source of her discomfort, revealing to Killian a slight roundness where once her waif-like figure had appeared trim and childlike. His stomach summersaulted, thinking back to why Ronan had been so upset. Had he got the girl with child after all? The thought filled him with trepidation, not only for Ronan but also for Cara. It suddenly dawned on him how close he had allowed himself to get to Cara and he wished that he had listened to his mother. For now, he could not simply stand down. He realised his feelings were not those of a brother but a potential lover, and the consequences would be life-changing.

It was unusual to see Sister Leonella sat at the kitchen table when he arrived home. His mother and father seemed a little tense, and his sister Bridget, or Bridge, as she was known, had tears in her eyes. Younger than the boys, Bridge was just fifteen, with dark hair framing her plain but nevertheless attractive face. Killian soon picked up the gist of the conversation and didn't like what he was hearing. It seemed that Bridge wanted to take her vows and become a novice nun.

"Sister, we appreciate all the help you have given the family over the years, but we weren't expecting to lose Bridge to the church."

Patricia held onto Bridge as if she were about to be taken away to the convent that very moment.

"Patricia, Ambrose, Bridge is a clever girl. We simply offered her the chance to further her education with us. She cannot take vows until she is at least eighteen, but she has proved herself to be a promising student. Would her talents not be wasted in service? She could become a teacher, or a nurse. We have posts abroad as well if she wanted to travel."

"I'll not have it. She's to go into service like the others and bring some money home. I'll not have it, do you hear? She spends far too much time up at that convent."

Ambrose had gone red in the face, his arms flailing, and Patricia could see that before long he would be shouting words that no nun should ever hear.

"Ambrose, darling, let's sleep on it. I'm sure Sister Leonella would like to get back to the convent before dark. Bridge, go upstairs and see if Kathleen has washed, there's a good girl."

Killian loved the way his mother could defuse a situation with the tone of her voice and a simple instruction. He offered to walk Sister Leonella back to the convent, leaving Patricia to placate her husband. Bridge went to Kathleen, who cuddled her and stroked her hair, not knowing the cause of her unhappiness but instinctively wanting to comfort her sister. Tomorrow would be the time to talk. Settling down that night, Bridge said three Hail Marys for purity. She had little idea of what was meant by purity, but the sisters had instructed her that this was for her own good.

Walking Sister Leonella to the large wooden gate of the convent, Killian wondered at the silence. He knew there were at least eighty boarders and roughly forty-seven sisters in residence. All windows were shut and the place looked dark and foreboding. There was no sound of laughter or movement behind any of the windows, although the children who boarded ranged from three to twelve years old. He said goodnight and left the sister to push the heavy door open and enter her outlandish world.

"It's a weird place, that convent, an unholy atmosphere if you ask me," said Killian on his return.

"Oh, hush now, Killian. What would Bridge say if she heard you talk like that?"

"I have to agree," said Ambrose, "I don't know what their motives are. She's being lured into that convent. They're filling her head with nonsense about education – what does a young woman need education for? I've heard bad reports of that place. I know they've been good to our children, but that's because we give them an income with the lace making and a backhander every so often. The poor buggers who board there with no family support are not treated the same way, I know that for a fact. Some of them are beaten and starved; old Ted the gardener up there has witnessed it."

"Oh, Ambrose, you shouldn't listen to local gossip. I'm sure that's not the case. Bridge would have said something."

"Bridge and Kathleen are in a different building on account of their age and their earning capacity with the lace making. They are seniors, and when ours were little, they never boarded; they were kept separate from the orphans. Send her off abroad! I've never heard anything like it. The answer is no!"

The subject was not brought up again, although Bridge did continue her education surreptitiously and continued to say her three Hail Marys every night.

Killian didn't visit Cara the following day. His mind was all over the place. Brandon was coming home exhausted every evening, unwilling to chat, so Killian was left with a dilemma which seemed insurmountable. He was unsure if Ronan had feelings for Cara; would he be stepping on his toes if he took up with her? The only thing Killian was sure of was that he missed Cara's company when they were apart and that of the children. He would have to confront her.

When he arrived at Cara's the following day, the children mobbed him. He threw Liam up in the air, much to the delight of Connor and the others. They all wanted a turn; however, Cara was looking dejected as she stood at the mangle, pressing out the water from her wash. She looked pale and unhappy. Killian couldn't bear to see her like that; she was far too pretty. He walked over and put his arm round her waist. It was the first time that he had touched her affectionately and she beamed.

"We missed you yesterday."

"I'm sorry, Cara, there was a bit of trouble with Bridge; I'll tell you later. We need to talk."

Cara's face dropped, for she anticipated trouble. Her heart sank at the thought of Killian going away for a while, or worse still, saying that he was not coming any more.

"Let's go inside. I'll make a cup of tea."

They sat drinking their tea, initially in silence, for Killian had no idea how to broach the subject, but he knew he had to get things clear. Did she have feelings for him, or did she see him as a father figure? He was ten years her senior, but he didn't think she saw him in that light. They had such laughs together and he had noticed how she looked at him occasionally.

"Cara, are you with child?"

There was no other way of saying it, but the shock took Cara by surprise. Her face dropped, and she looked like she was about to pass out.

"Cara, it's okay. You can tell me anything, you know that. I'm here to help you and the children. It won't alter things."

"I'm afraid it will, Killian. You should go."

"I'm not going until I know what we are up against here. Are you carrying Ronan's child?"

Chapter 14

Milldown

Much to the delight of the family, Maggie and Todd announced their engagement. The banns would be read in Coldingham Priory three weeks before the ceremony, which would take place in four weeks' time. Todd had been offered a job with the Ford Motor Company down south, so the couple would be leaving Milldown straight after the wedding. A job offer like that was rare, but Todd had been lucky enough to impress the company with his mechanical skills, and a letter of recommendation from Dr. Murray sealed the deal.

This revelation lifted the mood on the farm as preparations got under way. Beanie and Ellie planned a trip into Edinburgh with Maggie to buy materials for the wedding gown and trousseau. Maggie had quite simple requirements, but Ellie and Beanie were so excited they talked her into getting something quite special. They had a seamstress who was used for such occasions so the fittings started immediately. The gown, heavily laced at the high neck, seemed to flow over Maggie's trim figure like white icing over a cake, flaring at the hem. The trousseau was made up of a simple cotton nightgown with Maggie's name embroidered on it, towels, also embroidered, and linen tableware.

Helen, as mother of the bride, started her own preparations by making sure that the house was ready to receive guests. Todd's parents had agreed that the wedding should take place at Coldingham Priory and they had graciously accepted Helen's invitation to stay on the farm for the weekend. John's room, which had been left untouched since his passing, had now to be cleared out and cleaned, a job that nobody relished, but William undertook it with mixed emotions.

Ronan had heard from his family that Kathleen was out of hospital and on the mend so accepted an invitation to attend the wedding. He wrote, explaining that he would not be home for another month, much to Beanie's delight. The weeks rushed by in a flurry of excitement, then the day was upon them. Beanie and Ronan decorated their best wagon with flowers and ribbons and then started on Captain. His tail and mane were plaited and the long white hair on his fetlocks washed and brushed. He had never looked so handsome and would take the bride to the church.

Maggie was in a state of pure excitement one minute then floods of tears the next at the thought of having to leave the farm and her small white Pomeranian dog, Cora. It was difficult to keep her eyes dry long enough to put a bit of colour on them, so her lips were rouged, then the veil pulled over her face to disguise the imperfections of her distress. Todd's parents were wonderful, fitting into the family as though they were old friends, helping out where necessary or amusing themselves so as not to get in the way when things got hectic.

Helen had organised plenty of food and William plenty of drink. There was a local band of musicians playing and Ronan joined in with his drum, the tone of which was not to his liking after it had been re-skinned. Andrew had not been invited to the wedding, although several of the local lads were, but it was noticed that he had chosen a path running alongside the farm to get him to wherever he was going. Beanie smiled at the look of envy on his face as he walked on by.

The day was a complete success, but inevitably the time came for Todd and Maggie to depart. The cake had been cut and the bouquet thrown; there was no reason left to delay their departure. William hugged his daughter with a tear in his eye, knowing that he would not see her for some time. He slipped an envelope into her hand, which she knew would be money to give her and her husband a good start. He shook Todd's hand, wished them well and they were gone.

"Ronan, let's take a walk. I'm fair stappit."

"Fair stappit – what's the meaning?"

"It's Scottish for full up. Come on, I need to walk it off."

Ronan took Beanie's hand and they walked down the path to the beach to sit in the sand dunes. The moon was full, the evening breeze cooling and refreshing after the good food and wine. Captain had done a fine job and was back in his stall for the night, and William had employed help to clear up, so it was time to relax.

"What a wonderful wedding. Your parents are so warm and generous. You have a good life here, Beanie. I do consider myself lucky to be working here."

"I wish you could stay on. We certainly need the help now John has gone."

The seed was sown. Ronan hadn't considered the possibility of staying on permanently, but it was certainly an attractive proposition. He had no prospects back home in Ireland to better himself, and of course there was Beanie. Although he was young, only twenty-one, he had strong feelings for Beanie and dreaded the thought of returning home. He knew he would have Cara pursuing him and he had to admit that the thought of all the children filled him with a sense of horror.

"Come on, Beanie, we'd best get back or we'll be missed."

"Not until you've kissed me!"

Beanie was feeling playful after two or three glasses of wine, so by the time they got back to the farm, all was quiet. They hadn't been missed.

The following morning, a letter arrived for Ronan, much to his delight, for he thought it must be good news about Kathleen's recovery or his family would have phoned. On opening the letter, his face fell. He got to his feet and left the kitchen without a word. Beanie and her mother exchanged glances, thinking the news had to be bad or Ronan would have excused himself.

The letter read:

Dear Ronan,

I think that you must return home to sort out a problem which may or may not have been of your making. You remember the chat we had when you were upset? Well, I think you may have been correct in thinking that you have done wrong.

Yours,

Killian.

The letter was short and simple but spoke volumes. Ronan's heart sank. He was in a state of shock, knowing exactly to what Killian was referring. What on earth had he done? It didn't bear thinking about. For the rest of the day, he worked alone, not even stopping for refreshments. Beanie tried to approach him, but each time he made an excuse and walked away.

Later that evening, Beanie went to the barn to fill the water buckets up for the horses and saw the letter lying in the straw. She recognised the envelope. Obviously, it had been dropped by mistake, otherwise Ronan would have destroyed it or put it away somewhere safe. The letter clearly contained something that had caused Ronan considerable distress, so the temptation to read it was considerable.

She bent to pick it up but a voice behind her stopped her in her tracks.

"That would be mine, Beanie."

"I'm sorry. I was just picking it up to return it to you. Is something wrong at home?"

"Yes, you could say that. I'm going to have to leave tomorrow. I've got to finish helping your father with some fencing in the lower field today, so I'll plan to leave first thing in the morning."

"Is it something you want to talk about, Ronan?"

"No, no, it will not be concerning you, Beanie; something I have to take care of, 'tis all."

"Will you be coming back?"

"I can't say at the moment. We'll have to wait and see."

With that, Beanie left the barn in tears, totally confused and feeling rejected. But after a cooling off period alone in her bedroom, the anger set in. She avoided Ronan all day and ate in her bedroom. If he was going to take off with no explanation, he would have to do it without a goodbye from her. When she awoke the next morning, he was gone.

Chapter 15

Wicklow

Ronan arrived home, having been travelling for more than fifteen hours. The house was dark and he entered with a sinking feeling in the pit of his stomach. He was totally unprepared for the predicament that he found himself in, and the lukewarm reception he got from Kilian in the morning said it all. He was in trouble. Kathleen, however, threw her arms around him and started to talk twenty to the dozen, telling Ronan how awful the food had been in hospital and how the bed had been uncomfortable. Ronan made a fuss of Kathleen then told her that he had to go outside with Killian for a while.

"Cara hasn't spoken to me in days. She won't have anything to do with me after I asked her if she was carrying your child. She can't cope on her own, Ronan. The children will suffer if they haven't already suffered enough since the death of their mother."

"What do you want me to do about it? I can't become the father figure to nine children; I'm too young."

"You didn't think about that before you got her pregnant?"

"No. I gave it no thought at all, if the truth be known. I didn't set out to let it go that far. She just wanted some comfort and it just happened. I'm not proud of it."

Killian felt sorry for his young brother, knowing that temptation was a fierce adversary, certainly one to avoid.

"Ronan, you'll have to go and see her. You can't shirk your responsibility, you know that, don't you?"

"Of course I know that, but what will Ma say?"

Killian couldn't help but laugh at Ronan's fear of his mother's reaction. It confirmed to Killian just how immature poor Ronan was – surely that should have been the least of his worries? Killian was now not only concerned for Ronan but for Cara too. It was clear to him that Ronan was not the man to take on the upbringing of such a large family. If Ronan was in fact the guilty party here, which Cara hadn't confirmed, a solution would have to be found that was in the best interests of all concerned. Then in the middle of all this, Killian couldn't put to rest the fact that he had deep feelings for both Cara and her siblings and would be bereft if he had to concede to Ronan.

They had been walking for some time when their banter went quiet, and they found themselves on the outskirts of Cara's smallholding.

"Off you go, Ronan. You will have to face your demons."

Killian returned home and didn't see Ronan again for quite some time.

"Where's Ronan gone now when he's just got home?"

Patricia was busy in the kitchen making a large batch of colcannon to have with the corned beef hash she'd made earlier. Maybe she'd put a fried egg or two with it, as Ronan had just returned. A nice rice pudding with skin on top and a spoonful of apple compote would do for dessert. Ambrose was still condemning the convent as a place of entrapment and cruelty but no one was listening, so he stuck his head back in his newspaper.

"He'll be back soon, Ma. He's just gone over to see Cara."

"Talking of entrapment, is she going to take all my sons away from me? Haven't you spent enough time with her,

Killian?"

"I've told you, Ma, she needs the help at the moment."

"Well, I could do with some help here too. Will you set the table for me? And can you get Kathleen in? She's not long been out of hospital; we don't want her back in there with the consumption waiting to take her."

Killian set the table while Bridge went to find Kathleen, who was in the barn tatting, whilst Mary Beth helped her mother serve the food in the kitchen. Ronan appeared, hands in pockets, head down and shoulders slumped. Killian assumed that his meeting with Cara had not gone well.

As they ate lunch, Ambrose continued to denounce the convent, causing a heated argument; however, Ronan remained uncommunicative. Bridge could not stand the verbal attack of her beloved convent and the Sisters of Mercy so left the table with tears running down her cheeks. When lunch had finished, Killian took Ronan outside on the pretext of chopping some logs.

"Well, did you find out who the father is? Is it yours, Ronan?"

"I don't know – she was really strange. She wouldn't even confirm that she was pregnant and blames you for starting a rumour. She says she has no need of anyone's help and wants to be left alone. She looked very depressed. She's doing such heavy work and long hours looking after the children, who were grubby and miserable. There's something not adding up. I could see that she is pregnant, but she says it's not mine, or yours, for that matter. I don't know what to believe."

"Well, it's certainly not mine – I haven't been near her."

Killian was shocked that she would mention him as not being the father, as he had been nothing but a good friend to her. Rumours spread quickly in small villages, and as he had spent so much time with Cara, there was no doubt he would be implicated when word got round that she was pregnant. The boys had a dilemma on their hands.

"Killian, there is a possibility that I could go back to Coldingham and be offered a permanent job there, as they have lost John and now Maggie has gone as well. I would love to be able to do that. I love the place and I'm mighty fond of Beanie."

"Well, you can't go off and leave Cara until we know the truth. I have to tell you, Ronan, I've become mighty fond of Cara over the past weeks. Is that okay with you?"

"Of course, Killian, but what if the child is mine?"

"We'll cross that bridge when we come to it."

Cara's name was not mentioned for a few days, during which time Ronan wrote to Beanie. He kept the wording up-beat, not mentioning a return date or what the problem was that had sent him running home. He hoped she would forgive him for his sudden departure and said that he would write again soon.

The weekend gave Brandon time to rest up, as his work was arduous. His hands were scratched and rough and his back aching. The boys decided that a trip to The Fighting Cocks for a couple of pints of Guinness would do them all good. Ronan and Brandon set off, leaving Killian to catch up later, as he was busy helping Kathleen in the kitchen shelling peas, and she would not let him leave until the job was done. She was becoming precocious.

As he left the house in rare good humour at the prospect of having one too many with his brothers, two little boys holding hands came hurrying towards him. He instantly recognised Liam and Conor and by the look on their faces, something was wrong. They would not have strayed this far by themselves for any other reason than to ask for help.

"Boys, what's wrong? What are you doing all the way over here this time of the evening?"

The two bedraggled little boys spoke in unison, still clutching each other's hands.

"Cara's in bed and she's bleeding all over the place. She won't get up and we're hungry."

"Ma, Ma."

Killian took the boys into the house, where Kathleen took control. His mother wasn't to be seen.

"Kathleen, can you give the boys something to eat? I have to go to see if Cara is all right."

Kathleen took the boys under her wing, washing their hands and sitting them down at the kitchen table. Her mothering instincts came into full swing and when Patricia came into the kitchen, she was told that she wasn't needed.

"Well, what have we here?"

Kathleen introduced Liam and Conor, who sat very quietly, intent on seeing what Kathleen was going to give them to eat.

"Killian has gone to see Cara – she's bleeding. I'm to look after the boys," said Kathleen, full of self- importance.

"Well, I'll leave you to it then."

Patricia, who was indifferent to Cara's wellbeing, was put out by the fact that her food would be going to these children. Hadn't Killian done enough for them already without them now sitting at her kitchen table, eating her food?

Killian ran as fast as he could to Cara's house and flew in through the front door.

"Cara, where are you? I'm coming up."

Killian ran into the bedroom, finding Orla and Geraldine with their sister. She was white-faced and perspiring.

"Orla, have you sent someone for the doctor?"

"No, Cara says she doesn't need one. She won't let me go."

"Okay, can you two go downstairs and make Cara a cup of strong tea? I'll see to her."

The girls left the bedroom, which had once been their parents', leaving Killian to sit on the bed and hold Cara's hand. He had never been so scared.

"Cara, what's happened? The boys said that you're bleeding. Are you losing the baby?"

"Killian, please go, I don't want help. Don't send for the doctor."

"Cara, you could bleed to death, I'll send for the midwife."

"Killian, if I die, my prayers will have been answered. Please go."

Killian looked underneath the blanket and saw blood pooling between her legs, and fear gripped him. He ran downstairs and shouted for Orla to run and get Mrs. Doyle, the retired midwife, who lived not too far away.

"Geraldine, you run to the doctor and see if he can come quickly. Off you go, *now*," he shouted.

He returned to Cara, taking her hand again.

"Cara, are you losing a baby? Why do you say such things? You've got plenty to live for."

Cara gave a wry, weak smile. There was a buzzing in her ears and the room was spinning. She almost felt euphoric, thinking that her troubles would soon be over and that she would be taken simply and quietly like her mother had been, in her mother's bed.

"Killian, I wish the baby had been yours. I would have loved it."

Her mind drifted, and she spoke incoherently while Killian piled on blankets. Her hand was freezing.

117

Her eyes suddenly opened.

"Killian, don't send the children to the orphanage – promise."

"I'll not let anything happen to them, I promise. Cara, was it Ronan's baby?"

"No. I want to be buried without anyone knowing the truth, Killian. You'll all hate me; even the children will hate me if they find out the truth."

"What could be that bad, Cara? If you need to confess something that you have done, you can tell me. I love you, Cara."

Tears ran down his face as he professed his love.

"You love me, Killian? Then don't make me tell you."

Mrs. Doyle burst into the room, pushing Killian out of the way. She stripped off the bedclothes to assess the situation, bundling up a tiny, lifeless, blood-soaked form and putting it to one side. Massaging Cara's abdomen with firm, competent hands, the afterbirth that had caused the persistent bleeding finally slipped from her body, and Mrs. Doyle breathed a sigh of relief.

Killian sat at the table while Orla made the tea, his hands still trembling.

"Orla, do you know anything about this?"

Orla, who was fourteen, went quiet and looked down at her feet.

"Orla, I'll do my best to put things right if I know what has happened here."

He knew Orla was old enough to know about periods and pregnancy and thought that she might be able to shed some light on what this was all about. By the look on her face, his assumption was correct.

"Orla, you can trust me. I love your sister."

Orla looked up when Killian said he loved Cara, and he could see that she wanted to share with him something that was obviously weighing heavily on her young shoulders.

"I think my father hurt her."

Orla knew exactly what her father had done. She had witnessed it and heard the suffocated sobs from Cara. But how could she vocalise what had taken place when her father had been so drunk that he was capable of inflicting such an atrocity on his eldest daughter? It was too horrific and incomprehensible to allow any outsider to know what their father had become after the consumption of alcohol. The shame reflected on every member of her family, and she couldn't bear it. She loved her sister so much, and the pain she felt at not having been able to protect Cara ripped through her heart. She had even begun to think of ways of killing her father, the father she had loved and respected during her childhood. Their darkest, dirtiest secret was out.

Chapter 16

Milldown

Although still irritated at the way Ronan had rushed back to Wicklow with no explanation or farewell, Beanie missed him madly. At first, she refused to open the letter that he had sent, trying to convince herself that she wasn't interested in what he had to say. However, it took no longer than an hour before she could resist no longer. He still didn't speak of the emergency that had caused his departure. Instead, Ronan spoke of Captain and the farm, saying how much he missed everyone. He asked Beanie to reply by return of post, and he hoped he would see everyone soon.

"Just write whatever comes into your head, Beanie," he wrote. "That would be grand."

She replied:

"You asked me for something original,
Something from inside my head,
As I haven't got anything inside,
I'll give it from outside instead."

She enclosed a lock of her hair; no other words. She felt he didn't deserve any, but her warm feelings for him were restored. The three boys were certainly missed. The loss of John and then Maggie's marriage to Todd had left the farm extremely short-handed. Issy, the milk maid, was now employed for extra hours in the house, which freed up Beanie to work more outside with her father. William had asked Beanie what Ronan's intentions were with regard to coming back, but of course she had no answer.

"If he's not coming back, Beanie, I'm going to have to take on a lad from the village, I thought Ronan would take the job. He's a good worker and fitted in well; we had spoken about him staying on."

"I know, Father. Give him a couple of weeks, I think he'll be back. There was a family emergency; he didn't say what."

"I don't like to see you behind the horses ploughing, Beanie. It's hard work, and I'm not up to it now."

"With Captain up front I just plod along behind, especially when paired with Ivan. They make a good team."

Ivan, the farm's Clydesdale, was at least seventeen hands and as sturdy as Captain though a little older and not as spirited.

"We're going to enter the ploughing competition this year, did I tell you? I think we've got a good chance of winning. Perhaps we could host it here at Milldown. It would certainly cut down our workload if the fields were ploughed for us."

"Ah, Beanie, you're worth two boys from the village any day. You'll be rewarded."

"Can I have a motorcycle as a reward, Father?"

"I hope you're joking, lass."

But Beanie was not. She had her eye on a Harley Davidson strap tank for sale in Dunns. Beanie, being the tomboy in the family and liking speed, was attracted to the thought of being the first in the village to own a motorcycle, let alone the first woman to own one.

"Uncle Ralph, what do you think about me getting a motor-cycle?"

Uncle Ralph, a widower for many years, spent a great deal

of time up at Milldown if not out fishing. He strode over to give Beanie one of his strong, masculine hugs.

"Beanie, lass, I'd rather be out on the roughest sea than travel with you across the cliff tops in that pony and trap of yours, and I certainly would avoid any woman in charge of one of these new motorised cycles."

This was not the answer she wanted. He was not to be her ally in this matter. However, she hugged him, offering him tea and scones. His life at sea had been a tough one, and it showed now in his wrinkled, ruddy face and coarse hands. Beanie could almost discern the motion of the waves in his stride.

Later that afternoon during a quiet spell, she took Captain down to the beach. It was a beautiful autumnal day and the sea was calm. They were plodding along the shoreline with the gulls squawking overhead, Captain enjoying splashing his massive hooves in the water, when they were suddenly overtaken by a huge black dog, similarly enjoying the waves. It was Carro, from the shipwreck bounding along.

Captain threw his head up, acknowledging the interloper and broke into a trot in the wake of the dog. He seemed to be fascinated by the huge black beast and shook his head time and time again, making Beanie laugh. The trot was not a comfortable ride, so Beanie calmed him down into a walk. The dog doubled back and bounded alongside Captain, much to his delight and the amusement of Beanie. They came to a standstill in front of the dog's owner.

"He's a fine fellow. What do you call him?"

"This is Captain, one of the farm's workhorses. He seems to be enamoured of Carro."

"Oh, you know the dog?"

"Yes. A friend and I found him after the shipwreck, and we

handed him over to you."

"Ah, that's right. I'm very grateful – he's truly a wonderful animal, as is Captain here. I'm a great horse lover, you know, and keep a good stock in my stables, if you'd like to see them. Why don't the two of you come over to Kelso tomorrow? I have a Shire to match Captain. Perhaps you could persuade my son Alasdair to ride out? He's a bit of a bookworm and needs some fresh air."

"That would be lovely. I'll have to see to the animals first; say about eleven? I know the estate."

"Great. See you then."

Beanie arrived at the huge iron gates of the estate the following morning, soon after eleven as promised. This was a conundrum – she would have to dismount to open the gate, but then there was no mounting post. She didn't want to arrive leading Captain. She felt so small and inconsequential when walking beside him and thought it might make a bad impression. Thinking there was no other way, she was about to dismount when a young man approached.

"Hi, let me get the gate for you. I'm Alasdair, and you are?"

"Beanie. Your father invited me over."

"Yes, he did say someone was coming to try to get me on a horse. Good luck with that."

Beanie felt slightly awkward. The young man, although attractive, did not seem that friendly. He had crisp, thick, dark hair and blue eyes, a good, muscular physique, tall as far as Beanie could tell, although it was difficult to judge his height from on top of Captain.

"Come round to the stables. I think father wants to show off his horses."

The stable block was pristine with staff everywhere. The

house beyond was constructed of grey stone, four storeys with a large glass orangery to the side. Beanie began to wish that she had not accepted the invitation, as she felt her powers of persuasion in this case would be inadequate to coax this young man to ride out, as he seemed uninterested in horses altogether.

"Good morning, Beanie. I see you've brought the sunshine with you."

Carro ran by his master's side, tail wagging, his bright, intelligent eyes glistening in the sun. On recognising Captain, the dog rushed over with multitudes of enthusiasm, causing Captain to throw his head up and down in response.

"Hop down and I'll show you round the stables Alasdair, help her down."

Alasdair followed orders and came to stand next to Captain, waiting for Beanie to dismount. Rushing so as not to keep Alasdair waiting, Beanie threw her right leg over Captain's back and began to slide down, a manoeuvre she would not normally undertake because of the drop. Alasdair's hands found Beanie's waist and he lowered her slowly to the ground. Blushing madly, she found herself mute, let her hair fall over her face and just managed a mumbled thank you.

Following Alasdair's father, Beanie commenced a tour of the stables whilst Captain was led away by a groom. He didn't seem to mind, but Beanie felt lost without his huge presence. The horses were mostly fine thoroughbreds. There were a few polo ponies and a rare Arab bought for breeding, also a small Eriskay pony for children to ride. There were a few working horses, one of which was a large Shire being groomed to perfection, tail plaited and tied up.

"Here's Jimmy Key, named after a very intelligent horse, although the name doesn't befit this beast. I thought you could hack out with Alasdair – what do you say?"

"Yes, that's fine, if Alasdair would like that."

"I don't think it's a question of him liking it, but Jimmy Key needs the exercise. Harness him, could you, Pat."

The instruction was given to a groom and Jimmy Key was brought out, harnessed and ready to go.

"Am I to ride bareback too, Father?"

"Well, if Beanie can do it, so can you."

Captain was brought back and led to a mounting block for Beanie. Back on top of her horse, she felt more confident and less shy, knowing that Alasdair was obviously uncomfortable, especially without a saddle. However, Alasdair mounted like a professional, which surprised Beanie, and they set off with Carro in tow.

"Beanie, where did you say you were from?"

"Milldown. Do you know it?"

"Yes, I swim there in the bay."

"I haven't noticed you there."

"No, you wouldn't have."

What does that mean, Beanie thought, feeling it was some sort of rebuff. She didn't know what to make of this young man, whom she should have found pleasant but was somewhat aloof. She searched her mind for things to say, as the silence was deafening.

"Are you studying?"

"Yes, I'm studying land management. My father wants me to run the estate eventually. It's a costly place to upkeep. I think we will have to diversify in the near future to survive."

"How many acres do you have?"

"Fourteen thousand, give or take, not all farmed, of course." He smiled.

"That is a huge estate. We farm three hundred and sixty- five acres."

He didn't seem impressed, and the conversation went quiet again. She did, however, notice that he was sneaking the odd look at her. Whether he was liking what he saw or not, she had no idea. They plodded along in silence for some time, Carro running alongside, sniffing through the bracken. Up ahead, a herd of deer were grazing, unaware of their approach.

"Let's turn back. I don't want to disturb them. My father invites parties of stalkers to shoot them for sport – I think it's disgusting. I hate blood sports. If I do run the estate one day, I certainly will not permit it. I'd like to plant trees. Deforestation in Scotland has been going on for generations, mainly due to agriculture. There are very few forests hereabouts, and it's difficult to grow new trees because of the grazing, mainly by the deer. I'd like to reintroduce a few species of animals and birds that have become extinct here in Scotland too.

That took Beanie by surprise, as she thought him a country gent who would condone blood sports. He went up in her estimation.

"There's not much for young people to do round here. How do you amuse yourself, Beanie?"

"Well, apart from working on the land and tending the animals, I have to agree – socialising is a problem. We have the odd ceilidh, but it is difficult to meet new people."

"I'm having some friends for drinks tomorrow evening, if you would like to come. You could bring your sister if you want."

Another surprise. How did he know she had a sister? She failed to comprehend this young man at all, but against her better judgement she was beginning to like him.

Chapter 17

Milldown

Ellie's excitement was contagious when she was told of the invitation. They hadn't had the opportunity to dress well and meet new people for so long that preparations began late that afternoon. They both wore their hair rolled up and pinned at the nape of the neck and wore the clothes that they had worn for Maggie's wedding: high-neck blouses with plenty of lace work and long skirts. Great care was taken with their appearance. They had also polished their shoes, which was a rare occurrence. They were given permission to take the pony and trap even though Alasdair had offered to send a carriage for them. They thought that should they feel out of place or uncomfortable, they could make a quick getaway if they had their own transport.

Their arrival at Spylaw Park was heralded by a herd of skittish deer that bolted in front of the trap, running off across the lawns down towards a stream beyond the stable block. Staff were waiting to help the girls down and take the pony into their care before escorting them to the orangery. Ellie was intoxicated by the grandeur and a little intimidated, but their welcome was warm and she soon settled down.

Alasdair introduced them to two other sisters, Lorna and Faith, who lived nearby and two boys who were standing together, looking out across the gardens. A third boy was admiring a tall palm plant with his back to them. Alasdair walked

Beanie and Ellie over to introduce them.

"Andrew, I'd like to introduce you to Ellie and Beanie."

When he turned, Beanie almost swore. It was Andrew, dressed impeccably and looking, much to her chagrin, quite dashing.

"Andrew, how nice to see you here."

"Andrew has just taken a position with us on the estate. I find his thoughts on re-forestation are similar to my own. We're looking forward to working together on a few projects."

"Well, that's wonderful."

Beanie could think of nothing more befitting to say so left Ellie to make polite conversation with Andrew and Alasdair, whilst she went to talk to the two sisters, whom she found very companionable. The two other boys, Frasier and Tom, joined them, offering the girls a drink, and they struck up an easy conversation. Beanie didn't look back to see how Ellie was doing and felt rather guilty at having left her, but she knew she could handle the situation. Eventually Andrew came over to ask if he could have a quiet word with Beanie. He manoeuvred her away from the group, wanting her to himself, which she found quite disconcerting.

"Beanie, I know that you find me a bore, but I must get something off my chest. It wasn't me who damaged Ronan's drum, I can assure you. I know you think the worst of me and I have behaved badly, but it was only because I hold you in such high regard. My youthfulness made a fool of me. I'm sorry. The drum fell and caught on a sharp piece of wood; there were witnesses, if you don't believe me."

Beanie was holding back a laugh. She did feel sorry for Andrew, although she didn't want him to know. She thought he should suffer a little longer.

"The job here means everything to me, Beanie. Alasdair has such innovative plans for the estate, and he thinks that I can be of help. I've never been taken seriously before; my parents think of me as a labourer with no prospects. Please don't let me down."

"How did you meet Alasdair?"

"We met in the Plough and Horses over a pint and started talking about his estate and his plans to plant trees. He liked my ideas on protecting the saplings from the deer and other wildlife, and we just got on well. Then he offered me the job."

"Well, I won't tell him you're an idiot. Let him find that out for himself."

Beanie finally laughed and returned to the group, leaving Andrew slightly bewildered but somewhat relieved. He went back to talking to Ellie, who still seemed to be enamoured of him. Alasdair came to talk to Beanie.

"What a strange name for the house, Spylaw. Do you know how that originated?"

"It's a long story, Beanie, dating back to the reign of Mary Stuart. The rear aspect of this house was built in the sixteenth century and is said to have been used as a meeting place for Queen Mary and Lord Bothwell, her lover. At that time she was still married to Lord Darnley. Letters that were written between Mary and Bothwell were supposed to prove her complicity in the murder of her husband Darnley. The letters fell into the hands of the fourth earl of Morton and used in evidence against the queen.

"The letters were found in a silver casket here at Spylaw Park. The queen set about finding out who the spy was that had betrayed her and Bothwell and threatened to pass a law making it illegal to use the word of a spy as incriminating evidence in a court of law, thus the name Spylaw. The law was never passed, of course. It all sounds unbelievable but that is as legend would have it, passed down by our ancestors through the generations.

"They were savage times Beanie, Morton was executed in 1581 by the Maiden, an early form of the guillotine used here in Scotland. The casket was never found, but here at Spylaw we have a letter and a sonnet kept in a secret room, said to have been written by Mary Stuart. We have never asked anyone to verify the authenticity of these documents, as they would be confiscated; neither have they been translated. The sonnet is in French. Who knows – they might be original?"

"What an intriguing story. May I see the letter?"

"Not until I know you a great deal better, Beanie. I will show you the sixteenth-century façade at the back of the house but not just now."

"Alasdair, can I have a word?"

Lorna led Alasdair off, slipping her arm through his in a deliberate attempt to lure him away from Beanie. She obviously thought that they had spent too much time together and wanted to capture his attention for herself. Ellie was happily chatting to Andrew, which amused Beanie greatly, so she returned to the group discussing horsemanship and polo.

"Do you ride, Beanie?" asked Faith.

"I do indeed, I have all my life."

"Do you hunt?"

"I do not. I'm not fond of blood sports of any sort. I ride for pleasure, often bareback, and I use my horses for ploughing."

"Bareback, not side-saddle? Isn't that awfully uncomfortable? You don't mean that *you* plough, I'm sure."

"I do plough. We have three hundred and sixty-five acres and they nearly all need ploughing at some time during the year."

Beanie was becoming hot under the collar at Faith's persistent questioning.

"What do you do, Faith? Do you work the land?"

"Well, no, actually I don't do much at all. I have been invited to a polo match next weekend – that should be such fun."

The conversation finished there. Beanie had nothing in common with this woman and could not bring herself to make polite conversation. She wandered out into the garden, wishing that she could jump onto Captain's back and take him down to the beach to blow away the cobwebs.

"Having a tough time in there?"

"Nothing I couldn't handle."

Alasdair laughed.

"Come on. I'll show you the back of the house."

They walked off companionably, leaving the girls in the orangery watching from the window with envy, especially Lorna, whose green-eyed monster sat on her shoulder.

The grounds were beautiful, manicured to perfection. Rhododendrons grew in abundance, still holding their summer blooms. Huge trees that looked like they could have been there in Queen Mary's time ascended regally from the lawns, which were interspersed with rose beds and topiaries. A herd of deer lazed in the shadows of the trees and to make the picture perfect, Carro came bounding over.

"Hello, boy. No jumping; good boy."

By the look in Carro's eyes, he loved his master. How lucky he was to have survived the shipwreck and to end up living in such beautiful surroundings. He nuzzled Beanie's hand, demanding her attention, which she gave readily. He came up to her waist. She was sure a small child could have ridden him, he was so fit and muscular.

"See here, Beanie, this is the façade I was telling you about."

The three-storey fascia had wooden struts interspersed with

brick. The tiled roof and crinkled glass panes denoted the affluence of the building, for only the very wealthiest people could afford glass in their windows and tiles on their roofs in the sixteenth century. Houses were more commonly thatched except for in cities, where the risk of fire was too great.

"It's beautiful, Alasdair. How long have your family owned it?"

"We can trace our family as far back as the seventeenth century. Then it becomes a little vague."

"Can you just imagine Mary Stuart at Spylaw? She must have found solace here with her lover. She wasn't to have too many happy memories in her lifetime."

"You're right, Beanie. We like to think of her enjoying the delights of the house and park. The herds of deer would have been here, as would the plants and trees. The gardens have remained the same for centuries. There's also a small summer house that dates back to that era. Mary and Bothwell may have been lovers there; in fact, there is an etching in the wood of the summer house that looks like an M and a B."

"May I see?"

"Of course. Come on, Carro."

They walked across the lawns until they were out of sight of the house. Crossing a stream, they came across a pretty summer house that was in slight disrepair, a two-storey brick building with a tiled roof, not in the least as Beanie had expected. It had small, almost gothic-shaped windows and a round tiled turret on one corner of the first floor. The heavy wooden door was ajar and Beanie was invited in. It was dank and dark, smelling of a bygone era. There was a tiny fireplace with sticks and debris in the grate; birds had probably nested in the chimney over the years. A stone spiral staircase led to a single upstairs room with windows on all sides, wide oak plank flooring and a little round area that was the inside of the turret.

"There would have been a day bed in here for the ladies to recline on, having views across the park. The windows would have been open to allow a cool breeze in. I sometimes imagine Mary and Bothwell in here, away from the turbulence and intrigue of royal life, enjoying the privacy that this room would have offered them. See over here, in the turret where I imagine the day bed would have been, there is an engraving barely legible but there nonetheless. M and B intertwined – can you make it out? Look – this is the M and the curve of the B."

Alasdair had come up very close behind Beanie and she could feel his breath on the back of her neck, his leg pressing against hers. Her body tensed; she could no longer focus on the inscription, her face and body warming uncomfortably. Alasdair paused, intent on looking at the letters carved on the oak beam, seemingly unaware of the sensation and confusion he was causing Beanie.

"Beanie, I'm glad you appreciate history like I do. I'll show you the sonnet and letter one day if you want. You'll have to find the secret room first."

Beanie found it difficult to reply. No boy, or man in this case, had ever evoked such feelings in her before and she was a little bewildered. His maturity was becoming conspicuous against the naivety of both Andrew and Ronan.

"I think we should get back – I'm neglecting my sister," was all she could mutter.

Beanie found Ellie still engrossed in what Andrew was saying, the look on her face reflecting her infatuation with him. Beanie smiled, taking pleasure in Ellie's happiness, wondering where she would find her own, for now her feelings were indeed conflicted.

Chapter 18

Wicklow

The Fighting Cocks was aptly named, for when Brandon and Ronan arrived, the bar was empty except for the landlord. A raucous noise from the grounds at the back of the pub suggested that a fight was in progress. This almost weekly event attracted men from all over the county who would have bred a gamecock specifically for this purpose. Large spurs, pointed, claw-like growths on the back of the cockerels' legs, slashed at the opponent, inflicting sometimes fatal wounds. The cockerel's natural instinct to fight for a pecking order was exploited in this barbaric sport, the birds worked into a frenzy at the start of each fight. In nature one would be dominant, the weaker walking away; however, in a pit there is no escape. Out of the two Miner Blues fighting today, neither would be victorious, for the survivor of the fight would most probably be destroyed because of its mortal wounds.

Sometimes vast amounts of money exchanged hands and was then drunk away in the pub, either to celebrate or commiserate, leaving wives at home, short of money to feed their family. Ronan chose not to go and watch, ordering himself a pint of Guinness whilst chatting to the landlord, but Brandon thought that some of his hard-earned money could be put to good use out back. He soon returned, ordering himself a pint to mollify his losses. Several pints later, the boys walked home under a full moon, laughing and fooling around, listening to owls hooting and small mammals scurrying in the undergrowth.

The house was in darkness by the time they got home so they calmed their banter down, hoping not to wake anyone. However, Kathleen was in the kitchen.

"Killian's not come back yet. He went to see Cara – she was bleeding, and I had to feed the children."

It was only then that the boys recalled that Killian had not joined them for a drink at the pub.

"What are you saying, Kathleen?"

The boys were fuddled and could not piece together what Kathleen was trying to tell them.

"Killian went to help Cara, and the boys were hungry. I made them boxty to take home and put them to bed, but Killian said he was staying, so I had to walk home alone in the dark and it was scary."

"Okay, Kathleen, that's grand. You can go to bed now; we'll see to things."

Kathleen noticed that the boys were slurring their words and stumbling about the kitchen and rather doubted that they were capable of seeing to anything. She was used to seeing such behaviour from her father. However, she was relieved that they were home and felt happy that she could now go to bed.

"What in God's name is she talking about?"

"I don't know, but we're in no fit state to find out tonight. Killian will have to cope until the morning. Come on, we'd better get some sleep."

Morning came and with it a pounding head and photophobia. Ronan dragged himself out of bed and with a sinking feeling knew that he had to find out what was happening to Cara. He left Brandon to sleep it off, drank plenty of water then set off for

Cara's house, feeling nauseous and fearing what he would find there.

Several of the children were playing outside when Ronan arrived, but without saying hello he went straight into the kitchen. Mrs. Doyle was with Killian at the kitchen table and by the look on their faces all was not well.

"You – you've been sniffing around her like a dog on heat and look where it's got you."

Killian was taking an earbashing of monumental proportions, the look on his face subdued and accepting.

"As if that poor lass hasn't had enough grief in her short life, you have to come along and get her with child. It's just as well it's ended as it has."

There was no fight left in Killian. He looked like a defeated man taking what was due to him. No self-defence, even though Ronan knew he was innocent of the accusation. Killian put his hand to his forehead and Ronan thought he saw a tear run down his cheek.

"Don't worry, Mrs. Doyle, I'll take care of her. Please, let's keep this to ourselves for Cara's sake."

"That's grand, coming from you. Do you think I'd go chitter-chattering around the village? I keep myself to myself, unlike others." She glared at Ronan.

"No, no, I'm sorry. We're very grateful for all you've done." Which was the truth, as the doctor still hadn't arrived.

Mrs. Doyle stood up and left without another word, brushing past Ronan, collecting her bag, and was gone.

"What in God's name is going on, Killian? You know the baby wasn't yours. Are you taking the blame for me?"

"Ronan, I've been up all night and it's been very distressing. I'd rather not explain right now."

"Well, I think you're going to have to. I can't let you take the blame for something I've done. Not when it's this serious."

Just as an argument was about to ensue, Cara walked into the kitchen. Her hair was tangled and her face white. She walked crouched over, one hand on her abdomen.

"Cara, please go back to bed. You know what Mrs. Doyle told you. You must rest or the bleeding will start again."

"Killian, don't fuss, I have to feed the animals. Hello, Ronan."

She just managed to address Ronan, then she passed out. Killian grabbed her, lifted her and returned her to bed. When he came downstairs he was as white as a sheet with tears in his eyes again.

"Killian, sit down, I'll make some tea. I gather she's lost the baby. I'll stay – you go home and get some rest."

Ronan didn't know what to do for the best. He felt hungover and irritable but also responsible for this mess and the worry and distress he had caused his brother.

"Ronan, it wasn't your baby – let's get that clear."

"Then whose was it?"

"Cara doesn't want to say; it's her business. Let's leave it at that."

Killian refused to say any more on the subject but accepted Ronan's offer of help.

"You take care of the animals. I'll feed the children."

Just then Kathleen and her mother walked in with a basket of food.

"I'll feed the children."

Kathleen called the children in, sat them down and put potato farl and bacon on the table.

Patricia took Killian to one side and started her inquisition.

"Killian, I want to know what's happening in this house. I gather Cara is in some sort of trouble. Where is she?"

"She's in bed, Ma. You may as well know she's lost a baby."

"And the baby was yours, I presume."

"Well, you can think that, but you'd be wrong. It wasn't mine or Ronan's. She won't say who the father was and it's none of our business. She needs help and I'm offering, that's all."

Killian would not tell anybody of the abuse that Cara had suffered. If she wanted the truth to come out in the future then that would be her choice, but nobody would hear it from him.

"Where are you going, Ma?"

"I'm going to make sure that Cara is all right. She doesn't want men fussing around her not knowing one end of a woman from the other."

Well, that was one way of putting it and it brought a wry smile to Killian's face, but perhaps it was best that a woman should tend to her, although Killian wasn't sure that his mother was the best choice. She had not shown much sympathy so far.

"Are you comfortable, darling? Can I do anything for you?"

Patricia, although having a tough exterior, was compassionate and maternal towards other females. Cara looked so young and vulnerable that Patricia couldn't help being warm and affectionate.

"There now, how are you feeling, darling? Shall I get you a nice cup of tea?"

As Patricia leant down to adjust the pillow, the closeness of a sympathetic woman evoked feelings in Cara that she could not control. She put her arms round Patricia's neck and sobbed uncontrollably. Patricia held her and cried with her. She understood the loss Cara was feeling, not only for the baby but also for her mother, who should be there now to comfort her.

Patricia too had lost a baby many years ago, but the memory flooded back. Patricia didn't realise, however, that their circumstances were so very different, and that Cara's pain was born from abuse.

Patricia stayed with Cara until she fell into a deep sleep. Leaving her, she went back to the kitchen to find the children fed and the kitchen cleared. Kathleen had fine organisational skills when it suited her, and Patricia praised her.

"Come over here, my darling. Mammy needs a cuddle. Look what a fine job you've done. What would your brothers do without you?"

"Ronan's not well, Mammy. He looks green."

They all smiled at Kathleen's way with words. Because she had been born with Down's Syndrome, she seemed to see the world in black and white. There were no bad people; she loved everyone, and her feelings were reciprocated. They prayed that her world at least would never change. She was very precious.

It became obvious to all concerned that Cara was too weak to be left. She was unable to care for her family at present but they agreed that none of the children should be taken into care, for once taken they would not be returned. They decided to take it in turns to stay over, Patricia and Kathleen to take the first shift. The boys were either too tired or hungover so were sent home to rest. Their father, Ambrose, would not be pleased but the boys would have to deal with him if and when he noticed the absence of his wife and daughter. Killian volunteered to return that evening and sleep over.

Cara made a swift recovery. She was young and had a fierce determination to care of her siblings. Killian sponsored her efforts and two weeks later he married Cara quietly, with Patricia's blessing, in the village they had all been brought up in.

The ceremony looked more like a first communion than a wedding, as the small Catholic church was filled with laughing, happy children. Ambrose gave Cara away and Kathleen made a fine flower girl. Ronan, content that his brother and Cara were happy, now felt free to leave Ireland any time he chose.

Chapter 19

Milldown

The grand staircase in the centre of the oak-panelled hall led up to a suite of rooms devoted solely to Alasdair. Beanie followed him up; however, Carro refused to accompany them and was left howling in the great hall.

"He's afraid of the staircase; I can't explain why. Perhaps it has something to do with the ship he was on – the companionway leading below would have been too steep for an animal. He would have been left on deck; perhaps that is what saved him."

Alasdair led on, ignoring the pitiful noise from Carro and Beanie followed, slightly in awe of her surroundings. The invitation back to Spylaw had come as an unexpected surprise, a pleasant one that she had no hesitation in accepting, this time without her sister. Alasdair had promised to show her the letter and sonnet supposedly written by Mary Stuart, and he was as good as his word. He showed her into a room which was partly panelled, explaining that it was his study and apologised for the number of books scattered about. Light shone in through the open lead-latticed windows, the mottled glass of which made the lawn beyond undulate, seemingly out of focus. The room was not musty as one might have expected but smelt of fresh lavender polish and the earthy, fresh air from the garden.

"Now, Beanie, I told you that I would only show you the letters if you could find the secret room. I'll go and get some tea and when I get back, I'll expect you to have found it."

Alasdair left and Beanie took up the challenge. She circumnavigated the room, testing panels and looking for hidden handles to push or pull. She found neither. By the time Alasdair returned she was frustrated and baffled.

"Well, you win; I'm none the wiser. Where is it?"

"Let's have our tea and shortbread first, and then I'll show you."

"You're teasing me. I won't enjoy my tea unless you show me first."

Alasdair laughed and putting the tray down exposed what one would have assumed was a rope pull for the curtains, but when he pulled the rope, a click could be heard and a slight gap between two panels opened up. He pulled one of the panels open, revealing a stone staircase which led both upstairs and downstairs. One could hide in the room above or escape down the staircase into the garden. The door into the garden was hidden behind a trellis that could be pushed slightly away from the wall to enable an escape.

"Do you think it was once used as a priest hole? Can we go up?"

Beanie was anxious to see the room up above and maybe the letter in Queen Mary's handwriting.

"Scotland was Catholic under Mary and would have had little use for priest holes. They were mainly built in affluent Catholic houses in England, where Catholicism was outlawed and priests were pursued by pursuivants or priest-hunters. If caught, they usually came to a gruesome end."

Beanie bent her head low to enable her entrance to the passageway and walked up the cold stone staircase, the temperature seeming to drop a few degrees. It was a tiny, dark room with only one small window and was sparsely furnished. On an old oak table, two pieces of paper or parchment were encased in glass next to one another, one in English and the other in French. Beanie inspected them closely but could not make out a single word.

"What fascinates me is the fact that the casket letters were not signed, dated or addressed, but look here, Beanie, the letter is signed 'Mari R'. The sonnet is simply fourteen lines in French verse. Very difficult to make out any words, but look here, in the middle of the sonnet – what do you see, Beanie?"

Beanie studied the writing carefully, taking her time to look along each line, then she recognised something. In the middle of the sonnet were the letters M and B, intertwined as they were in the summer house.

"Oh, I see, how exciting! Has the sonnet not been translated?"

"No. My family are not known to be very scholarly, and of course they don't want to part with them – they belong to Spylaw. I think the room was more likely used as a hiding place not by priests but by Mary herself. Her Scottish crown was coveted by more than one person, and Mary was under constant threat. She would on occasion need a hiding place, and where better than here at Spylaw in a small safe room?"

Beanie couldn't take her eyes off the letter and sonnet. She totally believed the possibility that these were indeed in Queen Mary's handwriting and that she had used Spylaw as a sanctuary.

"Come on, Beanie, I have another surprise for you."

They went downstairs and back through the grand hall, where Carro was waiting.

"Hello, Beanie. Alasdair said you were coming. Has he made you tea?"

"Yes, thank you, and biscuits."

Alasdair's mother crossed the hall and was gone. Beanie was flattered that she knew who she was and thought what a friendly family they were, considering their obvious wealth and status.

Alasdair led Beanie over to the stables where she met Pat, a groom.

"Pat, will you bring the horses out and help Beanie with an apron?"

Beanie was a little bemused as to why she would need an apron, but it soon became clear. The horse that was brought over to her had been harnessed with a side-saddle. She had never used a side-saddle before but was more than ready for the challenge. She noticed that there was a balance strap as well as the girth for obvious stability but otherwise all looked familiar, apart from the pommels. Pat draped a long apron round her waist and fastened it at the back with a buckle.

"This is for your modesty, Mam."

Beanie was wearing a long skirt, which would obviously have to be hitched up to enable her to mount and put her leg around the top pommel; the apron would then conceal her legs. The horse she was to ride was called Hannah, an Irish Hunter with a glossy brown coat and at least seventeen hands. She mounted the steps and put her left leg in the stirrup then seated herself comfortably on the saddle whilst putting her right leg round the top pommel. It actually felt quite comfortable, with the left leg fitting snugly under the lower pommel. Pat adjusted the girth and straps and handed her a cane, or crop, to be held in her right hand.

Beanie felt totally invigorated and set off without even looking to see if Alasdair was ready.

"Trot on."

She encouraged her horse into a gentle trot but found that not being able to achieve a rising trot, having only one leg in a stirrup, made the motion quite uncomfortable. She clicked with her tongue and touched the horse with the cane to push her into a canter, eager to put the saddle and horse to the test. She found that she was laughing. The pleasure of being on this wonderful animal, riding in this unfamiliar manner was beyond all expectations.

"Hey Beanie, wait up."

Beanie grinned, and without looking back urged her horse into a gallop. The inclination of the ground made for a fast ride and she raced to the top, only then thinking of Alasdair. She slowed her horse down and finally came to a standstill, looking back to watch Alasdair canter up behind her.

"That was fun. I have to say, it makes a nice change to ride side-saddle."

"Beanie, are you crazy? I was going to take it slowly until you were used to the saddle."

"I've got strong thighs, Alasdair, no need to worry."

That was a slightly risqué thing to say, thought Beanie. He could misconstrue what she meant, but she was so happy she dismissed the impropriety, giving him her warmest smile.

"Let's walk a while, Beanie."

They walked the horses round the estate and chatted about his future plans to improve the land whilst Beanie explained the workings of her farm. Alasdair was impressed with the hard work she put in, suggesting new farm equipment and more help. Of course, Beanie and her family would like staff, but that was not an option financially, and as they approached the stables and saw the grooms coming out to take the horses from them, Beanie couldn't help thinking, how the other half live.

"Alasdair, I have enjoyed the day immensely, thank you. You must come over to Milldown some time soon."

"I'd like that, Beanie. As I said, I do swim in the bay there occasionally. I'll take the time to come and see you."

Beanie had had such a stimulating day with Alasdair that she felt quite morose returning to Milldown in her little pony and trap. Reaching her stables, she had the questionable pleasure of manoeuvring the trap under cover and brushing down the pony. The rest of the horses needed feeding, and so it began. Hard work. She felt tired and despondent entering the kitchen and her heart sank as her mother said, "Ronan's been on the phone – he's accepted the job. Aren't you pleased, Beanie?"

Beanie went to her room, collapsing on the bed. Her emotions were all over the place. She had loved her day with Alasdair so much that the thought of Ronan coming back filled her with a feeling of entrapment. How cruel, she thought. They had been the best of friends all summer, and now she felt nothing but duplicity.

The following morning, storm clouds were gathering. Literally. The North Sea was throwing large breakers up onto the beach and the howling wind was bashing on the tall landing window, making it rattle, splattering it with salt water and obscuring the view out to sea. The squall was persistent, preventing any outside work. Helen was up early, making jam from the last of the fruit from the orchard, and William was in the parlour, studying his accounts. The larder was full of compotes, chutneys and bottled fruit, enough to see them through the winter. It had been a good year both for produce and fair weather and the family was now reaping the rewards.

Although the weather was at its worst, Beanie still had to see to the animals. She had a piece of toast, liberally covered with plum jam, then dressed for outdoors. Ellie was not as robust as Beanie and preferred housework, which suited Beanie, who had no aversion to dust whatsoever. The stables were noisy, the wind blowing buckets and straw all over the place, the roof rattling. The horses were mostly quiet but Captain was not happy, stamping his feet and throwing his head up and down. Beanie fed and watered them then went to stand by Captain.

"What's the matter, boy?"

He blew out through his nostrils then came to rest by Beanie's face, allowing her to kiss his muzzle. Although Captain was predominantly black, with a white flash down his head, the muzzle was soft and pink, with the odd whisker. Beanie laughed, enjoying the companionship of this great beast, who had a soft heart.

"You want to go out in this weather?"

She slipped his bridle on and mounted, making sure that her head and legs were well protected from the storm. Captain seemed excited and rushed out of the warm stable, heading for the beach. Instead of his normal slow plod, his pace was brisk. He seemed to be enjoying the weather. Fair enough, thought Beanie, as he would be spending the rest of the day inside.

They walked down the path to the beach, his large hooves slipping occasionally, as the dry earth had turned to mud. When the beach came into view, they saw a circle of people looking down onto something that had been washed up, thrown from the turbulent sea onto the beach. As they got closer, Beanie could see it was a body. A passing man said he thought it must be a mariner from the sunken ship and asked Beanie if she would go back up and phone for the lifeguard and maybe an ambulance. She turned Captain and rushed back to her father, who would know what to do. The body was collected, and prayers were said. It became a sad day, and the storm was unrelenting. When Beanie looked that afternoon, the beach was strewn with debris, probably from *The Alfred Erlandsen*, which still lay on the Ebb Carrs Rocks, back broken and slowly sinking.

Chapter 20

Milldown

"Hello, Mrs. Thorburn, it's Ronan here. Would Beanie be about now?"

"Oh, hello Ronan, lovely to hear from you. No, Beanie is out with the horses. Can I take a message?"

"Can you tell her that I will be back within the week? There're a few things here that I have to take care of, then I will make my way back to you all."

"I'll tell her that, Ronan. We're looking forward to your return."

"Oh, that's grand, thank you. Can I still call you Helen?"

"Of course you can, Ronan. Now, hurry and come back to us."

"I will that. Goodbye, Helen and regards to William."

That evening, Helen remembered to pass on the message from Ronan to both Beanie and William. William was delighted that the cavalry was on its way; Beanie was apprehensive. Later that evening, the phone rang again.

"Now who could that be now?"

The phone was beginning to annoy Helen, as it made her jump each time it rang.

"Beanie, the call is for you – it's Alasdair."

"Hello, Alasdair."

"Sorry to disturb you, Beanie. I wanted to let you know that a friend of mine from Edinburgh University is coming here tomorrow to look at the letters I showed you. James is secretary of the Bibliographic Society at the university and may be able to translate some of the script. If you're interested, you could join us. He will be here for lunch. Say around one?"

"That sounds wonderful; I'll be there. Thank you for thinking of me."

"Father, Alasdair has invited me for lunch tomorrow. Is that all right with you, if I see to the animals first?"

"Aye, that will be all right, Beanie, but don't forget that you have to organise the ploughing competition if we are to hold it here at Milldown."

"I won't, Father., I've started putting the word around and it seems a popular choice for everyone to come here. It will mean that mother and Ellie will have to prepare a lot of bread and cheese and you will have to supply a barrel of beer, but it's worth it to get the fields ploughed. It will be a bit of fun."

Beanie went off to bed, excited at the prospect of seeing the letters translated and wondering what to wear for such an auspicious occasion. She was up and out, feeding the animals by six a.m., mucking the stables and the barn where the ten heifers were kept for the winter. The few cows that they did keep were for milking; they kept no bull or bullocks. There was an abundance of hay and straw, as the farming year had been exceptionally productive, so the animals were fed and clean in no time.

Taking the pony and trap after washing and dressing appropriately, she set off for Spylaw. James, Alasdair's friend, was already there and was introduced to Beanie, who felt a little shy in front of these two scholarly young men – Alasdair, looking very much the country gent and James, very good-looking in a suit and spectacles with blond hair parted down the middle.

"Let's have lunch then we can look at the letters."

Alasdair showed his guests through to a huge, warm kitchen, well stocked with every utensil that you could possibly imagine and a range that was twice the size of the one at Milldown. A wonderful smell of simmering soup was wafting through the kitchen, with fresh bread already on the table.

"Please, sit down. Is soup all right for you?"

Beanie's stomach was rumbling, as she had been up so early and not bothered with breakfast. She spoke loudly in an attempt to muffle the noise. She told James about the farm and the upcoming ploughing competition that she was organising.

"What a fascinating concept, Beanie. I've always fancied trying out a tractor."

"No, no. I plough with horses."

James exchanged a look with Alasdair that Beanie found a little disconcerting, but she let it pass.

"James, what are you studying?"

"I'm reading Elizabethan history, Beanie. I find the thought of a letter written by Mary Stuart fascinating, but I'm doubtful it is genuine."

"Oh, don't say that. I'm so hopeful that it is authentic."

"Then let's finish our soup and find out."

Alasdair led them up to his study and then further on up into the secret room. James took a long look at the manuscripts before speaking.

"Well, the writing certainly looks bona fide, although whether it was written by Mary is another story. I think the best thing that we can do is to start off by making an alphabet chart. If we can be sure of some letters, it starts to become easier to put words together. For instance, the letter 's' sometimes looks like an 'f', and 'y' is often used instead of 'i'. 'Mine' becomes 'myne', for example. 'V' and 'u' are often interchanged, and 'j' becomes 'i', and so on. 'James' would be written as 'Iames'.

"Mary also used a mixture of ciphers and codes if what she was writing was, for instance, treacherous; this was known as a nomenclator. The code was broken by Queen Elizabeth's top code breakers and resulted in Mary's death. Seriously, we can't begin to guess at the authenticity of this letter until we have a clue as to its content. It certainly looks like her signature. The best thing I can do is trace the writing and take the tracing back to the university, where I have the use of books of transcripts that will be of enormous help in deciphering this letter. Is that all right with you, Alasdair?"

Alasdair looked a little uncomfortable at the thought of the content of the letter leaving Spylaw, but what was the alternative? It had been in his family for generations without it having been translated. Now was the time, he thought, to find out if it was genuine. James had brought tracing paper with him and Alasdair allowed him to copy the letter. The sonnet in French they would leave for another time. Although the day had been pleasant, Beanie had found that their superior intelligence was rather demoralising. Alasdair had also studied at Edinburgh University – that's where he had befriended James. Beanie's education had been seriously restricted not only by finance but also by gender. She left Spylaw dispirited, wondering if this friendship with Alasdair would flourish or fail.

Back in Ireland, Ronan was planning his move to Scotland and wondered if it would be permanent or not. His prospects at home were very poor; the most he could hope for was a labourer's job like Brandon's, who came home each night exhausted, his only pleasure a drink down at The Fighting Cocks once or twice a week. Ronan was finding it difficult to imagine not seeing his mother or Kathleen for months at a time, but the prospect of living and working at Milldown and seeing Beanie every day was more than a little enticing. Now having accepted the job, he felt obliged to go, however torn he was. He thought that he would make one last gesture for his family, then he could leave with a clear conscience.

He had been meeting with Jim, his trainer, and had had a few friendly bouts with local lads, but Jim had arranged an illegal bare-knuckle fight with a competitor with whom Ronan was not familiar. It was to take place on private land nearby, and the stakes were high. A makeshift ring had been erected and it had pulled in quite a crowd, some familiar faces but mostly strangers, maybe from Dublin. Ronan always trained hard and was confident that he would receive no lasting injury; however, when he saw his opponent, his confidence wavered.

The man was stocky and muscular, slightly shorter than Ronan, his face solemn and his nose bent, obviously broken in some previous match, maybe more than once. There was no time limit to these fights; they went on until one was knocked to the floor and unable to rise, or one threw in the towel. Ronan was unsure if his stamina would match that of his opponent, but he would give it his best shot so that he could leave his family with plenty of money in their pockets.

They entered the ring and Ronan could feel the electricity in the air. The crowd was almost baying for blood for there was no doubt about it, this was indeed a blood sport. The intense, almost feral look in his opponent's eye was intimidating. His focus had honed in on Ronan and his determination to do him harm was palpable. The fighters had no sense of fear once the fight started, their whole being intent on annihilating their opponent. Ronan's advantage was that he was nimble; his adversary was broad and beefy but not as light on his feet. His tactic would be to get close to Ronan and start throwing punches with his uncovered knuckles, not giving Ronan a chance to dodge. Jim whispered to Ronan, "Use the first two knuckles; get in hard and swift. Don't let him corner you; use your legs."

The bell rang and the fight started. Ronan edged round the ring but the piercing eyes of his opponent never left his face. The man had obvious determination and rage in his soul. He threw a punch that tore Ronan's cheek and the first blood was spilt. Ronan got in several punches but none that did any damage until he targeted the bent nose of the combatant opposite him, with the desired effect. Blood ran down his chest, splattering the man's body but he seemed not to notice. He certainly had no sense of vanity, for his features were already disfigured. The crowd were in uproar as punches flew incessantly, then the bell rang for the first time.

Jim cleaned Ronan's face, giving him the usual pep talk, then the bell rang again. Neither man seemed to tire as round after round went on without a knockout. The tenth round was when Ronan took a punch to the side of his head that floored him, but he was up and punching again within the moment. By this time, both men were covered in blood, as were the crowd, who leaned over the ropes to roar at the fighters, whose faces were swelling around the eyes and forehead.

The rounds went on and on, the beatings more and more savage. An atmosphere of almost hysteria was whipped up as the crowd shouted for their preferred man. All Ronan could see was arms flying and mouths shouting through a blur of blood in his eyes. He could see Jim shouting; he too was covered in blood from tending to Ronan's wounds, his arms mimicking Ronan's punches. Ronan knew at this point that he was tiring. He was aware too that he had to use his brain instead of his brawn or the fight would be lost. The man opposite him in the ring was obviously stronger but lacked strategy. He threw more punches than Ronan but not all connected.

At this point, Ronan dropped his arms, feigning exhaustion, then when his adversary was off guard for just a split second, Ronan threw the left punch that he knew would win the fight. He put every ounce of strength that he had in reserve into the heaviest punch he could muster, flooring the man, who was semi-conscious before hitting the ground, unfortunately fracturing his left wrist at the same time. However, with the damage to his face and torso, he barely felt the pain in his hand. He stood panting, sweat pouring off him, unable to move another muscle.

Jim reclaimed him from the ring and tended to his wounds for some twenty minutes. They had been fighting for an hour and three quarters and Ronan could barely stand, but with the crowd congratulating him and a wad of money in his hand, he managed a wan smile. He had never fought a more brutal fight and promised himself that he never would again. The man he had fought had not recovered and lay prone and lifeless on the rough ground. His handler, indifferent to the man's condition, dished out money to his creditors, swearing and cussing as greedy hands threatened to engulf him in a sea of avarice.

"Holy Mother of God, Ronan, have you been hit by a train?"

Ronan's mother was aghast when her son walked into her kitchen. Kathleen burst into floods of tears and ran from the room when she saw her brother.

"It's all right, Ma. It's a leaving present for you."

Ronan handed his mother a large sum of money, but it did not placate her.

"Have you been fighting again? I'll not allow that Jim anywhere near you from now on. What in God's name is your father going to say when he sees you? Get yourself up to bed now. I'll bring you some tea."

It wasn't until the next day that the true extent of the damage done to Ronan could be assessed. He was unable to get out of bed, and his mother sent Kathleen to get Killian. Ronan's head was spinning, both eyes were closed and his left wrist was deformed and swollen. Bruises covered his face and torso. He refused to see a doctor, however, in case the fight was reported, so his mother sent for the priest.

"My son, you are going to have to get that wrist straightened or it will become useless. I'll ask no questions, but you must consider your mother's anguish at seeing you in this state, and there's no consoling our Kathleen. I think that you must have a concussion."

"It won't happen again, Father. Can I have your blessing now? I'm going off to Scotland to work soon. Will you watch over my family?"

"I will, of course. Now you need to rest, and while you're recovering, you can say ten Hail Marys and ten Our Fathers to cleanse you of your sins."

Killian and Cara arrived and went straight to Ronan's bedroom. Tears welled up in Cara's eyes but Killian just laughed.

"What a mess you've made of your pretty face. Beanie won't be impressed."

Cara went to the kitchen and with the help of Ronan's mother, devised a back slab to bind Ronan's wrist to. Killian held his wrist straight whilst Cara wrapped the slab into position with torn rags, hoping the fracture would heel without the need for surgery. It was clear that Ronan would not be able to travel for some time.

"Killian, will you go into town and phone Beanie? Tell her I've had an accident and that I won't be able to travel for a week or so."

"I'll do that, Ronan. You rest now. I hope this will be the last time I see you looking like you've been through the mangle."

Ronan placed a wad of money into Killian's hand.

"Buy something nice for the children and a ring for your wife."

Cara kissed his cheek and they left him in peace. He slipped off into a deep sleep, clutching the small pouch that contained the lock of Beanie's hair. He dreamed of riding Captain across Coldingham Bay with Beanie's arms around his waist.

Chapter 21

Milldown

"Ach, that phone again. Beanie, you get it. It'll be the death of me."

"Good morning, Beanie, Alasdair here. James has made some progress with transcribing the letter. Would you like to come over this evening? I can send a carriage for you."

"Oh, hello, Alasdair. No, I can't this evening, I'm sorry. I have something I have to do this evening."

"Oh, that's a shame. Well then, I'll show you some other time. Goodbye, Beanie."

"Goodbye, Alasdair."

"That was short and to the point. I thought you were getting on well with Alasdair."

"I am, Ellie, but I'm not in the mood right now. Mother has had a strange call from Brandon. Ronan has had an accident, but he wouldn't say what it was. Perhaps he's making an excuse and doesn't want the job here after all."

"Would that bother you? I thought you were courting Alasdair's affections these days."

"Well, you'd be wrong. We're just friends with a common interest. "Ellie, don't forget the ploughing competition – it's next weekend. You and Mother will have a lot of baking to do. You may need some help; I don't think you will be able to do it all yourselves."

"We've already thought of that, Beanie. We've put in an order with the baker."

Beanie went about her work but couldn't stop thinking about Alasdair's invitation. The whole story of Mary Stuart and the letter fascinated her, so by lunchtime she had phoned Alasdair back and accepted the invitation after all. She also accepted the offer of a carriage to pick her up, as the evenings were getting dark and chilly.

When she arrived at Spylaw, Alasdair and James were sitting at the kitchen table, concentrating on the letter.

"Good evening, Beanie."

James stood to greet her, as did Alasdair, making her feel very welcome.

"Alasdair, I never asked where exactly the letter was found."

"Sit down, Beanie. It was found on a ledge up the chimney when the secret room was being cleaned, many years ago."

"That accounts for it being so dirty and covered in water marks."

"That's right, Beanie. I've had a job transcribing the letter, but when you have comparable script, as I have at the university, it becomes possible. You see here, Beanie – you find letters that you recognise and fill them in on the tracing. You begin to see words taking shape. Some of it is of course guess work but look – we have enough to understand the letter."

James had written on a clean sheet of paper what he considered to be a true translation of the letter. It read:

Mon amour,

Quad Pro Quo "R" has been avenged.

I am with child, your child, and as Queen I do not want to give birth to a bastard. We must marry in haste.

Beware my brother, his eye has turned against me, as have

my Lords, he would raise an army against me. He has James, my son and I am not at liberty to go to him.

Should we be parted I have left your diamond and ruby hat pin shaped as a mermaid in the bosom of our retreat. Also "en tortue", the little turtle with ten rubies to be given to Joseph, "R"'s brother, as it was a gift from "R". My string of black pearls, so precious to me, is also there.

Take care mon amour, the walls have ears.

Marie R

"I have done my best to translate it accurately but of course I have had to fill in words here and there. What do you make of it?"

Alasdair spoke first.

"I think, and that is if the letter is genuine, that 'R' must be Rizzio, who was Mary's private secretary and close companion, who was murdered in front of her. Being avenged, she must have been referring to the murder of her husband, Darnley. This does seem to implicate her in her husband's death, but in fairness Darnley did thrust the knife into Rizzio. Her involvement, however, was always in question, as was that of Bothwell. It all adds up now. The part about her brother raising an army is also true. She was defeated at Carberry Hill then imprisoned in Loch Leven Castle, where she miscarried twins."

"Oh, that's so sad. Did she ever see her son again?"

"No, Beanie, she didn't, and he was taught to hate her, unjustly in my opinion. After she was forced to abdicate at Loch Leven Castle, in favour of her son, she never saw Bothwell or her son again. Bothwell was pardoned and went into exile where he died alone and insane."

"What do you think is meant by 'the bosom of our retreat'?"

"I think, and I may be romanticising, that she is referring to the summer house where the two could have met as lovers. What do you think, James?"

"Well, it's certainly intriguing. I guess we could authenticate it if we could find this so-called bosom in the summer house. If there were jewels there, all the better, but somehow, I doubt it after all this time."

"We should go down to the summer house before it gets too dark."

"You're very impatient, Beanie. Could we not wait until morning?"

"Alasdair, I won't be here in the morning, and I'm not missing out!"

"Very well. We'll take some lamps, as it's already dusk. Follow me."

"I wonder what she meant by bosom. The summer house is a one-up-one-down; where would the heart of the property be?"

"That we don't know. I'm surprised that none of my ancestors ever found anything, or perhaps they did and like grave robbers they've spirited it all away."

"Well, there aren't many places to search. There may be something under floorboards, but I'm not ripping them up – my parents would kill me."

Beanie was thankful that she had worn sturdy shoes, as the ground was uneven, and it was quite a distance from the house. The summer house came into view, and they studied the architecture. The dark red brick and the gothic-shaped windows made it look slightly eerie, most unlike a love nest, Beanie thought. The small turret with tiled roof stood out against the backdrop of the grey night sky. Animals rustled in the undergrowth and a spooked deer fled from a nearby bush, making Beanie jump.

They entered through the heavy oak door and stood in baffled silence, for there seemed to be no heart to the property at all. They almost expected to see ghostly apparitions from a bygone era, but all was quiet. They decided to start at the top and work their way down, and it didn't take them long. There was no hiding place. The bare floors and walls hid no secret however hard they looked. Their enthusiasm turned to disappointment as they made their way down the tiny stone staircase and back out into the open air again, pulling the door shut behind them.

"Well, that's a shame after all the work you put in, James."

"Well, I don't think that we should give up that easily. Because of the treachery of the time, people had to be ingenious and inventive. Communicating on paper was their only option, so hiding documents that could result in their death was imperative. Let's think about this."

They followed James' lead and stood for a while, looking at the building.

"We have to find a clue in the writing. What did she write? 'Bosom of our retreat'. Well, we think that this was her retreat, but what could she have meant by bosom?"

As she looked back at the building, deep in thought, Beanie suddenly had a theory. She was scrutinising the shape of the walls and turret when she noticed the rounded underneath of the turret. If she was not mistaken, it actually looked like a bosom or breast with a nipple pointing downwards. At first, she could say nothing. She had to be sure, as she didn't want to look foolish in front of the two scholars who stood beside her.

"Alasdair." She tugged his jacket. "Alasdair, I hope I'm not being fanciful, but to me the underneath of the turret looks like a breast."

"What do you mean?"

"Well, look. The underside of the turret is rounded with a projection pointing downwards. Could that not be interpreted as a breast or bosom with a nipple?"

"Well, you have to have a good imagination, but I expect you could be right. What do you think, James?"

James studied the silhouette of the building, and a smile crossed his face. The bright night sky illuminated the structure, and sure enough they were all looking at the outline of what could be described as a breast outlined by the light of the moon. Racing over, they circled the turret from below, touching the projection that resembled a nipple. It was solid wood, a good nine inches in diameter, but the dampness of the forest had made it swell and now it was impossible to twist or pull.

"We need a hammer to loosen it. I'll run back and get one."

Alasdair took off, leaving Beanie with James surveying the upturned dome and its protrusion. Soon after, Alasdair returned, this time with his father, Gordon.

"Now, what are you three up to? You can't damage the structure. Let me see."

Gordon came equipped with an old towel and a hammer.

"I must be mad, listening to your conspiracy theories, but it is a bit of fun. Let me get a grip of this and see if I can turn it."

Gordon wrapped the nipple with the towel and gave a couple of hits with the hammer. Nothing moved.

"Let me try, Father."

Alasdair took the hammer and, holding the towel in position, hammered softly around the circumference of the wood. He then tried twisting it, but it didn't want to budge. By this time the expectation of finding something had gripped Gordon, who took the hammer back and with the towel in position gave the wood a few good, hard taps. This time there was movement. He dropped the hammer and towel and started twisting the nipple that plugged the hole. Eventually the wood turned, and Gordon was able to pull the plug out.

The four of them stood in silence, as if expecting treasure to pour out, but nothing happened.

"Who's brave enough to put their hand inside?"

James volunteered and stepped forward to examine the interior of the turret. At first, he felt nothing, but then he grasped something quite large and pulled.

"Oh no – it's an old bone. It looks like it is from a cow or horse, it's so large."

"Is there nothing else up there?" asked Beanie, whose heart was pounding with anticipation.

"I can't feel anything. Does anyone else want to try?"

Gordon stepped forward, but however much he tried, he could find nothing else. Disappointment rolled over them like a wave as Gordon began to hammer the plug back into place.

"Why do you think someone would have put an old bone up there?" mused Beanie.

"They were full of superstitions in those days. Perhaps it was to ward off evil or something."

James picked up the bone to inspect it.

"I think it is the femur from an ox, it's so large. It's decomposed – look – it's hollow."

James suddenly went very quiet whilst examining the bone.

"Alasdair, I think there is paper rolled up inside. I'm wondering if it is another letter. Let's take it up to the house."

This time, Gordon sat at the kitchen table, as intrigued as the rest of them. He put an old cloth on the table and James laid the bone on it.

"Careful, don't tear it."

James slowly pulled a rolled piece of paper from the centre of the bone as everyone held their breath. Sure enough, it did seem to be a letter, although it was difficult to tell.

"We can't just unroll it. I've done this at university – we have to re-introduce moisture. Do you have a humidifier of any kind, Alasdair?"

"I don't think so, do we, Father?"

"No, I'm afraid not. I think your mother has an atomiser which used to be used for perfume. Would that do?"

"That would be perfect."

Gordon went off to get the atomiser. The room was quiet as they looked at the parchment in awe.

"This is made from calf or goat skin. You can see it's not paper. It really is old."

"Gosh, I wonder what it says."

Beanie hoped that they would be able to read it straight away, but James explained that it would take hours to soften.

"It has to be done under controlled conditions. I'll stay the night, if that's all right?"

"In that case I think that I'd better get home. It's late – my father will worry. Alasdair, could you call the carriage? Thanks."

Beanie arrived home to a kitchen full of sullen faces.

"Whatever is the matter?"

"It's Ronan. He's not coming back."

Chapter 22

Wicklow

Ronan knew every crack, water mark and cobweb on the ceiling of his bedroom. Since the fight, he had refused to get out of bed. The truth was, he couldn't get out of bed. Over the ensuing days and nights, bruises continued to surface on his torso, his eyes were closed and his laboured breathing was distressing to all who visited him. His wrist continued to be painful, but the most alarming thing for Ronan was the persistent weakness down his left side.

He had tried to get up and walk with the help of Brandon, but his lack of coordination, his swimming head and the pain in his chest caused him to collapse back onto his bed, feeling nauseous time and time again until he physically and mentally gave up trying. The thought of never seeing Beanie or Captain again sent him swirling down into a state of despair. Brandon tried to convince him that his injuries would heal, but Ronan was not convinced. He had seen other fighters end up in the same condition or worse, and that knowledge filled him with such a terror that life as he knew it would be over.

Kathleen was constantly by his side offering food, drink and entertainment, so much so that he had to ask her to leave him in peace for just a short while so he could sleep. However, sleep eluded him, and there was no escaping the nightmare he was in. If he did sleep, he would dream of the fight and wake, perspiring and panting. If he was awake, he lived every minute facing his worst fears, knowing that his condition was self- inflicted and life-changing. He still refused to see a doctor, and his mother was beside herself, cussing Ronan's trainer, Jim, with every breath in her body. His father's routine remained unchanged. He seemed unaware of the seriousness of Ronan's condition. Either that, or he blamed Ronan for causing an atmosphere of grief and misery in his house.

Killian and Cara were there every day, Killian washing Ronan and helping him to the toilet but noticing too that his strength and coordination were not improving. Whilst Cara was making the bed on one such visit, she found the pouch containing Beanie's hair under Ronan's pillow, and it hit home suddenly how Ronan's life had changed forever with the gravity of his condition. She was consumed with guilt, as she and Killian had benefitted financially from Ronan's misfortune. He always put other people first. He was such a loving young man, only now he was unable to participate in the rare gift of a loving relationship.

Sister Leonella visited regularly. She was the only person outside of the family that Ronan would allow into his bedroom. She prayed constantly for his recovery and helped him with exercises to help strengthen his muscles. She taught Kathleen simple games that she could play with Ronan to make him move, explaining that this was the road to his recovery. Kathleen didn't have to be asked twice to help her brother, turning out to be a strict taskmaster. She would never tire of throwing a ball to try to make him catch it, or putting a chicken feather on his nose to tickle and only allowing him to remove it with his left hand.

Days went slowly by, and Ronan's muscles seemed to wither. As much as Kathleen tried to encourage Ronan with his daily workouts, Ronan was drifting into a state of complete complacency. He seemed to accept his lot and became disinterested not only in his own life but that of his family too. He became uncommunicative and his appetite waned.

On a particularly bad day for Ronan mentally, he received a letter from Beanie saying that she wished him a speedy recovery and that she hoped that he would be well enough to return to Milldown before Christmas so that they might celebrate together. She told him that the whole family, including Captain, were missing him and that there would be employment for him when he was ready. Kathleen read the letter to him, and for the first time since the fight he gave her a smile. Kathleen rushed down to her mother to inform her that she had made Ronan smile, taking full credit for the miracle.

"Holy Mother of God, don't tell me he's going to put the smallest of efforts into getting himself back on his feet. It's about time. Go back up there, Kathleen, and take him this chicken broth, and mind you tell him this precious chicken didn't give up its life for nothing. He's to eat it all or I'll want to know why. We're one chicken down now."

"I will, Mammy. I'll make him eat it – I loved that chicken!"

Ronan's bruises were beginning to fade, and he took on a yellow hue, making him look jaundiced and even more poorly. The swelling around his eyes subsided, leaving his eyelids red and weeping. Sister Leonella bathed them daily in warm salt water and fortunately no infection set in. As days went by, he began to look like his old self and was showing a small amount of self-motivation in his recovery. He began to take his exercises seriously, and each day he found he could sit up a little higher without feeling dizzy. Patricia's motherly instincts came out of retirement and she fussed over him, constantly trying to find appetisers that would tempt him to eat.

"Kathleen, open that window and give the poor boy some fresh air in his lungs. Here, darling, eat this now. We'll have you up and about before the cockerel crows, for sure we will."

The cockerel didn't have time to crow, as he found himself in the pot. Ronan was now eating them out of house and home. He dreamed of huge roast dinners with Yorkshire puddings and all the wonderful food he was given at Milldown. He dreamed of Beanie too. Brandon replenished the brood of chickens and whilst Cara helped by making puddings to tempt Ronan, Killian brought home a puppy for Ronan and also one for Cara and her siblings to replace the dog they lost. Both families found that there was nothing like a puppy to bring happiness back into a household.

Ronan was certainly weak, but with the puppy's constant need of attention, he soon began to strive for some sort of normality, and once he had taken his first tentative steps there was no stopping him. He did constant workouts with Kathleen's help and encouragement. Her tatting, or lace making, had ceased and with it the income it brought in. However, the money that Ronan had given his mother after the fight was more than enough to last for several months. Sister Leonella gave her time and sometimes her overbearing energy willingly, hoping and praying to reignite Ronan's joie de vivre that seemed to have vanished along the way. The puppy certainly played his part, and Ronan's laughter from his bedroom soon became the norm.

Ronan received a second letter from Beanie, enquiring how his recovery was going, and this time he decided to reply. Fortunately, he had thrown a left punch to finish the fight, leaving his writing hand intact, so with his mother's help he wrote:

Dear Beanie,

I'm so sorry that I am unable at present to take up my

position on the farm. I do hope that you managed to find enough help in the village to tide you over. How are your plans going for the ploughing competition? No doubt you'll win with Captain and Ivan up front. I'm hoping that you're still taking Captain down to the beach. I long to join you; maybe one day I will."

At that point, Ronan became emotional and Patricia had to sign off for him, then she took the letter to the village and posted it. It was during this time of convalescence that Bridge started to confide in Ronan about her desire to become a nun.

"Bridge, what do you want to go and do a thing like that for? You're so pretty."

"Ronan, it's not a whim. I've thought about it long and hard. I don't want to go into a closed convent where I can't mix with the outside world. I want to be like Sister Leonella and help the poor and the uneducated people of Ireland. I could train to be a nurse and maybe travel a little. Ronan, what are the choices for a girl like me? I don't want to end up like a broodmare, producing lots of children until I'm old before my time. I want to help sick people and give my vows of poverty, chastity and obedience to God. I can't say that I have had a calling yet, but I'm sure this is the path for me to take. It is the only thing that makes me truly happy – accepting God's holy ordinance."

"Are you sure you wouldn't like to marry a nice young man? I've seen you chatting to boys, and when you are a little older your physical body may have needs. Do you understand what I'm saying?"

"I do, Ronan, but that seems to have so little importance in my life. I am only truly at peace when talking to God and praying with the other sisters. We share the same thoughts and we laugh and have fun; it's not a prison sentence. Please talk to Father for me."

"I will, Bridge, if that is really what will make you happy, and we can still see you. I'll talk to him tonight, though I doubt he'll listen to me."

Ronan did not choose his moment well to talk to his father that evening. Ambrose had been drinking whiskey, and he had lost money on a bet.

"Father, I want to talk about Bridge."

Ambrose didn't look up from his paper.

"Father, she's determined to become a nun. It's a choice that she should be allowed to make. She is nearly seventeen now and she's an intelligent girl. She wants to nurse and maybe travel a little. I don't mean leave Ireland – she's received a good education, and she wants to share that with young Irish girls that have no future without schooling. That wouldn't be so bad, would it?"

"Son, get out of here with your blarney. No daughter of mine is going to be a nun, and that's the last of it. That sister has filled her head with this nonsense and I'll not tolerate it. You can tell your Sister Leonella that she's not welcome here any more. Now get out of my sight, before your eye gets blackened again. What have I bred? You're all useless to me. Now get out, get out before I throw you out."

Ronan left the room in despair. His mother had heard the conversation from behind the door and was filled with sorrow. She knew how much this meant to Bridge, and she was ashamed of her husband's language. He was drinking too much and becoming used to being waited on hand and foot. It was left to her to try to keep the peace.

That night, Bridge packed a small bag and left the house for good. She had her mother's blessing and wondered if her father would even miss her. Children came into the world so easily, but it took a strong man and woman to become good parents. Bridge understood that large families, as were so common in Ireland, brought sorrow as well as happiness, poverty as well as reward.

She wanted no part in creating the next generation, for she was unsure if she could make a success of it with such restricted opportunities for women. Impoverished conditions were all too common. She wanted nothing more than to be given the chance to alleviate suffering and educate young women in God's name. Ronan managed to walk her to the convent gate and kiss her goodbye, but the journey took its toll on him. By the time he walked back through the kitchen door, his double vision had returned.

Chapter 23

Milldown

It was ten in the evening when Alasdair rang the phone at Milldown. Beanie had gone to bed; William and Helen were having a last hot drink by the range.

"Who would be phoning at this time of night?" Helen grumbled.

William picked up the receiver and was not pleased to hear Alasdair's voice asking for Beanie.

"Do you know what time it is? She's away to her bed. Is it important?"

"Well, to be honest, it's more exciting than urgent, Mr. Thorburn. I do hope you don't mind – I didn't realise what the time was."

"Ay, all right. I'll see if she's awake."

Before William could mount the stairs, Beanie was standing there in her nightgown.

"What is it, Father? Has something happened to Ronan?"

"No, no, lass. It's Alasdair asking to speak to you. Here, take the receiver."

"Alasdair, what's wrong?"

"Nothing is wrong, Beanie, it's just that James has managed to open the document enough to see that it is written in French and it is from Bothwell to Mary. We have translated it enough to know that they were going into battle. But that's not the best bit

– it talks of treasure in Coldingham Loch."

"Oh, I can't believe it! I'll be over first thing. Goodnight, Alasdair."

The boys stayed up late into the night going over the letter. It read:

Ma femme

Je vais défendre votre honneur et votre couronne.

Je me dirige vers nord-est avec une armée frontières.

Rejoignez-moi avec vos sujets fidèles à Carberry Hill.

Devrait défaire être la volonté de Dieu, alors,

J'ai jeté les bijoux dans Coldingham Loch à l'extrémité nord, marque par un cabeur.

La journée sera la nôtre, si Dieu le veut.

B.

"Let me see, let me see."

Beanie's enthusiasm the following morning was impetuous as she looked down onto the script. It was smudged and difficult to read, but the boys had done their best to write the translation.

My wife

I will defend your honour and your crown.

I am heading north-east with an army from the borders.

Join me with your loyal subjects at Carberry Hill.

Should defeat be the will of God,

I have thrown the jewels into Coldingham Loch

at the north end, marked by a caber.

The day will be ours, God willing.

B.

"So, they were already married when Bothwell left this message – see – he calls her his wife. Unfortunately, history tells us that they were defeated at Carberry Hill in 1567, soon after their marriage at Holyrood Castle. They never saw each other again. She was imprisoned at Loch Leven Castle; Bothwell was cleared of conspiring to murder Darnley but exiled.

"The most interesting part in my opinion is when he writes about throwing the jewels into Coldingham Loch. I'm sure that nobody has ever dredged the loch looking for treasure."

"Why do you think that he wrote in French?"

"Well, Bothwell didn't have to worry about his army from the borders; they were mainly illiterate farm workers. However, the nobles were often fickle, so secrecy was paramount to Mary's struggle for power. Any way that she and Bothwell could outsmart their enemy would have been taken. The nobles were very much against the marriage and wanted an annulment – it was a game of cat and mouse. You can see by how they were behaving that they knew there were spies threatening their struggle for power, so they took every precaution possible, and French was a second language for both of them. It may have thwarted some enemies, but certainly the nobles would have been well educated."

"James, what are you thinking about the jewels being thrown in the loch?"

"Well, it was the perfect place to ensure that the English as well as the Scots didn't get Mary's precious pieces of jewellery. A lot of it was sold or pledged for loans by both enemies and allies alike. It's fascinating to think that there may be some remnants close by."

"I know the loch well, James. I've been there recently and come to think of it, there was a strange piece of wood at the north end. It looks like lightning has struck it – it's black and distorted, as if it's been burnt."

"If indeed Bothwell did use a caber to mark the spot as he says he did, that would be advantageous, as cabers are made from larch wood, which is resistant to rot. Also, burning the wood gives extra protection, so if it had been struck by lightning for instance, or burnt deliberately, all the better."

"Well, there's no doubt we will have to investigate this, but who's up for swimming?"

"Beanie, I believe the loch is quite deep. I think maybe an attempt at dredging it may be safer. We have a small rowing boat that we use on the lake here at Spylaw. We could transport it to the loch in a wagon."

"Great idea, Alasdair. Then we need something heavy to do the dredging. I've got a piece of ploughing equipment that would do the job."

"Slow down, you two. Do you really believe that you will find treasure after all this time? If the jewels had been thrown in, they would be under layers of mud and silt by now. You'll never find anything."

"Oh, James, don't take the fun out of our discovery. You must admit there is a possibility of treasure in the loch."

"Sorry, Beanie, you're right. There are tangible clues, I'll give you that. However, I can't spare any more time on this. I must get back to Edinburgh – I have a dissertation to prepare."

Later that day, James phoned Alasdair with bad news.

"Alasdair, I've been doing some research into Mary's crown jewels. She did indeed have a strand of black pearls that were dear to her, but my books also confirm that Queen Elizabeth the First , Mary's cousin, got possession of the pearls. That can only mean one of two things. It could be that Bothwell never threw them into the loch, and they were confiscated after the battle, or someone was spying on him as he left Spylaw and retrieved the pearls and jewels from the loch when Bothwell left. Either way, they are not there now."

"Well, at least we have an authentic letter from Bothwell, but Beanie will be disappointed. Thanks, James."

Beanie was of course disappointed. She had had such plans for retrieving the jewels, but after receiving the news from James she now had to put those thoughts out of her head and concentrate on the ploughing competition. It would of course be a fun day meeting all the local farmers, but more importantly, the majority of the fallow fields on Milldown would get ploughed in one day. The work would have taken Beanie more than a couple of weeks and that was if she had help. Alasdair and Andrew offered to assist in marking out the fields that were put aside for the competition, and Gordon, as a figure held in high regard locally, offered to bring Carro along and judge the competition.

William had retained a photographer to commemorate the occasion, but he was commissioned mostly by the children, who wanted their photograph to be taken with Carro, who was becoming quite a celebrity, being known as the Danish dog from the shipwreck. Gordon was quite amused at Carro's popularity and the dog's obvious pleasure at getting all the attention. He took Beanie aside at one point, wanting to make it clear that the letter they found was to be kept secret.

"Beanie, if people find out that historic letters have been found at Spylaw, we are going to attract all sorts of unwelcome attention: historians, treasure hunters and even the press. I couldn't abide the disruption that would cause; do you understand that, Beanie? We will mount Bothwell's letter and keep it safe behind glass with the others. They belong to Spylaw."

"Of course. I fully understand and agree with you. They are an integral part of the history and ambience of Spylaw. I won't say a word."

Gordon laughed. "You have a sense of romance about you,

Beanie. You're a pleasure to be around."

Seventeen contestants had journeyed from far and wide to take part in the competition. They arrived in horse-drawn wagons containing their ploughing equipment and decorations for their horses and tack, highly polished brasses and, in some cases, plumes for the bridles. The horses rested from their journey before the ploughing started, and they were offered buckets of water and hay. The men took refreshments which Helen and Ellie had prepared, then they started to groom and dress their horses.

Some ploughed with one horse, others with two, and there was one farmer who had a team of four. Clydesdales, Shires and an unusual team of Percheron, a heavily muscled French breed not often seen in the Scottish Borders, stomped and snorted in anticipation. They were all at least seventeen hands tall, making a truly wonderful spectacle. Each team was given a number that corresponded to a field set aside for the competition, and they began to take up their positions. Beanie harnessed Captain and Ivan but had no intention of trying to win, as her competitors had made such an outstanding effort to take part, she thought that would be bad form. She was just delighted to watch her fields being ploughed free of charge, ready for planting potatoes and other winter crops in the coming weeks.

The atmosphere was wonderful. One of the villagers had made a tray of delicious pasties to sell, while another was selling ribbons and knitted socks. Others had come to chat and appreciate the skilful coordination of man and beast as the teams guided their horses in straight lines up and down the fields, churning the rich soil. Gulls riding the light breezes coming off the sea followed them, landing in flocks, ready to take any exposed morsel. The sight was truly wonderful. The patchwork of fields sloping down towards the ocean was ploughed to perfection, the dark brown lines of the newly sliced soil contrasting with the autumnal colours of the untouched stubble around the edges.

Suddenly a ballyhoo went up, as from the furthest field the Berwickshire hunt came galloping through unexpectedly, horn blowing, women riding side-saddle wearing black jackets and tall hats, men in pinks with white jodhpurs, following a pack of baying hounds. They thundered by far too close to the competitors, upsetting the working horses and making Carro bolt. He ran with the pack and was soon swallowed up in the melee. Children were crying whilst men settled their spooked horses, cursing the intrusion of the indifferent huntsmen.

Thankfully the day was at an end. The competitors had done their best, and an agitated Gordon, worrying about Carro, readied himself to present the prize. He thanked everyone for taking part and gave the trophy to the Clydesdales, which also received a rosette each. The day had been a total success until the hunt had gone through, and now Gordon's only thought was for Carro. The children were each placated with a toffee apple that Ellie had made whilst everyone else packed up to leave. When Milldown was once again at peace, Carro came limping back, to his master's delight.

Chapter 24

Wicklow

Killian, now a married man responsible for a brood of energetic children, found himself in his element. He was a good teacher and an affectionate father figure. the only thing slightly worrying was Cara's lack of warmth towards him. They had consummated the marriage, but since that one time there had been no desire on her part to repeat the bonding between them. Killian was a patient man, however, and understood that after what she had been through, it would take time for her to fully trust him and to become relaxed carnally. He thought the world of her and was prepared to give her as long as it took.

Killian also realised that with such a large family to support, he would need to be employed. Brandon confirmed that they were no longer taking on labourers at the docks, and the position of postman that Cara's father had left vacant had been filled in an instant. It was one evening when he was indulging himself in a rare pint of Guinness in The Fighting Cocks that Killian met a man named Arthur Forbes. The man was new to the area and welcomed Killian's local knowledge. Forbes had been commissioned to undertake the Avondale Project, and his enthusiasm was unmistakable.

He explained to Killian that the landscape cover of woods and plantations had been reduced to an area of approximately 1.6 percent in Ireland, the lowest point in historic time. Someone had to address this problem to achieve future wood supplies.

Forbes intended to lay down a series of field trials to determine the most suitable tree species for Ireland's forestry programme. He also intended to set up a forestry school for working foresters in which young men could be trained in plantation establishment and management. Landlords of large estates had introduced many tree species over the years, but there was no scientific information available on the best species or on how they should be managed.

Avondale Estate near Rathdrum, County Wicklow, had been chosen for the project. It was to be used as an experimental farm, as the diversity of the land was ideal. The land from Wicklow to Galway was blessed with valleys, lakes, sea, hills and mountains, ideal for experimental planting. Avondale already had such species as sessile oak, Spanish chestnut and walnut, European larch and Weymouth pine, all planted by Samuel Hayes, a historic owner of the Avondale estate, whose passion for trees was remarkable.

Killian found himself fascinated by such a study and put himself forward for a position as a labourer on the land. However, Forbes had a better idea.

"Killian, you're an intelligent young man with lots of local knowledge – don't sell yourself short. I'll tell you what I'm going to do for you. I'm going to personally sponsor you as my first student to be trained as a forester. If you do well, I'll give you a permanent job on the project. How does that sound to you?"

Killian couldn't believe his luck. The man seemed genuine, but jobs were so few and far between that Killian was dumbstruck, uncertain if this could be the answer to his prayers and that God had indeed listened. He had never dreamed that he would one day be able to further his education and be offered employment, but Forbes shook his hand, offered a small salary whilst he was studying but a fair wage once he was a competent forester. His salary would start straight away while he helped Forbes set up the school, and for the first time in Killian's life, a feeling of self-importance overwhelmed him, and he shed a tear.

Cara was over the moon when Killian explained what had happened at The Fighting Cocks.

"Cara, I'm going to be a student. Can you believe it? Me – a scholar!"

He threw his arms around Cara and swung her up into the air whilst the children screamed and giggled.

"My turn, my turn."

There seemed to be a hive of children all wanting a turn as they buzzed around under his feet, consumed with laughter. The puppy too joined in exuberantly.

"Do you know what we're going to do on Saturday to celebrate?"

The children all shouted their ideas of a celebration at once. "There's not a one of you that's right," shouted Killian over the raucous mayhem that was his family. "We're going to the seaside. I'll hire a wagon, and we'll take a picnic, and we'll splash in the sea and build sandcastles until the sun goes down. How does that sound?"

The children screamed their delight, but when he looked over to Cara, she was crying.

"Go out and play now, I'll see to supper." The children scampered off and Killian took Cara in his arms.

"What is it, darling? I thought you'd be happy."

"I'm so happy, Killian. I love you so much. It's just that I can't remember ever having fun, not until we got together, and I feel I've let you down. I don't feel I deserve you. I'm unworthy."

Cara broke down and sobbed. The pain and degradation of the past year seemed to flow out of her, and the sobs were pitiful.

"Cara, darling, don't cry so. You're perfect in my eyes. You're a beautiful person inside and out. Now, try to stop your tears, or I'll cancel the trip."

Although he was joking, it seemed to make the sobs even louder, causing Connor to come back inside and start to cry with her, clinging onto her skirt.

"There now, you two. Stop your wailing, will you? You'll set the puppy off."

And as if on cue, the puppy joined in, throwing his head up and howling like a wolf, lifting the mood until they were all laughing again and the puppy was bounding around, tripping Connor up.

That night, Cara lay in Killian's arms, and for the first time since their wedding night she felt relaxed. He held her close and kissed the top of her head as her arm went across his waist. She snuggled closer, pressing herself up against him, lifting her face so she could kiss him. His desire was instant and urgent, but he let her take the lead. There was no way that he was going to scare her or make her do anything that would compromise their fragile relationship, but her desire was as heated as his own. She sat up and removed her cotton nightshirt, revealing her silhouette against the moonlit window. It was perfect. Slowly, she lowered herself on top of him and passionately kissed his lips.

"Cara, are you sure you want to?"

He needn't have asked, for she made love to him slowly and tenderly, and there was no mistaking the pleasure that she derived from the act of lovemaking, with the man that she loved and who loved her with all his heart.

There was no stopping Kathleen when she heard about the

outing to the seaside. She had packed a picnic and was up in the wagon with the rest of the children by eight in the morning. The children were in a frenzy of excitement as the wagon rolled off, being pulled by an unfortunate old nag. The going was slow but the scenery was beautiful, hills and mountains covered in gorse and heather, yellows and purples merging into one, rolling down towards the sea.

However, Killian soon became aware of the austere landscape, devoid of trees on all sides. He pointed this out to Cara as they discussed his new vocation in life as a forester. They could see first-hand the effects of deforestation on the land, and Killian soon became as enthusiastic as his employer to reintroduce the most suitable trees for the land, mentioning spruce and pine as if he were already an expert on the subject, much to Cara's amusement.

The beach came into view and the children screamed. The old nag picked up his pace and they were soon on the sand. They tethered the horse, leaving him with hay and water and rushed towards the sea, Killian shouting warnings that they must change into swimsuits before getting wet. A large rug was laid out for the picnic and for once there was harmony. Swimsuits were in fact a spare pair of pants for both girls and boys, and soon piles of clothes were thrown everywhere. They rushed in unison to the water's edge, where they came to an abrupt halt, feeling the freezing Irish sea.

Kathleen, nearly in tears, complained bitterly that the waves were biting her toes.

"See, it's coming after me," she screamed, causing raucous laughter amongst the other children as the foamy waves engulfed their feet.

"Kathleen, come and fly the kite. See, I've been up all night making you a kite with a picture of a butterfly on it."

Gracie's enthusiasm spilled over as she ran up and down the beach, calling for the wind to come and fly her kite. Connor, Liam and Kathleen went about launching the kite whilst Cara and Killian set out the picnic. The fun they were having was unprecedented. Even the puppy couldn't contain his excitement, relieving himself rather too close to the rug then barking with delight at his achievement.

Sandcastles erupted from the soft yellow sand and deep holes were dug. The children exhausted themselves running endlessly up and down the beach with the kite and chasing the wind. Finally, when the food had been eaten by ravenous mouths and every child's imagination satiated, it was time to go. The poor old nag plodded his way home whilst each and every child slept. The puppy, his eyes and nose twitching as he dreamed, lay across Gracie.

Kathleen stayed the night, as no-one had the energy to walk her home, and in the morning, Patricia came to collect her. The children were still asleep, but Killian was up, preparing breakfast.

"I'm guessing you had a good day then. Was Kathleen all right?"

"Of course she was, Ma. She had the time of her life until she thought the waves were after biting her toes."

"You told me there was a green monster in the sea that put out his slimy green fingers to tickle toes!"

Kathleen had heard her mother and was down the stairs in a trice.

Patricia laughed. "And what else did your brother tell you, darling?"

"He told me that if I stood at the shoreline, I could see the whole world."

"And did you see the whole world out there?"

"I did, Mammy, but there wasn't much out there. I prefer Ireland."

"You do now? I'm glad about that, as that's where you'll be staying. Now come and give your mammy a cuddle. I've missed you something fierce."

Patricia enjoyed her very special hug then became serious.

"Have you spoken to Ronan lately?"

"I have, Ma. He seems to think that there will be no more improvement. I don't agree; I think he's a little depressed. I think he should finish his convalescence on the farm with Beanie. She's the type of woman that would get him back on his feet, no doubt. She'd stand no nonsense."

"Ronan won't hear of going back to Scotland, letting Beanie see him in his condition. He's adamant he won't go."

"Well, we can't force him, Ma. Give him a little longer."

"Okay, you're right. Now then, tell me all about this new job of yours. Your father is going to have a fisty-fit when he finds out that another child of his is going to receive an education instead of doing a hard day's work like he had to. I'll be that proud of you, Killian. Trees, is it?"

"Yes, Ma, it's trees. Now take your darling daughter home. She's that tired and there're far too many mouths to feed in this house. I'm not earning yet, you know."

Chapter 25

Milldown

The kitchen was quiet but had a jubilant atmosphere. Maggie had written to say that she was expecting a baby the following June and that she would like to come home to Milldown to give birth. Helen was over the moon; it was to be her first grandchild. The loss of John had left a gaping wound in everyone's heart. This would go some way to healing that wound. It took Beanie out of her reverie. She was missing Ronan and still had no conception as to what could possibly be wrong with him. Deciding to take Captain down to the sea, she left the leisurely banter in the kitchen, preferring her own company. Captain was as usual more than willing to be harnessed and rushed from his stable with Beanie mounted, as was now custom, bareback.

The sea was remarkably calm for October, and a warm breeze whispered across the sand, bringing in seabirds to feed along the shoreline. Out to sea, a steamship was passing slowly by on its way to Grangemouth to unload its cargo, the smoke rising almost vertically in the calm winds. Plodding along, lost in thoughts of Ronan, she didn't at first notice a man waving from some distance out to sea.

"Beanie, Beanie, it's me – Alasdair."

She broke into a wide smile as she saw Alasdair swimming towards her, making slow progress.

"Come on, Captain, let's go for a paddle."

She turned her horse and guided him deep into the sea until her boots were just touching the water's surface. The horse loved it. She marvelled at just how brave this wonderful beast was and patted his shoulder and neck in appreciation.

Alasdair had nearly reached them and was close enough to make conversation, in between spitting out sea water and puffing. He just about had the breath to let Beanie know that James had transcribed the French sonnet and was visiting Spylaw later to translate it into English. Both James and Alasdair could speak French, but the document was damaged and James had had to fill in letters that he could not decipher. It was of course written in Queen Mary's hand if they were to be proved correct, so the lettering was ambiguous and the paper water-marked, making the transcription somewhat conjecture.

Captain at this point thought that Alasdair was playing a game with him and snorted, throwing his head up and stomping his feet. He was visibly enjoying the treat of walking out into the sea, a pleasure he had not experienced before. Beanie laughed, telling Alasdair that she would come to Spylaw that afternoon. She thought it best to return Captain to the shore, but he suddenly developed a mind of his own. However much she coaxed him, he would not turn shoreward and started to go deeper. Alasdair tried waving his arms to turn him, but his mind was made up. He reared, unbalancing Beanie, twisting at the same time, causing her to slide unceremoniously into the cold grey water.

She was in hysterics when she finally surfaced, seeing Alasdair scramble to her rescue. Thinking she was in trouble, his wet, clinging arms went around her, unfortunately his grip falling upon her right breast as he gallantly tried to support her above water. He got such a fright at touching her breast that he dropped her and she went under again. This time she swam away from him, under water so confusion wouldn't lead to a repetition of his faux pas. Captain, at this point, decided to behave himself and walked to Beanie's side. There was just enough depth to the water to enable her to slide onto his back, her bedraggled clothes, thankfully summer weight, impeding the mount. Once again sitting upright, she turned to look back at a bewildered Alasdair.

"That was fun," she shouted. "I was in no danger, Alasdair. I have swum in the sea for as far back as I can remember."

"I'm so sorry, Beanie. I thought you were drowning."

"Don't worry, it's fine. I'll come over later."

Beanie laughed to herself all the way back to the stables. Poor Alasdair, she thought, he was so embarrassed. As she gave Captain a harsh rubdown with straw to dry him, she thought how glad she was that she had not waited to see Alasdair come out of the water in a wet, clinging swimsuit. The picture in her head was distracting and amusing at the same time, causing her smile to linger. As she walked in through the kitchen later, passing the family sitting round the table, they barely gave their dripping, cheerful daughter a second glance. This was Beanie at her best.

Beanie did her chores still with a smile on her face and a skip to her step. The sea had washed away her blues, and the thought of her sister being pregnant was an exciting prospect. She dressed casually to go to Spylaw, as the family were used to her by now, and she no longer felt the need to impress anyone.

"Hello, Beanie."

Gordon greeted her with a hug, holding onto the reins of one of his stallions. "The boys are up in Alasdair's study. Go on up."

"Thanks. What a beautiful horse. What's his name?"

"This is Barkley the Third; he's a fine beast, isn't he? I'm hoping he will sire a stallion that I can race. Pat is one of the best trainers. We've got high hopes for both Barkley and his descendants."

"He certainly is handsome; too much for me to handle."

"With your horsemanship skills, Beanie? I doubt that."

He laughed with a lifted eyebrow, making reference to her dip in the sea.

"I forgot to ask how Carro is after running with the hounds."

"He came limping home with a tear to his hind leg, but Pat has patched him up. He's good to go."

Beanie let herself in through the kitchen and went up to Alasdair's study, finding the boys lounging in armchairs.

"Hello, Beanie. You've come for the unveiling of the sonnet, I presume."

"I have indeed. How far have you got with it? Can I see?"

Alasdair seemed a little reserved and couldn't quite look Beanie in the eye, but she was too excited to be concerned about his awkwardness over the faux pas in the sea.

"Well, here's what James has been able to do by tracing the original then transcribing it. I know that you don't speak French, but I thought you would like to see how it was written before we translate it. Take a look at this."

The sonnet, now in James' handwriting, was laid out on the table. It read :

Pas les vents du temps je ne suis pas encore détruit
Bien que les nuages soient froids et gris
Mes seigneurs et mon frère conspirent dans la nuit
Mais dans leurs visages perfides, je ris.
Vous m'avez enveloppé dans votre manteau
Mon corps et mon âme sont à vous
Sous quelle étoile allons-nous sur ce berceau
J'espère que c'est un chanceux pour nous.

Je vais élever un verre devant notre feu
Dans la bosom de notre retraite
Je prie pour un ciel toujours bleu
Et la terre écossais sans défaite.

Bonne chance mon amour, je vais monter à vos cotes.

Nous sommes dans les mains de Dieu, il décidera notre destin.

M

"To me, it almost seems like Mary had written down her thoughts the night before they went into battle against her lords and her brother at Carberry Hill. I know I'm a romanticist, but I think it could have been written in the summerhouse. See – she refers to the bosom of our retreat. We've seen that reference before, if you remember. And where she uses the word 'berceau' for bed instead of 'lit', which would have been the normal translation, I think she is referring to a tiny day bed of sorts.

"By using the word crib or cradle, as it translates, she's almost making fun of a piece of furniture so small it would have fitted into the turret. That is where she and Bothwell could have been lovers. Also, when she says 'I will ride by your side', she seems to be accepting Bothwell as her king. It was royal etiquette that nobody should ride alongside or in front of a queen unless it was her king. I think that they were truly in love."

"Oh, how exciting. It is becoming more certain that these documents were actually written by Mary. But how sad that we know from history that she is imprisoned, miscarries twins and never sees Bothwell again after the battle. Are you going to translate it now?"

"Yes, Beanie. We've kept you waiting long enough. It should

be possible now James has done some work on it. You read the French version, James, and I'll write it down in English."

"Okay, here goes."

By the winds of time, I am not broken yet
Though the clouds are cold and grey
My Lords and my brother plot in the night
But in their treacherous faces I laugh
You have shrouded me in your cape
My body and soul are yours
Under which star do we lie on this bed
I hope it's a lucky one for us.
I will raise a glass before our fire
In the bosom of our retreat
I pray for a sky that is always blue
And Scottish soil without defeat.

Good luck, my love, I will ride by your side.
We are in the hands of God, He will decide our destiny.
M

"Oh, I'm sure she wrote it."

Beanie was awestruck to be in the presence of Queen Mary's documents written in her own hand. She was convinced entirely that Mary and Bothwell had used Spylaw as their hideaway and that the writing was genuine.

"Well, thanks to James we finally know what the documents say. The question is, what do we do with them now? If they are genuine, they prove or maybe disprove, if you like, some historical facts, but do we want to expose ourselves to an investigation?"

"No is the answer to that."

Gordon came into the study at that point with a tray of tea and shortbread biscuits for them.

"I'll have to put my foot down. It's a wonderful thing that we finally know what the documents say, and that's mostly thanks to James, but that is for us to know and not the public. When your mother and I have departed and you are in charge, you can do as you see fit, but not while your mother and I are still around, and hopefully that will be for some time yet!"

"Very well, Father. We've done what we set out to do – translate them. We'll leave it at that."

"Case closed. Oh, I wanted you to read this article in the *Farming and Agriculture* magazine, Alasdair, I think you'll find it quite interesting. I was thinking about your vision of re-forestation. This is an article about a project in Ireland called the Avondale Project. It's all about re-forestation and educating foresters. I thought Andrew might benefit from some training, if you're serious. Just a thought."

Gordon left with a tray of empty cups and saucers, leaving the magazine for Alasdair to read.

"Well, that's excellent. My father is taking me seriously about overseeing the estate. He could relax, training his horses with Pat, and I could manage the land. Andrew is proving to be a valuable member of the estate staff, I have to say. I might just consider him for a sponsorship."

Chapter 26

Wicklow

Killian rose early, ate a hearty breakfast and prepared himself for his first day of employment. He polished his boots, determined at least to start the day resembling a student rather than a labourer, then he took his best flat cap off the stand and left the house. Cara was there to wish him good luck and give him a peck on the cheek.

Avondale itself was constructed of yellow brick with a slate roof. It was double fronted, with a large columned porch centrally positioned with a window each side and three small windows above. Several huge chimneys rose majestically from the shimmering grey of the slate, and it was encircled by magnificent, ancient trees. The whole estate probably covered the best part of three and a half thousand acres. This excluded tenanted holdings and land unsuitable for forestation.

Arthur Forbes was there to greet Killian and showed him to one of the outbuildings put aside for his use.

"This is where I intend to establish the school, Killian. I advertised for students in *Farming and Agriculture* magazine and have had fifteen applicants, one from as far away as Berwickshire. If they are suitable, we will get started straight away. I have acquired some desks from an old school that was closing down, so if you wouldn't mind, your first job will be to pick them up. Is there a lad you know whom you could take along to help you?"

"I could take my brother. Is there a horse and wagon?"

"Of course, of course – it's ready and waiting. The school is on the road to Bray – do you know it?"

"I know it well; it's not far from where I live. A lot of the Irish round abouts have emigrated, leaving schools empty, and the Welsh have moved in, but they prefer to build their own schools and churches."

"I see. Well, you take the wagon and I'll start planning the lessons. When you get back, we'll walk round the land and see where to start laying out the experimental plots. I'm surprised that the Dublin and South Eastern Railway runs round the outskirts of the estate; I didn't realise that it was so close. It might provide a service for the applicants – they are quite a diverse group."

Not half an hour later, Killian arrived home with the wagon, thinking that it might be good to get Ronan on his feet and out of the house for a while.

"Ma, where's Ronan? I need a hand to pick up some old desks for the Education Centre where I work."

When Kathleen saw the horse and cart pulling up close to the back door of their house, she was out like a shot.

"Can I come with you, Killian? Oh, I love the horse. What's his name?"

"I don't know, Kathleen; you give him a name. Ma, Ma – where's Ronan? I thought he could give me a hand, get him out and about a bit, take his mind off things."

"Oh, for sure. Ronan! Ronan!" she shouted. "Your brother wants you. Kathleen, get away from that horse. You're too close to it; it will stamp on your toes. Ronan, come down here."

"Woman, in God's name, what's all the shouting for?"

Ambrose had a sore head and didn't appreciate all the noise, but nobody answered him, so he left, going back inside to read his paper.

"Killian has come for Ronan. Kathleen, have you seen him?"

At that point, Ronan slumped from the kitchen door, took one look at the imploring look on Killian's face and jumped up beside him.

"Killian, the horse is called Myrtle," Kathleen shouted after them.

"Kathleen, it's a boy. Try again."

"I thought we'd never get away. Are you okay, Ronan? Do you think you're up to giving me a hand?"

"Anything to get out of that house."

The boys laughed and took up an easy banter.

Killian instantly became aware of the progress that Ronan had made over the past week or two. His speech was normal, and his sense of humour was back with a vengeance. The journey gave the boys a chance to have a really good chat, and Killian was pleased with what he was hearing. They picked the desks up from the caretaker, a Mr O'Loughlin, and set off back to Avondale where Ronan could lend a hand unloading.

"Do you see those pears there, Ronan? Do you fancy one? They look mighty juicy. Do you fancy a bit of scrumping? I'll pull the wagon over to the fence and you grab a couple."

Ronan had just plucked two of the ripest pears off the tree when a ruckus started.

"I'll be having your guts for garters! Get out of here, stealing my pears! Do you hear me?"

A shot was fired into the air, causing Killian and Ronan to burst into fits of laughter. They knew the shot would not be aimed at them, but Killian struck the horse on the rump, and they fled the scene of the crime at full speed. It was the first hearty laugh that Ronan had had since the fight.

It soon became the norm for Ronan to accompany Killian to the estate to help with the laying out of plots of land for planting and generally help out where necessary. It had been explained to Mr. Forbes that Ronan was recovering from an accident, so instead of putting him on the payroll, Mr. Forbes would slip him some money every so often. He was a very generous man and treated Ronan with kid gloves. It wasn't long before Ronan was pulling his weight though and doing a full day's work.

Naturally, working on the estate, the boys became familiar with the owner, a Mr. Parnell, whose children were now grown up and living in grand houses of their own. Ronan, if not helping out on the land somewhere, was spending a lot of time with a small pony, which appeared somewhat neglected.

"Good morning, Ronan. How are you this fine day?"

"Good morning, Mr. Parnell, I was just tending to the pony. I think she's in need of a farrier – her hooves are a little overgrown. They would benefit from a good trim. I could recommend someone, if you like?"

"Ronan, that's kind of you. She hasn't even been shod. The truth is that now the family have gone, there is nobody to ride her or make a fuss of her. I'm ashamed to say that I have neglected her with everything that's going on."

"Oh, that's a shame, for sure. Would you like me to spruce her up a bit? I'd be happy to spend some time with her."

"Ronan, if you want to take her off my hands, I'd be grateful. I wouldn't want payment; I would just be pleased that she's gone to a caring home."

Ronan's heart skipped a beat. Was he really giving him the beautiful little pony?

"I'd be glad to take her, Mr. Parnell, but are you sure you don't want payment?"

"Ronan, you would be doing me a favour, I couldn't send her to market – she's too old. I dread to think what her fate would be, and she is, I'm afraid, overlooked here. There is a small saddle and bridle that goes with her."

"I'll take her for sure, and I'm very grateful, I have a sister that will think that she has died and gone to heaven when she sees her."

That evening, Ronan walked the little white pony home and hid her in the barn with the milking cow. He left her saddled and bridled.

"Where's Kathleen, Ma? I have a surprise for her."

"She's tatting in the snug. What have you got for her?"

"You'll have to wait and see, Ma. Kathleen, come out here."

Kathleen joined Ronan and their mother in the kitchen.

"Kathleen, what would you wish for if someone said to you that you had been such a good girl, you could make a wish and it would come true?"

"Don't be silly, Ronan. I'm never that good."

"Oh, darling, your mammy thinks that you are always that good."

"Well, tell me anyway, and we'll see if you are the best sister ever, or not."

"Well, you know I'd wish for my very own pony to ride."

"Well, that is a big wish. We'll have to see if you have been that good. And where would you find a pony if someone had granted you that wish, Kathleen?"

"Ronan, stop teasing your sister."

"It's all right, Ma. Kathleen, where would you find it?"

"I'd probably find it in the barn."

Ronan raised an eyebrow. Kathleen dropped her lace and rushed from the kitchen with Ronan and Patricia on her tail.

She entered the barn to see her little white pony groomed and saddled, ready for her to ride. Coming to an abrupt halt, she stared in wonder then burst into floods of tears, sobbing and trying to catch her breath.

"Come here to Mammy, darling. Now, why all the tears?"

"Mammy, I've not been that good. They will take the pony away again."

"Kathleen, look at the saddle – it has your name on it. Nobody can take her away. She's yours."

Ronan had carved her name carefully into the leather on the saddle, knowing that Kathleen insisted on having her name on all her possessions, whether that be books, clothes or toys. She had a generous nature and was sharing, but at the end of the day she liked to keep a close eye on what was hers. When she saw her name on the saddle, her mood soared. She walked over to the pony and held her head, kissing her muzzle.

"Mammy, it is my pony. See – my name is on it. Ronan, is this horse called Myrtle?"

"She's called whatever you want her to be called, darling. She's yours."

Myrtle became Nelly, after Sister Leonella, and Kathleen's life took on a new sense of self-worth as well as responsibility. She had never been happier, and both she and the little pony thrived.

Ronan was offered a permanent job at Avondale but declined, preferring to work ad hoc, as he still had a burning desire to return to Milldown. He was abruptly reminded of his life in Berwickshire one day when he walked into the Education Centre to be confronted by a familiar face.

"Hello, Ronan."

"Andrew, what in God's name are you doing here?"

Chapter 27

Milldown

Alasdair was in turmoil. He found himself besotted with Beanie ever since holding her lithe, young body in the cold North Sea. His concentration had lapsed, and he lay awake at night fantasising about her. Her slim waist, long auburn hair and dark blue eyes seemed to bewitch him. He had noticed James studying her but had thought nothing of it at the time. Now he felt a desire that precluded any other suitor.

His parents were to host a cocktail party to herald the start of the fox hunting season the following week, so he decided to ask Beanie to be his guest. There were few enough people to socialise with in the surrounding areas, so the members of the Northumberland and Berwickshire Hunt, or NBH as it was known, were the sole source of his family's entertainment. He knew that Beanie did not approve of blood sport of any kind, but at social events it was not usually a matter for debate.

"Beanie, there's a phone call for you – it's Alasdair."

Ellie raised her eyebrows and grinned at Beanie as she handed her the earpiece from the wall-mounted telephone.

"Hello, Alasdair. Have you found any more historical documents for us to translate?" she teased.

"No, no. I just phoned to see if you would like to come to my parents' cocktail party on the seventeenth? It will be quite a formal affair but it's usually quite good fun. I could send the carriage for you?"

"The seventeenth." Beanie paused to consider the invitation. Did she really want to go to a formal evening at Spylaw as Alasdair's guest? And what on earth could she wear to such an occasion?

"Beanie, are you still there?"

"Yes, sorry, Alasdair. That would be lovely, thank you. What time will the carriage come?"

"Say, around half past six for seven?"

"That's kind of you to think of me. I'll see you then."

As soon as she put the earpiece back into the holder, she regretted her answer. Ellie's persistent teasing didn't help, but she didn't react, as she thought that Ellie might be a little jealous, as she hadn't received an invitation.

"What can I wear, Ellie? They are all so well dressed and glamorous. I have nothing suitable, and it's on the seventeenth. That only gives me a week and a half."

"Mother has that green dress that she wore to the Young Farmers Ball last year. We could take that in and add some lace."

"No, I didn't like that when mother wore it. Oh, I'll think of something. Perhaps I can get one made in time; I'll ask the seamstress in the village tomorrow. Come on, let's feed the cattle."

William and Helen were most impressed that their daughter had been invited to a cocktail party, especially so as the daughter was Beanie, the tomboy of the family, who hated dressing up. Helen rushed into Coldingham to the seamstress to see what fabrics were on offer.

"Beanie, darling, you must go straight away to see Mistress Brodie – she has a swathe of ivory satin and some chiffon. She has lace too from Ireland. She says that she can cut a pattern and have a tea dress ready in time. Your father says he will pay. Go on now, put your corset on, and hurry."

Beanie screwed her nose up at the thought of the whalebone corset that her mother was referring to. She enjoyed her freedom from such cumbersome articles of clothing and couldn't remember when she had last worn a corset.

"Ellie, you come with me. I don't know which design to choose."

Helen, having been shown a pattern, had already discussed the style of dress that Beanie should wear, so the choice had, in effect, already been made. It had to be said that the satin was beautiful, and the pale grey chiffon, which would be made into sheer sleeves, slightly cut away at the shoulders and rising into a high-laced neckline, would be quite audacious for the time. A heavily laced belt cut into a low V shape at the front of the dress would be the pièce de résistance.

Beanie submitted to having her corset tightened then being measured from head to toe, an experience that she did not find pleasant. Matching stockings were chosen and decorated hair combs bought. Helen was obviously intent on showing her daughter off to her best advantage. Bidding Mistress Brodie goodbye, Beanie and Ellie returned to Milldown, threw off their best clothes and returned to their chores, forgetting all about the dress.

The days flew by, then on the sixteenth of the month, Beanie was reminded that she had to go for her final fitting and if the dress fitted, she could bring it home. Ellie and Helen went with her to make sure everything was perfect.

"Don't worry, darling," Helen whispered to Ellie, "it will be your turn soon enough."

Beanie went behind a curtain in the tiny, cramped shop,

strewn with off-cuts of fabric, ribbons and threads, and had Mistress Brodie dress her. The fabrics against Beanie's skin felt wonderful, giving her a sense of femininity that she had rarely experienced before, and when she revealed herself, both Helen and Ellie gasped. Beanie looked like she had stepped out of a Parisienne magazine.

The colour and texture of the satin was sumptuous and the sheer chiffon sleeves, exposing her straight shoulders, were inimitable, if a little daring. The high lace collar, which tickled the underneath of her chin, made her stance both upright and elegant. The low V-shaped belt sat well on her nineteen-inch waist, exaggerating the lower flare of the skirt. Beanie had never felt more like a woman. The thought of wearing this beautiful garment to Alasdair's house was daunting to say the least.

The following day, Beanie bathed and washed her hair. When it was dry, Ellie heated her curling irons and began to style it. When the curls had been put through every strand, Ellie piled the hair on top into a chignon, creating an effect of thick, lustrous hair, held up with decorated combs. Her corset tightened, stockings and shoes on, Ellie lowered the dress onto Beanie. She had not put too many petticoats on, so the satin fell dreamily to the ground. She was ready. All of a sudden, Beanie welled up. "I wish John was here to see me, Ellie. I do miss him."

At six thirty, the carriage drew up. Beanie took an umbrella, as fashion dictated, and left the sanctuary of her home. The plodding motion of the carriage churned her already fragile stomach. Pulling up at the front door of Spylaw, Beanie saw several of the carriages had been taken over to the stable block to await their return journey, all being tended to by Pat and several young stable boys.

She had a sudden preference to spend the evening in the

stables with the horses, but Alasdair arrived to escort her into the house. His eyes said it all: he was stunned by her appearance. He gave her a peck on the cheek, took her arm and led her inside. She was aware that she looked beautiful, which gave her the courage to mix with this unfamiliar set of people. Alasdair had not mentioned that the party was to celebrate the start of the hunting season, and he hoped it wouldn't be mentioned.

She was presented to Gordon, who gave a low whistle of appreciation. "This is not the Beanie that I know and love. This young woman is far too elegant."

Beanie blushed and allowed him to give her a peck on the cheek. Gordon's wife was also brought up short, admiring Beanie's dress, and with a look of envy she noted her youth and elegance. Champagne was served in the great hall to Beanie's delight, as she was unused to such luxuries, then the guests filtered through into the orangery. Alasdair never left her side. He couldn't take his eyes off her.

"Beanie, I have to say you look delightful. You're going to be the envy of many of the guests here this evening. I hope you're prepared."

At that very moment, Lorna walked over.

"Hello. It's Beanie, isn't it? I have to say, I love your dress. You must have bought it in Jenners in Princes Street – I've seen one just like it. Are you not cold with your shoulders uncovered like that?"

Off the peg, naked, Beanie appreciated the dig, seeing the envy in Lorna's eyes, not only for her dress but also because she was on Alasdair's arm.

"No, Lorna, this is haute couture, and your concern is heart-warming, but I have Alasdair to take away the chill in the air."

Touché, thought Alasdair. No need to defend Beanie.

Although Beanie had valiantly upheld her dignity, it had not pleased her to find that so early in the evening she had made an enemy.

"I'm sorry, Alasdair. I think Lorna is upset by my invitation."

She stood closer to Alasdair whilst sipping her champagne but did not feel sheltered. These people were not of her class, and although her beauty could stand up to any one of them, could her social standing? Alasdair introduced her to many of the guests, all of whom were welcoming, but a sinking feeling was permeating her subliminal sense of equality.

Just as her initial high spirits were evaporating, Gordon made an announcement. Alasdair hoped he wouldn't mention the hunt and fortunately he didn't. He was going to do his usual trick of making the men a cocktail called a "Blue Blazer". They had been led into the orangery for this purpose, as the floor was flag-stoned and wouldn't stain or burn if his trick went wrong.

He invited the men to gather round and the ladies to stand back for their own safety. Beanie was intrigued, and she temporarily forgot about Lorna's verbal attack.

"Now," announced Gordon, "I'm going to take one wine glass of Scotch whiskey and one glass of boiling water." Both were prepared and handed to him by his wife.

"I'm putting the whiskey and boiling water into one mug – please observe carefully – and I'm going to ignite it with this taper." He lit the contents of the mug, and flames instantly shot up into the air to gasps from the onlookers. "Now, if you watch carefully, I will pour the blazing liquid from one mug to the other several times."

It was becoming very dramatic.

"And you will see a continuous stream of fire going back and forth."

The audience applauded and congratulated Gordon, who took a theatrical bow. The show was over, and the warm whiskey was served to the men in small tumblers, sweetened with one teaspoon of powdered white sugar.

"A 'Blue Blazer'," he announced to each delighted recipient of the cocktail.

The show had lightened Beanie's mood, and she and Alasdair chatted easily in a corner of the orangery, mostly about the documents that they had translated.

"James did have another theory about the jewels in the loch. He thinks that the black pearls belonging to Mary Queen of Scots may have been retrieved, but the other two pieces could still be in there, too small to have been found – 'En Tortue', the little turtle with ten rubies and the diamond and ruby hat pin shaped as a mermaid. He thinks we're still in with a chance of finding them."

"Gosh, wouldn't that be wonderful? What would you do with them if you did recover them?"

"That would be up to my father. We should hand them in, but he would probably be worried that it would cause speculation. Would you like another champagne?"

They wandered back into the vast empty hall, where Carro lay sleeping.

"Here, take your glass and we'll retreat to my study for a while, get away from the noise."

The study was warm and quiet, the champagne making Beanie relaxed and happy. She really enjoyed Alasdair's company and respected his parents immensely. The night was a pleasure after all. Chatting companionably, they didn't notice the passage of time.

"It's ten thirty – our guests will be leaving. We'd better go down."

As they stood, Beanie lost her balance slightly and found herself leaning on Alasdair, who took a chance and tilted her head and touched his warm lips to hers, his body reacting violently.

"Alasdair, what are you doing? I'm sorry, that is not what I was expecting. I thought we were just good friends."

"Beanie, you must know that you are more than just a friend. I can't stop thinking about you. You are on my mind night and day."

"Please, Alasdair. Don't spoil a wonderful evening."

"I'm sorry, Beanie, it must be the drink. I'm so sorry — forgive me."

The atmosphere became a little awkward as they left the study to return to the party. Descending the stairs, they saw Lorna and Fiona loitering in the hallway. Beanie got a cramp in the pit of her stomach, noticing two young men by their sides watching them come down the stairs.

"Alasdair, we wondered where you were. Beanie, your lovely dress is crumpled."

There was no doubt as to what Lorna was insinuating, and the hackles on the back of Beanie's neck began to rise.

"Tell me again, won't you Beanie, how many acres do you farm? The boys were interested."

The boys looked on, wondering where this line of conversation was going, for it had not been mentioned before.

"I farm three hundred and sixty-five acres, Lorna. Why do you ask?"

"Have they been in your family long?"

Beanie became suddenly fully aware of what Lorna was getting at. She felt like she had fallen into a pit of fire and there was no way out. Alasdair clasped her hand in support, feeling the tension of conflict as the others looked on.

"We are tenant farmers, Lorna, as I'm sure you are well aware, or you wouldn't have asked the question. My family may not have the wealth of your family, but if your demeanour is representative of your lineage, we are richer by far."

On hearing that Beanie was a tenant farmer, Alasdair dropped her hand. Shocked at his response, she turned to face him. What did she see in his eyes? What was that look? Had he not realised that her family were not landowners? Was he disappointed? Would he really terminate their friendship because of her status?

"Alasdair, I'll walk to the carriage alone, if you don't mind. I'll leave you with your friends. Goodnight."

Gordon was at the stables, seeing his friends into their carriages and was surprised to see Beanie unchaperoned.

"Beanie, where is Alasdair? Could he not see you to your carriage? I do hope that you had a pleasant evening?"

"Gordon, thank you, I enjoyed it immensely. Alasdair .is caught up with his friends. I'm perfectly all right."

Gordon didn't seem convinced as he handed Beanie into her carriage and saw the look of distress on her face.

"I'm so pleased you came, Beanie. I hope we'll see you again soon. Perhaps you can ride out with Alasdair again – it's good to get the horses exercised."

Inside the carriage, as it rumbled across the uneven road towards Milldown, Beanie was near to tears. The thought of being embarrassed by a vindictive, jealous girl in front of Alasdair and then to have her family's standing scorned was too much for her to cope with, but she could not let her parents know how the evening had ended. On entering the warm, familiar kitchen, she found her father sitting by the range, a small tumbler of whiskey in his hand.

"Father, you didn't have to wait up for me."

"That's all right, lass. I just wanted to see you safely to your bed."

William looked at his eldest daughter and emotion overwhelmed him. He was so proud of her. Since John had passed away, she had worked tirelessly, and the farm hadn't suffered. He knew that he could rely on her and it took a weight off his shoulders. However, tonight, seeing her for the first time as a woman, and a beautiful woman at that, he wondered how long it would be before she found herself a husband and left Milldown for good.

Giving her father a kiss, she thanked him again for buying her such a beautiful dress and told him that she had been the belle of the ball and what a wonderful evening she had had. She described how Gordon had made "Blue Blazers" for the men and how the women had drunk champagne out of dimple cut bowls with slender stems, then giving him warm hug, she went up to bed. She was exhausted, emotional and yearning for Ronan to return to Milldown so they could ride on the beach without a care in the world. She hadn't realised just how much she missed him.

Chapter 28

Wicklow

Out of the fifteen applicants that were accepted for the Forestry School, only one was English. Although Andrew lived in Berwickshire, all his family had come from Middle England, having moved to where they could find work. Andrew's father was a baker by trade, and his mother served in the small grocery store in Coldingham. Twelve of the applicants came from Southern Ireland, one from Ulster and one from Belfast.

It was a troubled time in Ireland. The Irish Republican Brotherhood, or IRB, had been revived, and Sinn Fein (We Ourselves) was established. The talk in public houses was anti-English, although the Protestant population of Ulster in particular was keen to remain part of the British Empire.

"Andrew, I think for your own safety you had better say that you are Scottish, not English."

"Why's that, Killian?"

"The British are mighty unpopular. Ireland wants its independence, and if word got out that you were English, you'd stand out like a sore thumb if there was any trouble."

Andrew had no political knowledge or views on the subject and didn't take the warning very seriously, although he would never mention his English roots. His goal was simply to learn as much as he could on the subject of reforestation over the six-week course and then take his skills back home to share with

Alasdair.

One hundred and four experimental plots were to be laid out over the following years with eighty-four tree species, to determine the cost of production, yield in timber and the comparative market of the species planted. The work would begin on the slopes leading down to the Avonmore River and across the Great Ride, a picturesque mountain range. An arboretum would be planted near to the Education Centre, to discern which trees would be suitable for private gardens. This was to become Ronan's task, as the work was a little less labour intensive. The positive reputation of the school encouraged more and more applicants, the course providing the background and expertise needed to develop a successful state forestry programme as well as private forestry initiatives like that of Alasdair.

Andrew had not been educated to a high standard. However, he threw himself into his studies and soon became one of Mr. Forbes' star pupils. Ronan, although not officially a student, was allowed to sit in on the classes as long as he made the tea and coffee and did any preparation necessary for the lectures. There was also a small canteen run by staff, providing lunch and snacks for the hard-working young men, whose standard uniform was long trousers, long-sleeved shirt, waistcoat, flat cap and the obligatory muddy boots.

Ronan and Andrew forgot their differences, and one evening, Andrew was invited to go home with Killian and Ronan to meet their family.

"And who would this fine young man be?" asked Patricia.

Ma, this is Andrew. I told you, he works on an estate near to where Beanie lives."

"Ah well, that's grand. Will you be staying long in Ireland,

Andrew?"

"Just for two more weeks – I've nearly finished the course. I was only booked for the six weeks of lectures. I won't be staying to see the hard work start."

At that point, Kathleen joined them. Suddenly she was coy, completely out of character, and couldn't take her eyes off Andrew.

"Come here, Kathleen. I want you to meet Andrew. He lives near to Beanie, and he's met Captain, the huge horse I told you about."

Kathleen's cheeks had turned pink, and she clung to her mother.

"I thought you could show Andrew Nelly. He loves horses."

Kathleen turned and left the room in a state of flustered confusion.

"I think she likes you, Andrew," Ronan teased.

"Andrew, she has Down's Syndrome. She's a little shy – don't take offence."

Patricia tried to excuse her daughter's sudden departure, but Andrew just laughed.

"I had a sister with Downs. I'm afraid we lost her before we moved to Scotland. She was born with a heart defect and other complications. I think we moved partly to help my mother recover from losing her, and of course the prospect of work."

"I always thought you were an only child. I'm sorry for your loss, Andrew."

Ronan was starting to see another side of Andrew and was beginning to like him. Patricia did her best to impress him with her culinary skills, but the food was not what he was used to in Scotland. He missed the beef stews with dumplings and apple crumbles, but he complimented Patricia nonetheless, then the boys left for a pint of Guinness in The Fighting Cocks. Brandon joined them on his way home from the docks.

The bar was not packed, but a table of five young men was becoming rowdy, their language distasteful. They were not local boys or they would have been recognised, but nobody, including the barman, knew who they were. They seemed furtive, but their alcohol consumption was making them loud, their conversation travelling to Killian's group.

"Bloody English – they should get out of our country. They've pilfered enough over the years. My great grandparents had their land stolen. We've been left with nothing but rotting potatoes and arrogant bastards occupying our grand houses."

"Whilst we live ten to a croft, no jobs, starving children. My God, they're going to pay."

"And those Protestant bastards in Belfast and Ulster – they've got it coming too."

The unrest was spreading, the animosity palpable.

Andrew, don't rise to it. They're full of liquor; it could become ugly."

The boys decided to forego their Guinness and moved towards the door. Unfortunately, Andrew bumped into one of the chairs that they were sitting on, and before thinking, he spoke.

"Oh, I do beg your pardon. I've made you spill your drink. I'm so sorry."

"Beg my pardon? What accent would that be, now?"

One of the troublemakers rose from his chair, sliding the feet noisily across the floor. He would have taken the confrontation further had Brandon not stepped in between them.

"Calm down, now. He's a guest of ours from Scotland. Do you have a problem with that? Do you want to take it outside?"

Fortunately, Brandon was taller and obviously more mature

than the angry youth, so he stood down, or rather nearly fell down, losing his balance due to the alcohol he had drunk. The barman gave Brandon a grateful look and the boys left the pub.

"They're trouble if ever I saw it. There is a lot of resentment towards the English, Andrew. It goes back centuries, but it seems to be bubbling to the surface again with this generation. Take no notice."

Wise words, but Andrew had got a shock at their hostility and wished he could return to the safety of the Avondale Estate. The boys bunked down in the same room, something Andrew was not used to, but the mattress was clean and comfortable and he dozed off.

A little later, all four boys were awoken by a commotion in the barn. Both the horse and the cow were obviously alarmed by something so the boys went to investigate. The pony had her saddle hanging to one side but no bridle, and the cow had pulled loose from her tether and was frantically stumbling around the barn. The dog was nowhere to be seen.

"What in God's name has happened here?" asked Patricia, who had followed the boys out.

"I don't know, Ma. Why is Nelly half saddled?"

"Where's Kathleen? Ronan, go and fetch Kathleen."

Patricia was alarmed, thinking that something may have happened to Kathleen."

"She's not in the house, Ma. When did you see her last?"

"She was away to her bed two hours ago, Ronan. Where is she?"

Patricia was becoming hysterical as the boys searched the barn.

"She's not here. Where the hell is she?"

Voices were now raised as panic spread like wildfire

213

amongst the family.

"Ma, you search the house again. We'll spread out and search the woods."

Patricia was by now in floods of tears, screaming for her husband and shaking. The boys went off in different directions, north, south, east and west, Killian towards his own home. He found no trace of Kathleen so rushed in to wake Cara.

"You stay here, Cara, in case she comes to you. Lock the doors though. There was trouble at the pub."

With no further explanation, Killian turned and ran off again, shouting Kathleen's name. No one had seen any sign of Kathleen as they regrouped back at the house.

They searched for the best part of four hours, intermittently meeting back at the house, but the search proved to be in vain. The boys were convinced that it had something to do with the drunken youths in the pub, and their imaginations were running wild. Patricia was inconsolable, and Ambrose was running through the forest with a loaded rifle. A return visit to The Fighting Cocks also proved to be futile, as the bar tender, woken from his slumber, simply confirmed that the group of boys were strangers to the area, and he had no idea where they had gone at closing time.

In the depths of despair, their frustration turned to anger and focused on Andrew, who had revealed his English origins in the pub.

"If you hadn't spoken to those bastards in the pub, none of this would have happened," Killian yelled at him.

"You'd best get yourself back to Avondale, Andrew, we've no need of you here. Ma, I'm going into Bray to the Garda Siochana."

Andrew was beside himself with grief, reliving the loss of

his sister and praying that nothing had happened to Kathleen. He would have thanked Patricia for her hospitality and said his goodbyes, but no one was listening. He turned and left, not knowing exactly how to get back to Avondale but realised that he was no longer welcome. How fickle the Irish were, he thought. On this occasion, however, perhaps his feelings were unwarranted.

He made his way along a footpath that seemed familiar, walking until the first light of dawn presented him with an alien vista. He had no idea where he was and seemed to have strayed off the footpath. As he stood for a moment, trying to get his bearings, he became aware of a quiet sobbing. The noise was coming from a derelict barn over to his right.

He prayed to God that it would be Kathleen and he could take her home, so he went to investigate. Quietly, he went to the back of the barn where he could peep in. The five thugs from the pub lay on the floor asleep, vomit pooled next to one of them. Kathleen was sitting up, quietly sobbing, her face puffy and red. She was not restrained, so Andrew wondered why she had not made an escape. Her clothes were intact, thankfully, so he concluded that she had not been molested and wondered what the boys' intentions were.

He crept round to the front of the barn and tried to get Kathleen's attention. However, her dog, which had obviously followed her, began to bark. Kathleen stopped sobbing as one of the youths began to wake up, but then she caught sight of Andrew.

Andrew put a finger to his lips in order to quieten Kathleen, but on seeing a familiar face, she got up and ran towards him, followed by the dog.

"Oy, where do you think you're going? Get back here."

Kathleen took no notice and ran into Andrew's arms.

"Kathleen, we have to run very fast. Do you understand?"

"Yes."

She took off like a bat out of hell with Andrew and the dog on her tail. However, the youth who had woken up was right behind them. He lunged at Andrew and catching his legs, floored him, knocking the wind out of him.

"Run, Kathleen, run home."

Kathleen and the dog ran as fast as they could through bracken and thorns, stumbling and gasping for breath. Kathleen began to recognise the landscape and after some time found herself at the convent. She burst through the gate and ran along the cloister towards the room where she knew Sister Leonella would most likely be. Sister Leonella leapt to her feet with fright at the sight of Kathleen and her dog.

Kathleen threw herself into Sister Leonella's arms, crying wildly.

"They stole me, Sister, and now they have Andrew."

"What on earth has happened, child? Where is your mother?"

"Please keep me safe. Don't let them take me again. Lock the gate, Sister, quickly."

"Sister Anne, go and find Bridget for me, quickly now."

Kathleen cried until her sister was found and held her close.

"What has happened, Kathleen?"

Through the sobs, she managed to tell Bridge that some boys had stolen her and said if she moved, they would kill the dog, so she had sat very still.

"Sister Anne, run to Patricia's house and tell the family that we have Kathleen safe and sound. They will be beside themselves with worry. Hurry now."

Forty-five minutes later, the whole family rushed into the convent, a member of the Garda and an exhausted Sister Anne in tow. Ambrose had been persuaded not to bring the loaded rifle with him into the sacred grounds of the convent, even though he was in the mood to shoot someone or at the very least something.

Kathleen managed to explain that she was practising saddling her pony when some boys had taken her.

"How on earth did you get yourself to the convent, darling?" asked Patricia, holding onto Kathleen tightly whilst they both sobbed.

"Andrew told me to run as fast as I could, then the boy got him."

"Andrew?" asked Brandon.

"Yes. He saved me, but then they got him."

Chapter 29

Milldown

The farm was always less industrious in the autumn and winter. The calves were fattening for the spring market and the winter crops propagating. On a quiet day, Beanie and her father went to the market in Dunns to purchase a dozen turkeys to fatten up for Christmas. Turkeys were given to the workers and of course one kept for their own consumption. Helen and Ellie were spending their morning baking, and life seemed to be getting back to normal. Beanie had not heard from Alasdair and at present had no wish to.

The market was bustling with stalls selling all manner of goods: wools and fabrics, cheeses and meats, black pudding and of course, fish. Bakers had been busy and were selling breads, cakes and singing hinnies, a sort of griddle cake whose name was derived from the sound of the butter and lard singing when it touched the hot flat griddle pan on which it was cooked. Kitchen utensils, farm tools and all manner of household products and gadgets were also being displayed. Of course, some livestock were crated, ready for the diverse consumer.

"Father, I just want to go into the milliner's, if you don't mind."

"Ay, lass, you go ahead. I'll wait here."

Beanie stepped into the milliner's shop. It was dark, as the day was gloomy, but the hats fascinated her. After getting a taste for wearing elegant clothes, she couldn't resist trying on the largest hat in the store.

"Would you like any help with that, Madam? Here, let me."

The assistant annoyingly began to change the tilt of the hat on Beanie's head.

"There now. That looks perfect."

Whilst the assistant was fussing over Beanie, giving her advice that she didn't appreciate, a finger tapped her on the shoulder.

"Beanie, how nice to see you again. What a lovely hat. Are you going somewhere special to wear it?"

"Hello, Lorna. Err, yes, I do have a special assignation as it happens, but this hat is not what I was looking for. Excuse me." She had no idea why she had said that, as she had no occasion to wear such a hat at all.

The assistant looked disappointed at not making a sale to Beanie so instantly proceeded to put into practise her selling skills on Lorna.

Outside, Beanie met with her father, who could sense that her mood had changed and not for the better.

"What is it, Beanie? Is something wrong?"

"No, Father. Let's just pick up the turkeys and get home. I just bumped into someone I know, that's all."

"Was it Lorna? I saw her follow you in. I know her father."

"It was. How do you know her father?"

"Och, lassie, he's a ne'er-do-well. I've seen him in the Plough and Horses over in Kelso. Thinks he's high and mighty just because he won some land gambling. He fair ruined a man's reputation who lived here in Dunns. The man and his family had to move away."

Beanie fumed. To think that this girl with no refinement had spoiled her friendship with Alasdair. Petulantly, Beanie thought of how she would one day get her own back.

The turkeys were housed in a barn that Beanie had prepared earlier for that purpose. It was clean and waterproof, the floor covered in straw. She fed them and returned to the house.

"Beanie, a letter arrived for you this morning. I forgot to give it to you."

It was from Alasdair, apologising for Lorna's behaviour at his parents' cocktail party and for not being in contact sooner. The fact was, he had had to travel to Edinburgh to consult with the family's accountant and had stayed a few nights with James on campus. They had delved further into the possibility of Mary Queen of Scots visiting Spylaw but had found nothing new to confirm her using the house as a sanctuary. Beanie found that she had almost lost interest in the historic documents and put the letter to one side.

The following morning, Alasdair phoned.

"Good morning, Beanie. My father has bought a new horse and wants me to try him out. How do you fancy a ride over to Coldingham Loch?"

"I don't know, Alasdair. I'm a bit tied up this morning. Perhaps this afternoon?"

Alasdair sensed a lack of enthusiasm. She was not as good humoured as she usually was, but he persisted.

"This morning would be better, as the hunt is out later. It's up to you."

Beanie was not going to be restricted by the hunt, especially as she knew that Lorna would be out with them and stubbornly stuck to her preferred time.

"I'll meet you at the loch around two."

"Thanks, Beanie, I appreciate that. I value your opinion."

Beanie left Milldown, mounted on Captain, with a sense of foreboding. It wasn't that she didn't want to see Alasdair. She couldn't put her finger on it, but she wasn't at ease. There was a low Scottish mist over the heather and gorse, and the air was damp. Captain, however, was excited and frisky, his loud exhalations of breath forming their own cloud patterns in front of him as he shook his huge, heavy head, rattling his harness. The squelching, rhythmic sound of his massive hooves sucking on the mud lulled Beanie into a false sense of security. The afternoon was ominously quiet, no gulls screeching and no sound from the ocean. Beanie wondered what lay ahead.

Then she saw Alasdair at some distance on top of a fine thoroughbred, but something was obviously wrong. His arms were frantically waving, and his horse was prancing and showing signs of distress. At first, she thought that Alasdair was having trouble controlling the animal, but it soon became clear that he was not the one in trouble.

The loch was behind him, but as Beanie approached, she could see the water erupting and a horse's head flailing madly, the noise of it screaming in terror sending goosebumps up Beanie's back. She urged Captain on with difficulty, as he was not built for speed, but he seemed to be aware that a horse was in distress and broke into a canter.

The scene was terrifying. The horse was obviously stuck in the loch, trapped by its legs in the thick mud and silt, panicking and sinking deeper, its eyes wild as its body thrashed.

"It's Lorna's horse, Beanie. She was out hunting today. She must have taken a fall and the horse has bolted. She could be injured. I'll have to check the surrounding area."

Alasdair was shouting over the noise of the horse in the water and also the whinnying from his own mount.

"What about the horse? We can't leave it – it's going to break a leg if we don't help."

"Beanie, you stay with the horse. I'll look for Lorna and see if I can get some help."

With that, he galloped off, leaving Beanie to cope with the traumatised horse in the loch. She could do nothing unless she dismounted, which left her vulnerable, but a decision was made, and she slid from Captain's back with a thud. Captain was still wearing his leather collar, as Beanie had been working him that morning, and she wondered if she could get Captain to pull the horse free. It was impossible to formulate a plan, however, with the noise and commotion, and Beanie let out a sob. She couldn't bear to witness the distress of the poor struggling beast, but she was the only one there to help.

Captain stood still, thankfully, so Beanie slowly paddled into the loch, whispering to the terrified animal, at the same time trying to protect herself from its thrashing head. She tried to approach, but that seemed to make it panic even more, then Captain slowly plodded forward and joined Beanie in the water. That had a calming effect on the horse, which suddenly quietened down, although its nostrils were flared, its breaths still coming in gasps and its wild eyes darting from Beanie to Captain.

Beanie stood still for some time, whispering to the horse, the freezing water chilling her to the bone, then Captain stepped further forward into the loch and touched his muzzle to the muzzle of the panic-stricken horse. They almost seemed to whisper to each other, and the horse became still. Beanie was mesmerised, with no sense of the cold or of passing time until Captain threw his head up and brought her out of her reverie.

The horse's reins had been thrown forward and floated on the water in front of its head, so Beanie picked them up and looped them over Captain's collar, where usually his harness would be attached. She urged Captain to turn slowly, but that caused the horse to start thrashing again. They were moving too fast, so Beanie brought Captain to a standstill again.

They spent some more time trying to gain the horse's confidence then tried again. Beanie managed to slide her hand down into the water, trying to ascertain how deep the horse's legs had gone into the mud, but she was in danger of sinking herself. It wasn't good. The mud was halfway up its legs, preventing the horse from freeing itself. Although the mud was soft, it seemed to have suction almost like quicksand.

By this time, Beanie was giving up all hope of freeing the animal. She had no tricks left up her sleeve and was becoming desperate herself. Then she heard galloping hooves. She breathed a sigh of relief as she saw Alasdair and Pat racing towards her with ropes.

They leaped off their mounts and Pat took charge. He threw a rope behind the horse and under his tail so it lodged between the round of the buttocks and the hocks. Alasdair took one side, Pat the other and asked Beanie to guide the horse while they pulled. It wasn't sufficient to free the horse. Captain had to do his part, so while the men pulled from the back, Beanie encouraged Captain to pull from the front. It was disastrous – the horse fell sideways and its head went under.

"Quickly now, pull as hard as you can now. His legs are free. We'll have to slide him out."

Captain took the strain, and, as if he were pulling a heavy plough, with all his might he slid the horse to the edge of the loch. The horse seemed lifeless, and Beanie wondered if it had suffered a heart attack. Captain's head came round, and once again he blew into the horse's muzzle. He pushed and cajoled the horse's head until at last the horse showed signs of life.

"He's freezing. Everyone – rub him down as hard as you can; get the circulation back in his legs."

Pat was wonderful, his lilting Irish accent throwing out orders that no one could disobey, for they came from the power of conviction. He felt for breaks in the horse's legs – there were none. However, its legs then went into spasm.

"It's the cold and shock. Keep rubbing; harder now; he'll be fine."

All the while they worked on reviving the horse, Captain continued to nuzzle it, aware that the horse was in trouble. Finally, the horse slowly came round and tried to sit up. It took it several attempts, but it managed to sit for a while then struggle to its feet, its legs trembling and weak. It came to rest, head hanging low with its nose against Captain.

"Beanie, you must be freezing. We must get both you and the horse back home and warm. Spylaw is closest; we'll go there. My mother is tending to Lorna. She took a fall jumping a hedge on the hunt, and her horse bolted. She's okay, just shaken. Let me help you to mount Captain."

He cupped his hand and effortlessly propelled Beanie up onto Captain's back.

"I must say, Captain did a fine job reassuring Lorna's horse. He deserves a medal."

"Alasdair, I'll go home, if you don't mind. It's been quite an ordeal. I'd rather go to Milldown and take a hot bath."

Alasdair was visibly disappointed, but Beanie had no desire to be tended to alongside Lorna. She wanted to get Captain into his stall, reward him with carrots and extra oats, then feel the warmth of her family around her. It had been a bad day from start to finish. She wanted it over.

Chapter 30

Wicklow

The family found it difficult to believe that it had been Andrew who had rescued Kathleen. Kidnap was a serious offence, and the Garda wanted to get his facts straight so questioned Kathleen over and over whilst taking notes. Bridge had prepared a tray of tea to soothe everybody's frayed nerves, and the family gradually calmed down. Kathleen was able to give a good account of what had happened, and the Garda complimented her on her bravery. Brandon gave a description of the five youths, and they were then free to go home. A search party would scour the woods and roads to locate the offending boys.

Back home, Kathleen began to talk about what had happened to her. She had been talking to her pony when the boys approached her. They had made fun of her then tried to tempt her away with chocolate.

"I think they thought I was stupid, Mammy. I know I mustn't go with strangers. I tried to run to the house, but they grabbed me and told me they would shoot Bracken if I didn't go with them. They had a gun. They dragged me through the forest, but they were drunk, and one had to stop to be sick – it was disgusting. We got to the barn, and they pushed me around and made fun of the way I look and called me names. They told me it was bedtime and that I should take off all my clothes, but I told them I was too cold. Bracken growled at them, but they kicked him, Mammy, and he cried."

At that point, Kathleen broke down and sobbed in her mother's arms, at the same time looking for her beloved dog, which had remained by her side.

"Come here to Mammy, my darling. You're the prettiest girl in the whole of Wicklow County, for sure you are. Those boys don't have a mammy that loves them like you do. They have been brought up to be mean and nasty. If you're not loved, you don't know how to love and be a good person. We must pray for them so that God will love them; for sure nobody on earth will."

"That's sad, Mammy, that no one will ever love them until they get to heaven."

"That's right, darling. We'll ask Sister Leonella to pray for them, for if the Garda catch them, they will be in all sorts of trouble."

Brandon had had enough of his mother's soft talk.

"Boys, what do you say we go looking for these eejits, and we'll see if God loves them enough to protect them. Come on."

"Ronan, don't you go fighting now – you'll get hurt again," Patricia shouted.

At that, Kathleen burst into floods of tears again at the thought of Ronan getting hurt, and Patricia broke down too. Ambrose took up his gun again and followed his sons, leaving the two women sobbing in each other's arms, the dog with his head resting on Kathleen's lap.

Their tempers, that they had so far kept under control, now flared. They travelled quickly with determined strides across the rough undergrowth, Ambrose following the boys, trying to keep up. A bullet was fired, and a squirrel dropped from a tree up ahead.

"Pa, you'll just be warning them that we're coming if you

shoot off a few bullets. We've got to find Andrew – who knows what's happened to him? The Garda were only interested in catching the boys, who are probably on the road by now. We'd better locate Andrew; he may be hurt. Let's stick together, and Pa – not so trigger-happy."

They came across the barn where the boys had held Kathleen, and a quick search outside revealed a boulder on the ground with a congealed pool of blood on it.

"I don't like the look of this," said Brandon. "We'd better find Andrew quickly."

They rushed on and in the distance saw something unusual under a huge oak tree.

"Oh my God – is that Andrew?"

Andrew had been tied naked to the tree. His head was hanging, and they feared the worse.

They swarmed round him, throwing questions at him.

"Are you hurt, Andrew?"

"What have they done to you? Where did the bastards go?"

"Untie him, for God's sake, Ronan."

He was untied, and he stood, a little shaken, his mouth and nose bleeding, but no other wounds were visible. Brandon covered him, and they helped him to sit on a fallen tree trunk.

"Andrew, what happened? Are they still in the area?"

Andrew seemed bewildered but managed to tell them that after Kathleen had run from the barn, one of the boys had rugby-tackled him and brought him down. However, in doing so the boy had smashed his face on a boulder and lost his two front teeth. His friends were so incensed that they had given Andrew a good thrashing then tied him to the tree. His clothes were scattered around. Ambrose gathered them and helped him dress.

"How long ago was this?"

"About an hour or two; I'm not sure, but I'm bloody freezing."

"Ronan, you take him home. We'll continue to search, but if it was that long ago, they'll be gone."

Andrew was in some considerable pain, especially around his ribs. The blood on his face had dried and he looked dishevelled and pale. The two boys walked slowly, Ronan supporting his friend. However, their troubles weren't over. Two of the vagrants had split up from the group to avoid capture and were sitting under a tree ahead of Ronan and Andrew, obviously lost.

"In God's name, what now?" said Ronan under his breath.

Andrew felt sick to the stomach, knowing that he was incapable of putting up a reasonable fight in his condition and knowing that Ronan was recovering from an injury, leaving the two of them completely at the mercy of the youths.

"What have we here? They've come back for more, Sean."

The boys stood slowly up with a look of feral aggression in their eyes, blocking the path of Ronan and Andrew.

"Calm down now, boys. We just want to get home – back off." Ronan knew his words would mean nothing, but there was no harm in trying."

"Get home to your mammy. I don't think she wants you, do you, Sean? I think we'll take care of them. What do you say, Sean?"

"I'd say they want another round. That one must have enjoyed it, specially showing us his little willy."

Andrew's head started to spin, and he knew he was about to pass out. The forest lost colour, everything went grey, then he slipped to his knees. He wasn't fully unconscious and tried to focus on the two boys approaching. He struggled to his feet in an attempt to fight beside Ronan but knew his effort was futile.

Ronan let go of Andrew and brought his fists up into a fighting position. The boys laughed as they mimicked Ronan's defence stance. They crept closer, spreading out slightly so as to attack Ronan from both sides. They were baiting him, but Ronan was ready. As Andrew swayed with his fists held high, Ronan threw two swift punches with his right hand. Both boys hit the ground simultaneously and Ronan smiled.

"Now would you look at that Andrew – I've still got it!"

They would have walked on and left the two boys on the ground, but Brandon, Killian and Ambrose arrived. Ronan was grinning from ear to ear and the boys could see why.

"Well done, Ronan. Leave them to us now. You get Andrew home – he looks like he could do with a strong cup of tea."

Ronan was a little reluctant to leave his father and brothers alone with the vagrants. He wondered what their intentions were, for if they should do further damage, they would be committing an offence. But then again, he thought, the eejits deserved whatever they had coming to them.

When Ronan and Andrew were out of sight, Ambrose spoke to his sons.

"Well now, boys, I'm going to turn my back for two minutes. See if you can do for me what I'm no longer capable of. Think of your sister whilst you're attending to these nice young lads, would you?"

Ambrose whistled, pretending not to hear the punishing thuds of fists against skin. When the boys had finished, the lads could no longer stand.

"Now, I'll just be waiting here with my gun while you go and fetch the Garda. Tell them that Andrew threw a few heavy punches in self-defence before he was stripped and beaten. Isn't that right, boys?" The boys nodded, knowing that they were defeated and would in all probability serve a prison sentence.

Ronan and Andrew walked in through the kitchen door and Patricia let out a fearful gasp.

"God help us – what's happened to Andrew?"

"He's been beaten, Ma. Can you make him a hot cup of tea? He floored the bastards and saved me from a beating, sure he did."

Andrew looked vacant, not understanding why he had been painted as the hero, but Ronan's wink in his direction quelled his objections.

Patricia looked at Ronan suspiciously, unimpressed with his description of events. Andrew did not look like the type of boy who could throw a punch.

Ronan, could you take this for me now?"

Ronan put out his right hand to take the fictitious object from his mother, who instead grabbed his hand.

"Now, let me see." She turned his hand over, revealing red and bruised knuckles, especially the first two knuckles on his right hand.

"That Jim taught you well, Ronan. I gather there are no more bruises."

"Not a chance, Ma. There were only two of them." He grinned and winked at his mother, who shook her head but couldn't hide a smile.

Kathleen then entered the kitchen with Bracken in tow and took one look at Andrew, but instead of crying she went over to him and touched his face.

"You're a very brave boy, Andrew. You saved me from those bastards."

"Kathleen, you mustn't use such words; God will hear you."

"But Mammy, they are bastards. Look what they've done to Andrew, and I bet God saw. I'm not surprised that nobody loves those boys. I think God will find it difficult to love them too!"

Kathleen could always make them laugh.

The men arrived back home having left the offenders in the custody of the Garda Siochana, who had already apprehended the other three. Brandon went straight over to Ronan and ruffled his hair.

"Back in action, boyo!"

The three brothers laughed and joked. Ambrose too was in rare good humour, having seen all three of his sons capable of taking down those who would hurt his family. He was proud of them and tearful knowing that Ronan had made a full recovery.

"Andrew, we have a lot to thank you for. You got our Kathleen back home safely."

"Well, it was purely by accident that I found her. I did my best, but I did take a good beating."

Kathleen was listening intently and would hear nothing of his modesty.

"But Andrew, you saved Ronan as well as me."

"He not only saved me, Kathleen, but he knocked the two front teeth out of one of them then floored the two who tried to beat us again on the way home. It's a fierce shame that I mustn't fight any more after my injuries."

Kathleen was in awe of Andrew, whose heroism sat uncomfortably on his shoulders. However, he went along with the story, even embellishing it, as he was aware that the version of events was important to the family for some reason, and Kathleen certainly enjoyed having a hero.

Andrew was soon patched up and sustained no lasting injuries. He resumed his studies with Killian and Ronan on the Avondale Estate and found that the course had gained him enough knowledge to take back to Spylaw and help Alasdair with his vision of reforestation on his land. Ronan, now fully fit, was anxious to speak to Beanie to see if he would be welcomed back to Milldown, or if life had moved on and he was no longer needed.

Chapter 31

Milldown

"Beanie, hello, I've just sent Alasdair off on a fool's errand to fetch my hat so we can have a chat, if that's all right with you?"

"Yes of course, Gordon, if you can help me down."

Beanie threw her right leg over Captain's neck and slid down into Gordon's arms. Thankfully he was as strong as his son and Beanie landed gracefully.

"Take a walk with me, Beanie. Pat will take Captain." Beanie was beginning to wonder where this conversation was heading but was comfortable with Gordon. In fact, she was very fond of him.

"Beanie, if we can talk in confidence, I would very much appreciate it. Is that all right with you?"

"Of course."

"Beanie, Alasdair is very fond of you as you are probably well aware. He has discussed with me the possibility of courting you. Now, being my only son, there are implications to that. He will in the future run this estate, and I would expect nothing less of him. You know he has an interest in reforestation."

"Yes. I know that he has sent Andrew to learn to be a forester, but..."

"Beanie, let me finish. Now, I've got to know you well recently and both my wife and I are very fond of you. However, we would like you to think carefully about what you would be taking on before you get Alasdair's hopes up. You can appreciate that we feel protective towards him, I'm sure. Beanie, you may see our lives through rose-tinted glasses; the obvious affluence and status, but it can be a lonely life and difficult sometimes.

"You've seen the people we socialise with, and I know that you find their company not altogether to your taste, and I don't blame you. But these people will be coming to Spylaw well after my wife and I have departed. Spylaw is not just our home – it's an institution. It has traditions and commitments to these people. Alasdair will continue to do business with them, employ them and host the annual Hunt Ball plus other events well into the future. We rely on their friendship and cooperation. We are a close-knit community. Do you see where I'm going?"

Beanie was confused. Should she be flattered or insulted?

"Gordon, I think you are jumping the gun. I'm several years younger than Alasdair and certainly not ready to accept a proposal. I am of course very fond of him but only as a friend. I haven't led him to believe otherwise. I'm not saying that in the future my feelings won't change, but at the moment you have nothing to concern yourself with."

Her last words were spoken as a soft rebuff, as her hackles had risen slightly, and Gordon was remorseful.

"Beanie, please don't take this the wrong way. My wife and I agreed that you may need a little guidance. Have I said the wrong thing? I haven't upset you, have I? Alasdair would never forgive me."

"Father, your hat was nowhere to be seen, sorry. Hello, Beanie. Father wants me to ride Lorna's horse back to the loch. If he is skittish around water, we won't be able to keep him, as he will no longer be fit to hunt. Lorna has given up riding after the accident. She's got what she wanted – social acceptance. She never was a horsewoman; now she wants rid of the horse. It's tough mucking out a stable with painted finger nails."

"Oh, I see. That's why you invited me over." She gave a sideways glance at Gordon, who was now looking slightly uncomfortable. "All right, let's go. I have to be back to do the feeding; the nights are drawing in."

She gave Gordon a curt farewell and did not look back. Alasdair as usual was left in her wake. The horse, although a thoroughbred, was strong and well trained, so the ride across to the loch was fun, as the horses remembered one another and initiated some sort of race. Beanie, bareback as usual, couldn't help laughing as she was bounced up and down by what Captain thought was a reasonable canter. The thoroughbred, however, surged forward in a gallop that Captain was not willing to emulate.

Slowing down alongside each other, they took in the vista of the mackerel sky reflected on the rippling surface of the loch. It resembled small shoals of fish scudding across the water, and it filled them with a sense of tranquillity. The sea too was a calm backdrop to the loch, empty of fishing boats, clear to the horizon. The horse, however, got the smell of the water and heard the familiar lapping sound at the water's edge, which evoked memories of the trauma it had suffered in the loch. It started to whinny and prance, shaking its head violently until Alasdair accidently dropped the reins then slid off to regain control. Captain pranced too, positioning himself between the horse and the water, allowing Alasdair to grab the reins.

"Wow, boy, wow, it's all right. We're not going in the water."

Alasdair's voice and Captain's reassuring nuzzling quietened the horse down until it stood, relaxed, by the shore line.

"Beanie, dismount and we'll walk them for a while."

Alasdair helped Beanie dismount and they strolled slowly around the loch to where the accident had happened. The horses quietened down, giving Alasdair the confidence that his mount had suffered no lasting phobia from its accident, and that he would be able to hunt again after some time out. They had reached the spot where the caber stuck ominously out of the water, and they stopped to study it. They reminisced about how they had hoped to find Queen Mary's jewels there in the water and laughed at their own sense of romance.

The shore line was disfigured where the horse had been dragged out of the loch, the mud having a slightly unpleasant odour. Suddenly Alasdair went down onto one knee, and Beanie's stomach summersaulted. She took several steps back, completely speechless, thinking that Alasdair was going to propose to her and not knowing how to reply.

"Alasdair, please, I…"

"Beanie, come here quickly. Look, there in the mud. What's that?"

Beanie calmed herself and followed Alasdair's instructions. She loosened her hold on Captain's reins and bent by Alasdair's side.

"Look, Beanie. Something is sparkling in the water. I can just about reach it."

He pulled the object out of the mud and rinsed it until it was clean.

"En tortue," gasped Beanie.

"The little turtle with ten rubies. The horse must have disturbed the sediment and mud and brought it to the surface. You know what this means, don't you, Beanie?"

"It means that the documents at Spylaw are genuine. They really were written by Mary and Bothwell. I can't believe it,

Alasdair."

Beanie's heart was beating so fast that she felt quite giddy and leant on Alasdair's shoulder.

"Beanie, this is wonderful. It also means that somewhere in the mud down there is the hat pin shaped like a mermaid with diamonds and a ruby."

"That could be deep in the mud. We may never find that, but how wonderfully unbelievable to find en tortue. May I hold it?"

"Of course – here."

As he passed Beanie the brooch, he grabbed her, lifting her off the ground and swung her around. Beanie squealed and clung on tightly, then he planted a kiss on her lips. It was just a peck, but it left her bewildered. His strong arms and the mood of elation at finding en tortue threw her off balance. Had she enjoyed the kiss a little too much? Was the feeling of his strong arms around her a little too desirable? The moment passed as they were taken up by their find.

She had to hold back tears. To think that she was actually holding a prized possession of Mary Queen of Scots. She thought of the young woman and her heroic struggle to regain the throne of Scotland, the loss of her twins and the separation from her only living son and husband and ultimately her execution. Suddenly Mary became a real person, not a historical character who sometimes seemed no more than a fictitious personality in a storybook. She actually rode to Spylaw. They held the proof in their hands. They had authenticated her writing, so what would Alasdair do with it?

When they were back at Spylaw and the excitement had died down, the little turtle was put away in Gordon's safe. Beanie and Alasdair retreated to his study to discuss the implications of the find.

"Will you tell James?"

"Although I would love to share this with James, I don't think it's a good idea, not yet anyway. Before we found the brooch, it was a tall tale to tell. Now we have authenticated the letters, we should probably relinquish ownership. I'm thinking of the future of Spylaw though, Beanie. Having met with the accountant, I realise that we will have to diversify to survive. I have my ideas regarding timber, but I don't think in the near future that is going to be the solution.

"I have been thinking of opening the house to the public, although my parents would disapprove, but it would bring in some money, and what if we incorporated the letters and had a small museum dedicated to Mary Queen of Scots? We could do guided tours of the secret room and the summer house. All this is just a pipe dream at the moment, but my father is only interested in his horses, and mother has never participated in the business side of things. What are your thoughts, Beanie? How do you fancy sharing that dream?"

Caught off guard once again, Beanie stumbled over her reply.

"Well, I think that you are very enterprising, Alasdair, and I think that under your management Spylaw most definitely will survive. I do admire your passion. However, I really must go now; it's past feeding time. I'm neglecting the livestock."

"Oh, I forgot to tell you; I've had a letter from Andrew. He will be back in a week, and he is travelling with Ronan. Apparently they are best buddies now. Did you know?"

"I did not – how strange. Look, I really must go, Alasdair. I'll see you soon."

Reaching Milldown, she got Captain settled in his stall and fed the calves, poultry and horses. She was tired, emotionally drained and felt a little depressed. Entering the warm kitchen, the atmosphere lifted her and she hugged her mother.

"Och, what have I done to deserve such attention?"

"Nothing, Mother. It's just nice to be home."

"There's a letter waiting for you. Will you change for supper?"

Beanie had mixed emotions about opening the letter. She wondered, after all this time, if Ronan still had feelings for her, and more importantly, did she still have feelings for him? The letter read:

Dear Beanie,

I'm so sorry that I wasn't able to speak to you on the telephone to discuss my return. I had an injury and it has taken this long for me to recover. Killian and I met Andrew studying on the Avondale Estate and we seem to have become mates. He's become quite the hero here in Wicklow. I'll explain when I see you. Andrew and I will be with you by next Friday, God willing.

Love,

Ronan.

Beanie took the letter into Ellie's room and let her read it.

"What do you make of that? I can't imagine Andrew being a hero."

Ellie was delighted, as she still held a torch for Andrew and was pleased to hear that he and Ronan were now friends.

"Ellie, I think Alasdair wants to be more than friends, but now Ronan is coming back to Milldown, my emotions are all over the place. Alasdair kissed me today, Ellie. It was only a peck but, if I'm honest, it melted my heart."

"Beanie, you haven't seen Ronan for so long. See how you get on when he gets back. I can't wait to see Andrew, my hero." She laughed.

Chapter 32

Milldown

The family had a big farewell party in Wicklow, then Ronan and Andrew travelled via Edinburgh on their return journey to Coldingham. Ronan wanted to open a bank account and make a deposit into the Royal Bank of Scotland, as he had accumulated quite a large sum of money from his fighting, especially from the last fight when his winnings were substantial. His trainer, Jim, had also had a collection for him when he had been so badly injured and that resulted in another lump sum in his kitty. The boxing fraternity looked after their own, and Ronan had been set up for life.

"Would you like to come and meet my family, Ronan? They'll be glad to see me back on Scottish soil. It's the first time that I have left Scotland, and Ireland seems so far away to them."

"If it's all the same with you, Andrew, I think I'd like to get up to Milldown before dark. I'm mighty weary, and there's a lot I have to get off my chest when I see Beanie and her family again."

The boys parted in the village and Ronan made his way up the muddy track to Milldown in the twilight. The house was in darkness apart from the warm light from the kitchen, which Ronan found both familiar and welcoming. At the table, the family were sharing their supper and nattering before an early night, as was the custom on the farm, as everybody was up at the crack of dawn to tend to the livestock.

A knock on the door made Beanie's heart skip a beat, as they were expecting Ronan to arrive that evening.

"I'll go," said Beanie, jumping from her seat to open the kitchen door.

"Ronan!" She jumped into his arms, making him drop his case, and the two hugged.

"Ronan, have you put on weight? There is something different about you."

The family noticed the difference in Ronan too as he came into the light from the cold to sit at their table. It was difficult to pinpoint the change, but he had left the farm as a boy and returned with a manly persona. His hair was shorter under his flat cap, revealing several thin scars, one traversing his eye and brow. There was less of the blarney about him. He was serious, obviously tired, and his speech a little slow. However, the family were pleased to have him back, and by the grin on Beanie's face, she was too.

"Did Andrew come back with you, Ronan?" asked Ellie.

"He did indeed. He is away with his family down in the village. He's mighty pleased to be home. I think he thought Ireland was – how shall I put this, now – a wee bit rough for his fair hands."

The family laughed and served Ronan with bread, ham, cheeses and homemade chutney, all swilled down with a large mug of tea.

"And how is Captain? I've missed him something fierce."

"Och, he's fine, still loving his walks to the sea. In fact, he's almost taken up swimming."

"Can we go and say hello, Beanie?"

"Of course. I'll get my coat."

The horse remembered Ronan instantly, stamping his feet and throwing his head in the air then resting it near to Ronan's face to nuzzle. Affection from a Shire horse was a fleeting gesture; however, the moment was always precious.

"Aw, I've missed you too, Captain." Ronan stroked his neck and blew on his nostrils until the horse was pacified. He then turned his back and returned to munch on his hay. The smell of the barn was everything that Ronan had remembered when he was at his lowest ebb after the fight. Imprisoned in his bedroom, unable to move, it had been the one thing that had kept him going, and he was mighty glad that he was here now with Captain and Beanie, although he knew he wasn't staying.

"Beanie, there's so much I have to tell you. So much has happened to me since I last saw you. I was in a fight and although I won, I was badly injured. There was a time that I thought I wasn't going to recover, and I would never see you again. That's why I didn't contact you."

"Ronan, are you all right now? You do seem to have changed. You've lost that roguish charm that I loved so much."

"Did you love me, Beanie? I've grown up since then, that's all. I have plans too; big plans for the future. I'm hoping you will be part of those plans. Beanie, I'm going to America. I've bought a gymnasium with my trainer, Jim. We're going to start a boxing school in New York. I want you to come with me. I have tickets on *The Campania* leaving from Liverpool to Ellis Island, New York in a week's time. Will you come with me, Beanie? We have to be in Liverpool two days prior to departure."

Beanie's ears started to ring, and she thought she was going to faint. She moved away from Ronan, as her perceived hopes and dreams for the future evaporated into thin air.

She found herself unable to answer Ronan, the impact of his

words too great for her to comprehend. She fled from the barn, rushing through the kitchen, unable to look at her family. Ellie ran after her into Beanie's bedroom and sat beside her on the bed.

"Beanie, what has happened? What has Ronan done? Did he hurt you?"

"No, of course not, Ellie. It's just that, he's going to emigrate to America, and he wants me to go with him."

Shocked and upset, Ellie relayed this news to the family downstairs, and they looked at one another in bewilderment. Helen contemplated the separation from another daughter, whilst William fretted at not only the loss of another daughter but the one he relied on to help him with the running of the farm in John's absence. Ellie was beside herself at the thought of a life without Beanie in it and started to cry. At that moment, Ronan entered the kitchen to a wall of silence.

"I guess I should have at least waited until morning to let you in on my plans. I'm so sorry. It seems to have come as a shock to you all. I'll take myself off to bed now, and hopefully we'll all see things more clearly in the morning. Goodnight, and thanks for your hospitality, Helen."

Although a small fire had been lit in Ronan's bedroom, the ground floor of the farm was bitterly cold. Ronan lay awake, imagining his exciting new life without Beanie. Perhaps it had been the shock of his proposal, but Ronan had seen no enthusiasm on Beanie's face at the prospect of starting a new life with him in America. Had he been a fool to think that she thought enough of him to pack her things, leave her beloved farm and family and cross the Atlantic to a strange, new world? And for what? A life in an unknown country, surrounded by men who made a living fighting. Was she too refined? Had he misread her feelings for him?

The morning was bitterly cold. A hard frost covered the yard and the cattle behind their enclosure bellowed for food, creating white plumes of breath with each exhalation. Beanie was first out. She hadn't slept and was miserable and impatient with the livestock, throwing the poultry their grain, topping up the hay for the cattle and breaking the ice on their water trough with a kick from her boot. Entering the stables, she relaxed slightly with her horses, the warmth from their bodies taking some of the chill out of the air. They would have no work today, the ground being too hard, but would be put out later to exercise when the frost had melted. She fed them and gave them each fresh buckets of water, cleaned their stalls and put more bedding down. Ronan came up behind her.

"Beanie, darling. I'm so sorry I blurted out all my plans. I know I gave you and your family a shock. But it will give us such a good future, Beanie. I will be able to support you and your family if necessary. Jim and I have jointly bought a huge building in New York with living accommodation upstairs and a gymnasium downstairs. I could never do the same in Scotland or Ireland – it's a once in a lifetime opportunity, Beanie, and my fighting days are over. Would you think about coming with me?"

"Ronan, I don't know how you can ask that of me. With John gone, Maggie moved away and my father growing old, how could it possibly work?"

"Beanie, we are going to be rich, rich enough to send for your family and look after them in their old age. I've given my word to my family too; we will be able to send money to them until they are ready to join us. Our Kathleen has refused to leave her pony, or they would be coming with me now. Will you discuss it with your family, Beanie? Please?"

"I'll explain what your intentions are, Ronan, but you would be asking too much of them. They are Scottish born and bred, as am I. We enjoy a good life on the farm."

"But I do love you, Beanie. It will be mighty hard to leave without you."

He had never actually said that he loved her before, and Beanie's emotions were soaring one minute then plummeting the next. He stood tall, his hands on her cheeks, and he gently kissed her. He seemed so much more masculine than he had done, and her heart was melting, the thought of him leaving tearing her apart. They kissed again, but she pulled away.

"It's cold, Ronan. Let's go inside."

Breakfast was laid on the table, but the atmosphere could be cut with a knife. William's feelings towards this young man had diminished considerably, for how could he plan to take his daughter away from her birth place to a foreign country, and so far away? Helen had warned her husband that they must not influence Beanie; she must make her own decision. She was an adult and perhaps truly in love with this young man.

"Ronan, sit down. Tell us what your plans are."

Ronan laid out his plans and his future prospects. Jim had been in New York for some time, and the opportunities were immense. Living quarters for three or more families were above a gymnasium that Jim had kitted out with a boxing ring, punch bags and all the facilities necessary for training young boxers. Boxing was apparently even more popular in America than it was in Ireland, and they had big plans for future expansion. They anticipated the accumulation of great wealth in America.

"And you think that Beanie would fit into this metropolis, surrounded by multi-racial entrepreneurs reaching for the sky?"

"William," Helen admonished, "let Ronan finish."

"Well, William, I can only tell you that I love your daughter.

I would take great care of her and hopefully do her proud. I've told Beanie that we could accommodate and support you and your family if you should want to join us. My family have had the same offer. In fact, Brandon is booked on the same crossing. I don't know what else to say."

"Well, I think Beanie should have a say now, don't you?"

"Father, I don't want to have a say just yet. I can't believe all this is happening."

"Well, I'll say one more thing, if that's all right."

William looked at his wife, who, with a sinking feeling, thought that no one was going to like what he was about to say.

"Ronan, I've spent my whole life here on Milldown Farm, as have my family before me. My blood and sweat are in the soil. Scottish soil. My ancestors are in the Priory. John is there, and you think that I would uproot myself to follow your pipe dream, which may or may not succeed, and be beholden to you? What state of affairs do you think we are in to want to follow you to America? Do you think because I'm a tenant farmer I can't look after my own?"

"William, I'm sure that's not what he meant."

Beanie could take no more seeing her father and mother so distressed. Ronan had offended William and pricked his pride. He was, after all, a dour Scotsman and very proud of it. She ran from the room in tears, plucking her coat off the peg to seek sanctuary in the stables. She harnessed Captain and took off on impulse before anyone could stop her.

Chapter 33

Milldown

Cantering across Coldingham Bay, deep in her heart she knew that she could not be parted from this place. This was her life, here on this beach, the fertile land of Milldown Farm behind her, the cold North Sea in front of her with its trawlers and shipwrecks. It was in her soul. No man could tempt her to give up what was so precious to her. Her thoughts became clear. Ronan did have a place in her heart, but it was not big enough or strong enough to tear her away from her beloved farm and family. She was Scottish; it ran through her veins. The sea air was in her lungs, and like Mary Queen of Scots she would not easily give up her birthright.

Slowing Captain down and letting him splash along the shoreline, she saw Alasdair with Carro at the other end of the beach. Not wanting him to see her with tears in her eyes, she would have turned, but he called out.

"Beanie, hey, wait for us."

Carro bounded towards them, and there was no escape. She brought Captain to a standstill and waited for Alasdair, who jogged along the sand towards her.

"Beanie, I'm glad I've caught you. There've been some developments over at Spylaw. I suppose you know that Andrew is back? I was hoping to discuss some plans that I thought you might be interested in. They could be beneficial to Milldown.

Can you come over some time?"

Men and their plans, thought Beanie. All I want is to be left alone.

"I can't today, Alasdair. Actually, I'm tied up for a couple of days. Can I give you a call when I'm free?"

"Yes, I'll look forward to that. Are you on your way home, or do you want to walk along for a while? Are you all right, Beanie? You look a little flushed."

"I've caught the wind in my eyes, that's all. I have to get back, but I'll give you a call in a couple of days."

She had to head back towards the farm, as that is where she had told Alasdair she was heading, but at the top of the path she turned left, away from the troubles, towards Eyemouth and Killedraught Bay, where her Uncle Ralph lived.

He was a man of few words, but when he did speak, he was both intelligent and pragmatic. Beanie dismounted on his dry stone wall next to where he was mending lines.

"Beanie, what brings you here? Are you all right, lass?"

"Well, my father thinks that I have brought a wolf to our door, and the wolf in question wants to whisk me away to New York to start a new life with him."

"I see, and your father wants to get his gun out, I presume?"

"Pretty much so."

"Is it one of the Irish boys? Your father told me that one of them had a crush on you."

"It is, Uncle. He has captured my heart, but I'm afraid he is going to have to leave without me."

"Are you sure, lass? If you love a man enough, you'll follow him to the ends of the earth. If you can't do that, then you don't love him enough. "

"Then I don't love him enough, Uncle. But how can I tell

him? It will break my heart and his."

Beanie fell into his strong arms and sobbed. Could she actually bear parting from Ronan, knowing that he loved her and she him? Her heart told her to follow him and let him fulfil his ambitions, but at what personal cost? She knew that he wanted her to be part of his future and that he was desperate for her support, but although he now looked physically strong, emotionally he was just a boy following a dream.

"You have to be truthful. Be clear, so he's not left in any doubt. You owe him honesty, Beanie. And your father needs to calm down. He's a fair man until he is riled; then there's no telling what he'll do."

"You're right, Uncle. I'll go home and sort things out."

Beanie kissed his whiskery old cheek, dried her eyes and mounted Captain, returning home feeling a little better but still torn apart. Her father was waiting for her at the kitchen table.

"Beanie, darling, I've been worried sick. I thought you might have done something silly after all the arguing. I've spoken to Ronan, and the decision is of course yours. He's a good lad. We've all been very fond of him, and if you do love him then we must let you go. It would be selfish of me to want you to stay. He's out mending some fences. Why don't you go and talk to him?"

"I will, Father, but I want to talk to you first. You know I have fallen for his Irish charm. He is a lovely man, and I do love him, just not enough."

With that, Beanie burst into tears again and fell into her father's arms.

"There, lass. I know, I know."

"Father, I don't know how I can tell him."

"Well, I can't do that for you. Are you sure of your feelings,

Beanie? You won't change your mind once he's gone?"

"No, Father. I want my life to be here on the farm with my family. I'm sure I'll marry one day, but just not too soon."

"All right, Beanie, stop your crying now. I think it best you tell him as soon as possible. He's all over the place. He's been in tears himself."

She found Ronan in the lower field, working away as if he belonged there. If only he thought as much of Milldown and Scotland as she did, he would never leave. Beanie composed herself, thinking that she could tell Ronan her decision calmly and sensibly. However, looking into the wounded expression in his eyes, she broke down again. Ronan grabbed her and pulled her close. His smell and the reassurance of his hug melted her heart once again. She lifted her head and kissed him as she had never kissed anyone before, clinging onto him, not ever wanting to let him go. He felt like the man she should spend the rest of her life with, but not in America.

"Beanie, I love you. Please come with me. I can't fight any longer – my body is too damaged. I could work the fields for the rest of my life, but I long for so much more. I want to make you proud of me, not see me become old as a field hand. Is that what you want, Beanie? That I should become old before my time, full of arthritis?"

"No, Ronan, of course not. I love you too much for that, but I can't go to America. I want you to go and fulfil your dreams. I want you to remember me and Captain and the wonderful times we've had together. I don't want you to have any regrets. Let's part now while we are strong enough to do it."

"Beanie, I can't let you go."

Ronan sobbed, but Beanie pulled away.

"Ronan, we've both made up our minds. We can't prolong

this any longer. You'll have to go – it's too painful."

"Beanie, I'll write."

Beanie ran off towards the shore and didn't look back. She found a deserted place in the sand dunes, lay down and let the tears fall. She was aware that she would never see Ronan again, and the pain gripped her heart, her mind not accepting the finality of their parting. She drew her knees up, lying on her side, knowing, however, that the pain of leaving Coldingham would have been far greater than her present suffering, and she tried to calm herself. Tears flowed, but the sobbing subsided as she focused on the mackerel sky and the gulls overhead.

Ronan gathered his things and said a tearful goodbye to the family he had hoped to become a part of. He went to the stables, breathing in the wonderfully familiar smell of horses and hay. As he took Captain's head in his hands and kissed his muzzle, pent-up tears flowed. He suddenly remembered his precious drum left behind in the parlour, but with a heartfelt desire to one day see Milldown again, he turned to begin his journey without the two things he held most dear to him: Beanie and his father's Bodhran drum.

Author's Note

Although the Thorburns of Milldown Farm are indeed my ancestors, Beanie being my grandmother, the story that I have created around them is a figment of my imagination. It is, however, interspersed with memories of stories told to me, by my grandmother, as a child.

Through research, I found certain things that she told me were not simply stories but fact. For instance, Beanie recounted to me the story of the shipwreck of *The Alfred Erlandsen* and her seeing the sea awash with pit props. She also told me of the surviving dog, Carro, which became something of a celebrity. Shipwrecks were not uncommon in the sea off St. Abbs Head, and today it has become a popular dive site.

Sir James Simpson's daughter, Eve, befriended Beanie, who, on occasion, took her into Eyemouth shopping in her pony and trap. Eve presented my grandmother with a biography of her father, and it is now held in the Royal College of Anaesthetists in London, signed "Eve Blantyre Simpson".

Elements of truth run throughout the book. To me, they almost seem like inherited memories from my grandmother's wonderful times on the farm. Of course, life in the early twentieth century had its disadvantages. Beanie's brother John did die of diabetes in his early thirties, as there was no insulin, and Queenie, the horse, died of tetanus. It was a hard life for the working horses labouring in the fields before tractors took over their drudgery. It would have been in Beanie's lifetime that all the farm horses were commandeered for the First World War, none of which returned. Thankfully, Captain was imaginary.

Epilogue

Marie R
March 1567

The Palfrey was tired. His huge hooves plodded down the slope to the little stream at the bottom of the incline. The dog, Tétu, paused to drink and to cool himself after the long journey south, from the outskirts of Edinburgh. Tétu, translated as "stubborn," belied the true nature of the beast, who was both staunchly loyal and a true defender of the young queen of Scotland. His breed, Irish Wolfhound, saw him standing more than two and a half feet tall with harsh, wiry coat, long eyebrows and beard, a truly intimidating spectre.

"Tétu, viens ici, Tétu, viens.

Mary's upbringing some miles west of Paris led her to revert to the French language when she found herself alone in her thoughts, or when her temper flared. Now, as her mind wandered, lulled by the motion of the horse's slow gait, she reflected on her two unsuccessful marriages. Francis, whom she had loved as a friend and confidant since childhood, had died in pain and delirium from an ear infection at the young age of sixteen, their adolescence impeding the protocol that made necessary the consummation of their marriage. Lord Darnley, however, whom Mary had fallen in love with when she had first set foot on Scottish soil, had a weak spirit, enjoying the consumption of alcohol and the company of men a little too much. Mary had given him a son, James, but like Francis, Darnley proved to be little interested in the pleasures that the marriage bed could offer. He was gullible and disloyal with no interest in satisfying the passion that came so naturally to Mary.

"Walk on Héros."

The black stallion flinched at her command but walked obediently towards the small summer house, outlined so perfectly against the late afternoon sky, pink and cloudless, miles away from the atmosphere of corruption and contempt that permeated the very walls that threatened Mary's freedom.

Bothwell's horse, tethered lightly to a sapling, allowing him to graze, lifted his head and whinnied a greeting. Mary's mood lifted at the thought of an hour or two in the arms of her lover Bothwell who, waiting upstairs, reclined on the small day bed positioned in the circular turret. The windows, carelessly flung open, indulged him with scented breezes from the abundantly stocked gardens of Spylaw, the estate owned by his friend The Duke of Lochober, who, loyal to the catholic faith, was of course a true sponsor of Mary's cause.

Bothwell lay exposed, his taught muscles a complete contrast to the delicate frame of Francis and the odious body of Darnley, whose own hygiene went unchecked for days at a time, until Mary could no longer have him near her. Raising himself onto one elbow, Bothwell's lazy gaze perused the attire that Mary had chosen to wear. She had dressed as a young lad so she could ride astride, unrecognisable, but the breeks did nothing to hide her femininity. She removed her clothes and stood without discomfiture in front of her lover, the ravages of childbirth having done nothing to rob her of her vivacity. The only thing she now wore was the small dirk, inlaid with a black pearl and tied at her thigh, a gift from Bothwell. Crossing the room, she dropped into his arms and their lips met.

"Tétu."

The dog ran at speed across the room to accept the huge ox bone that Mary had brought with her to occupy the dog whilst she and Bothwell appeased their mutual desires.